SCALPELS & PSYCHOPATHS

Dr. Maxwell Thornton Murder Mysteries

By S.C. Wynne

Dedication

I ran a poll in my readers group to help choose the title of this book, and I told my readers if I used their title I'd credit them in the book.

Eric Thornton, a reader and author pal of mine, suggested a title that I loved, Sutures & Psychopaths. Although I ultimately didn't pick that title, I still wanted to thank him for his wonderful suggestion.

Not only did Eric deserve a shout out for the great title suggestion, but he also has a great last name, don't you think?

If you'd like to join my reader's group, it's called the Wynner's Circle on Facebook.

Chapter One

Maxwell

Rainy Dale's gossip network operated a lot like a rash; it spread fast and was impossible to ignore.

Not that I thought the murder of Mayor Penelope Granger's beloved father should go unnoticed. But the minute it was discovered someone had shoved a hatpin through his chest at Penelope's birthday party, paranoia and accusations flew like packing peanuts caught in a twister.

I hadn't witnessed the actual murder. Royce and I had been making out in another part of the house. For once, I'd actually been having a good time at a party. Of course, the moment the murder was discovered, Royce had gone into full-on sheriff mode. Seeing as a man had been murdered, I'd had to pretend not to mind that Royce was suddenly all business and no pleasure. He'd arranged for one of his deputies to give me a ride home from the party, planted a distracted peck on my mouth, and closed the door in my face.

Groaning, I kicked off the covers because sleep was impossible, and it was almost time to get up anyway. Tugging on my robe, I made my way down the creaky stairs toward the kitchen. Not only had I not been able to spend the night of the party with Royce, I hadn't even spoken to him for two days. I was feeling decidedly grumpy this morning.

Entering my kitchen, I expected to find a pot of piping-hot coffee to lighten my mood but instead found the counter covered in water and coffee grinds. "Good Lord," I hissed, unplugging the machine. "Has the world gone mad?"

The sound of the front door opening came to me, followed by a cheery "Good morning!" as Girdy entered the building. Her footsteps neared, and she came into the kitchen. "How's it going?"

"Peachy," I grumbled, pressing the button on the coffee maker over and over, as if that might help. "Coffee brewer is broken."

"Oh, crap." She came closer, undoing the buttons of her jacket.

"Do you suppose any of the stores in town carry coffee makers?" I grabbed a wad of paper towels and began to mop up the water and grounds.

She laughed good-naturedly. "Of course."

Sighing, I tossed the wet towels in the trash and leaned on the counter. "How am I supposed to function today without caffeine?"

"Tell you what, I'll go into town right now and buy you a new coffee maker." She studied me. "Will that cheer you up?"

I shrugged. "I can't promise I'll be cheerful, but it'll be safer for all concerned if I get my coffee."

"Yes. I don't doubt that." She buttoned her jacket back up again.

"Is it cold out?"

"A bit nippy. It is October."

I frowned. "Did Todd drop you off this morning?"

"Yeah."

Guilt nudged me. "That means you'd have to walk into town to get the coffee maker?"

"I don't mind."

"I'd loan you my car, if I had one." I kept talking about buying a car, but I rarely needed one. Maybe when winter hit, I'd change my mind.

She smiled. "I know you would, but walking is good for me."

"I guess."

A few months ago, I wouldn't have thought twice about her walking into town in cold weather to do me a favor. Unfortunately, Royce was rubbing off on me a bit, and I actually felt *guilt* these days. I wasn't pleased about his saintlike influence on me. Guilt often interfered with me getting what I wanted.

"Never mind. I'll just have a cup of tea. I can get a new coffee maker on my lunch break."

She lifted her auburn brows. "But I truly don't mind going now."

As tempted as I was to take her up on her offer, I could hear Royce's voice chiding me for being selfish. "No. That's fine. Tea will do nicely."

She smiled and leaned toward me. "My goodness, Maxwell. I do believe you're growing a heart."

My face warmed. "Nonsense." I sniffed. "If you get sick, I'll have to run this place by myself. I have enough to do, without answering the phone and filing too."

"Oh."

I went to the cupboard above the stove, grabbing a box of Earl Grey tea. I filled the teakettle, aware of her still watching me. "Did you need something?" I asked gruffly.

"No. I was just thinking about what happened Saturday." She shifted uneasily. "Nasty business poor Bob Cunningham being murdered."

"Indeed." I turned the stove burner on and then tore open the tea bag packet.

"Did the police question you yet?"

"No." I glanced at her. "You?"

She nodded. "Royce brought me and Todd in yesterday to get our statements. Not that we were any help. We didn't see anything."

I frowned. "Huh. Wonder why he hasn't dragged me in yet."

"Oh, he will. He's pissed someone dared to murder Bob right under his nose." She sighed. "I've rarely seen him this angry. When we were at the station, he even snapped at his deputies, and that's almost unheard of."

She was right. Royce was one of the most even-tempered people I'd ever met. He generally reacted to stressful situations with thoughtful consideration. If he was losing his temper, he must truly be frustrated. We'd only been seeing each other a few months, but if not for his patience and easygoing attitude, I doubted we'd have lasted that long. Not that we were an official couple or anything. We slept together and spent days off with each other if we could. But we'd yet to put a label on what we were.

"I'm sure Royce's pride is involved. But he'll figure out who the murderer is." I faced her, crossing my arms.

"I hope so." She shivered. "It creeps me out to think another murderer is wandering the streets of Rainy Dale. I mean, it could be anyone."

"Well, anyone who was at the party."

"True." She bit her lower lip. "We never have violent crime around here. I can't believe it's happened again so soon after Ned Tinkerson's murder."

I nodded but had nothing to add really. I'd only lived in Rainy Dale a short time. Where I came from, the murder rate was huge in comparison, but I guessed it was relative. With only around 1,001 people in this town, two murders in a few months probably felt like a major crime wave.

"It's so depressing knowing one of us is a cold-blooded killer," she said softly.

"I don't know anything about Bob Cunningham. Maybe he was a man with a lot of enemies."

"Even so, you can't just go around killing people because they're unpleasant."

"No. Of course not." The teakettle whistled, and I turned quickly to shut it off. I filled a large mug with hot water and murmured, "I'm sure you're safe, Girdy. You're very likeable."

"Did you just compliment me?" She sounded amused. "If so, would you mind repeating it so I can record it on my phone?"

I ignored her and dunked my teabag in the hot water. "Do we have many appointments today?"

"A full book, I'm afraid. I hope your tea does the trick." She moved toward the hallway that led out into the waiting room. "The offer to go get a coffee maker still stands."

"Thank you, but it can wait."

Making sure I truly could function without my coffee, I drank three cups of tea before the first patient arrived. It didn't give me the same kick I was used to from coffee, but it was better than nothing.

My first patient was David Grant. He was in his mid-fifties, with white hair and startling blue eyes. His eyes weren't the only startling thing about him, which was revealed to me when he spoke.

"Dr. Thornton, my heart and liver are missing." He sounded a hundred percent convinced as he took a seat for our consultation.

"Excuse me?" I raised my brows in surprise.

"It's the truth. They're gone."

I frowned and sat behind my desk, studying him. I didn't want to overreact, so I made sure my expression was emotionless. "What makes you say that, Mr. Grant?"

He touched his chest. "I can't feel my heart beating anymore, and I just know my liver is gone too. I can feel just tell."

I cleared my throat. "It's highly unlikely you're missing either of those organs. If you were, you wouldn't be sitting in my office right this moment. You'd be unable to breathe or talk without a heart." I couldn't believe I was having to say those words, and yet, he looked unconvinced.

He blinked at me. "That's what you think."

"Come again?" I scowled.

"Doc, can you keep a secret?"

"Uh… sure." I was apprehensive as I held his glittering gaze. I knew instinctively something crazy was about to come out of his mouth.

"I believe I've turned into a… zombie."

I couldn't help the gruff laugh that escaped my lips. "A zombie?"

"It's not funny, Doc." His face was flushed, and he glanced around the room.

I grimaced. "No. It's not funny. How about you give me more information. Why… why do you feel as if you're a… zombie?"

At times like these, it was hard not to miss my practice back in Los Angeles. I'd never had to deal with crackpots who thought they were zombies back then.

I'd kept my head down, performed brilliant cardiovascular procedures, and accepted the kudos due me. Then disaster struck, and I'd fallen into a personal and professional tailspin I'd been unable to pull out of. Because of that *one* failure, I now had to deal with people who truly believed they were the walking dead.

God help me.

Twisting his hands, he said, "I had a stroke last year, and ever since then, I've noticed little things."

"Such as?"

"I smell rotting flesh constantly, and I'm positive it's coming from me."

"Really?" His comment jogged my memory. In medical school we'd briefly touched on a condition called Cotard's Syndrome. It was a mental illness where people literally believed they were dead. Unfortunately, I hadn't paid a lot of attention at the time or even thought of it since.

He sighed. "My wife is ready to divorce me. She insisted I come see you. I told her you wouldn't believe me, but she made me an appointment all the same."

"It's good that she did. We can't have you wandering around thinking you're... dead." I laughed.

"I should have known you wouldn't listen."

"I am listening. But I believe there's another reason for what you're experiencing."

He wrinkled his brow. "Like what?"

Frowning, I said, "You mentioned you had a stroke last year?"

He nodded. "Yes. I almost died, and everyone told me how lucky I was to have survived." He swallowed hard. "But the thing is, Doc, I don't think I did survive."

"Mr. Grant, you must know how crazy it sounds to say you're dead, but still walking and talking?"

He hung his head. "Yes. But I swear I can't feel my heart anymore. Believe me, I've tried."

I tapped my chin, trying to decide how to proceed. Logic wasn't his strong suit, seeing as he didn't seem to grasp that interacting with others, while deceased, wasn't a thing. I leaned forward, clasping my hands. "Mr. Grant, I believe you may be suffering from a mental condition called Cotard's Syndrome. It's possible it was brought on by your stroke."

He frowned. "Cotard's Syndrome?"

I nodded. "Sometimes when a person suffers a stroke, they can develop certain psychological issues. Are you taking any medications for anxiety or anything like that?"

"No. Just blood thinners."

"Hmmm. I'd like to schedule you for an MRI."

He squinted at me. "MRI? You mean a brain scan? Are you saying I'm crazy?"

"No. I'm saying your mental abilities might have been affected by your stroke."

"How is that different from crazy?"

I frowned. "Well…"

He stood. "I knew you wouldn't believe me. No one does." He gritted his teeth. "I'm telling you I'm dead. Why won't anyone listen?"

I stood too and instinctively moved to the examination table. I could feel he was about to bolt, and I didn't want that. "How about I give you an exam?" I said cheerfully, desperately trying to think about how I could get him to understand he wasn't actually a walking corpse. I patted the table. "Come on. You came here for my expert opinion, correct?"

He hesitated. "Yes."

"Well, I can't give you that unless I examine you." I pretended not to notice his frustrated demeanor as I pulled on gloves. "Sit on the table for me, please."

He stared at me.

"Come along. I don't have all day." I used my most authoritative voice because often people would obey without question, if you were bossy enough.

Slowly, he moved toward me. "So, you do believe me?"

"I'll let you know my prognosis after my examination." Stalling was the best I could do at the moment. Of course I didn't think he was a walking corpse. But I needed *him* to believe that.

He got on the table, watching me warily. His nostrils were flared and his gaze suspicious. "Okay, I'm on the table. Now what?"

"Please unbutton your shirt." I put the earpiece of my stethoscope in my ears.

He obeyed, undoing his shirt slowly.

Once he had his top undone, I pressed the metal diaphragm against his bare chest. He hissed and wiggled a bit but stayed put. I was oddly relieved to hear the loud thump of his heart. While I knew he wasn't dead, he'd been eerily convincing.

"So? Is my heart gone?" he asked breathlessly.

I cleared my throat. "No."

He scowled. "What?"

An idea came to me, and I took the earpiece out and held the stethoscope out to him. "Put this in your ears."

"Why?"

"Just do it," I ordered.

He obeyed and pushed the buds into his ears. Then he closed his eyes and scowled. "That's my *heart*?" He flicked his eyes open.

"It most certainly is."

Pulling his white brows together, he looked nonplussed. "But… why can't I feel it beating?"

"I'm not sure. But it's definitely there."

He examined the stethoscope. "You sure these aren't rigged?"

Narrowing my eyes, I took the equipment from him. "How would I have planned for that? I had no idea what your ailment was until you told me."

"Oh, yeah."

I hung the stethoscope around my neck again. "I'm willing to bet your stroke has done damage that went undetected. I want you to have that MRI as soon as possible, and we can discuss your options from there. Once we know exactly what we're working with, we can begin treatment."

He nodded, looking less suspicious. "Promise my wife didn't put you up to this?"

"What?" I scoffed. "I have a waiting room filled with hypochondriacs and the likes. You seriously think I took time out of my busy schedule to hatch an elaborate plan with your wife?" I laughed humorlessly. "I assure you, I did no such thing. I'm sorry to disappoint you, but you're alive, Mr. Grant."

He scratched his jaw. "Well, I'll be damned."

I returned to my desk and pulled up an appointment app on my computer. "I'm sending in a request for the MRI. You should get something in the mail in a few weeks. Don't ignore it. If left unchecked, this condition could get much worse. You're lucky your wife cares about you enough to make you come to see me."

He buttoned his shirt, looking sheepish. "I suppose so."

"There's no supposing about it. Don't take her love for granted. She could easily have ignored you, and you'd have just continued to go downhill." I almost couldn't believe those sappy words were coming out of my mouth. Don't take her love for granted? Since when did I spout such drivel? What was next? Would I be hanging posters of adorable puppies in the waiting room?

"I… I won't take her for granted."

"See that you don't." I stood and led him to the door.

Before he exited the room, he turned to me. "You weren't nearly as horrible as I thought you'd be."

I frowned. "Pardon me?"

He shrugged. "Everyone says what a dreadful ogre of a man you are. I mean, could you be a little more tactful? Sure." He smirked. "But overall, you weren't a total asshole."

"Gee, thanks."

I watched him leave, wondering why I even bothered trying to connect to the nutty people of Rainy Dale. It certainly was a thankless endeavor. What did these dolts want from me? I'd even reinstated the coffee and cookies to try and soften them up. Truth was, if I didn't care so much what Royce thought of me, I'd have given up trying to ingratiate myself long ago.

I sighed, eyeing the crowded waiting room. Babies screeched, and housewives whispered to each other, giggling. There were seniors with walkers parked next to their chairs, and a few teens thrown in for good measure. I had a long, dull, irksome day ahead of me, and no guarantee I'd get to see Royce.

It was disconcerting how depressing that thought was.

Chapter Two

Royce

Sitting in one of the interview rooms at the station, I held the surly gaze of Sal Brenner. He'd been at the party the night Bob Cunningham was murdered, and he'd argued with the victim. I had a few more questions for him, but problem was, Sal didn't seem to be in a cooperative mood.

"Now, Sal, there's no need to give me the stink eye," I said calmly. "A man has been murdered. Do you think I can just ignore that fact?"

Sal grimaced. "No. But I already told you everything I know the day of the murder. Don't you remember you interviewed me already?"

"I did talk with you, that's true, but this is your formal statement. I want to get your account of things on the record. See that camera up there?" I pointed to the red blinking light in the corner of the room.

"Yeah."

"That's recording what you tell me today. That way you can be assured I didn't write things down incorrectly or twist your words. Okay?"

"Got it."

"Great." I tapped my pen on the notepad in front of me. "Why don't you tell me again where you were when you heard Rita scream."

He exhaled roughly. "I told you, I was over by the punch bowl. I was trying to cool off a little."

"Because you'd had a fight with Bob?"

He pointed at me. "See, when you use that tone, Sheriff, it makes me feel like you're accusing me of murdering Bob."

I raised my brows. "I'm not doing anything of the sort. You admitted you'd had an argument with Bob. Even if you hadn't admitted it, everyone heard you two. I'm just trying to get the scene straight in my head. There are a lot of moving pieces."

He looked unconvinced, but he didn't respond.

"Now, what was it you argued with Bob about again?" I knew what he'd argued about, but sometimes people's stories changed when they were lying. I had no idea if Sal was the killer or not. I didn't think so, but at the moment, he was the main person with a reason to kill Bob.

He groaned, leaning back in his chair. "How many times do I have to tell you the same damn story?"

"Come on, Sal. Work with me."

Gritting his teeth, he said, "Bob promised me that vacant lot on the west side of town. That prime corner next to the gas station. It would have been perfect for my tire store relocation. When he reneged on the deal, I had every right to be pissed."

"No one said you didn't."

"Well, everyone is looking at me like I'm a cold-blooded killer lately. You should hear the gossip in town." His cheeks were flushed, and he rubbed a hand over his balding head. "I didn't kill Bob. Was I mad that he lied to me and gave that location to my competitor instead? Hell yes. But I didn't murder the guy."

"You said to Penelope that Bob 'Wouldn't get away with this.'" I lifted one brow. "Even I heard you say that."

"People say things in the heat of anger. I didn't mean it literally."

"Hmmm."

"I was livid when I found out he'd given the space to my competitor. I simply let Bob know my displeasure."

"Definitely. Could you remind me of the name of your competitor?"

"Lydia Gonzales. She owns Red Wheel Tires." He scowled. "Bob knew I needed that spot, and he still gave it to her instead. That's bullshit. She already has six locations all over Texas. I have my measly one location, and I needed a better spot. He *promised* me I could have that space, but he pulled a fast one."

"I can hear how frustrated you are."

"Damn straight," he growled. "I mean, who does that? Who lies right to a person's face like that?"

I hated to break it to him, but lots of people lied to your face. The ones who didn't were the rarity. "Bob had a reputation for dealing people dirty. Didn't you know that?"

He sighed. "Yeah, I knew. But truth was, Bob was a real smooth talker when he wanted to be. He had a way of making you believe he was your best friend. Until he stabbed the knife in your chest."

I winced at his choice of words.

"Anyway, I didn't kill him. Was I mad enough to take a swing? You betcha. But it was Penelope's birthday party, and I didn't want to ruin the day for her."

"I see. That was nice of you."

He shrugged. "Well, I'd already argued with her dad. I didn't want to fuck up her entire day by keeping it going."

"I'm sure she appreciated that."

"Maybe." He scowled. "You know, maybe I argued with Bob at the party, but he was alive when I stomped away. Not to mention, I'm not the only person in town who had a bone to pick with him."

"I've definitely heard things."

"I'm sure you have. It wasn't just business where he fucked people over either, if you get my meaning."

"You sound like you know a lot about his personal life."

He chuffed. "The guy couldn't be faithful to save his life."

"So, you're saying he messed around with other women?"

He started laughing. "Come on, surely you already knew that."

I shrugged. "I tune gossip out most of the time."

"Well, if you'd been listening, you'd know he fucked around, whether he was in a relationship or not. The guy had no morals. He slept with his friends' wives, enemies' wives, strangers' wives. He didn't give a shit. In fact, I think he liked it better. He enjoyed the thrill."

"He didn't strike me as… the classic philanderer type." Bob had been easily over three hundred pounds. Not that a morbidly obese person couldn't find love, but it sounded like Bob had been a real Lothario.

"Like that matters when you have tons of money and power."

"Fair enough."

"I guess what I'm saying is, instead of just deciding I killed Bob, pay attention to the fact that Bob had a lot of enemies."

I narrowed my eyes. "I hope you know me well enough to know, I'd never just pin this on you because it's easier that way."

He avoided my gaze, looking a bit sheepish. "I've never really seen you in action. It's not like I've ever been dragged in before for a murder investigation."

"No. I don't suppose you have. But I've been the sheriff years now. I'd hope you know my character enough to trust me."

He flicked his gaze to mine, and some of his anger seemed to drain away. "Let's just say, I hope you're the man I think you are, Sheriff Callum."

"I am."

He shifted in his chair. "Was that it? Can I go now?"

"Just a few more questions, then you can take off." I pursed my lips, trying to read him. He was nervous, and there were sweat marks under his armpits. He didn't like to meet my gaze, but lots of people didn't like looking cops in the eye. I didn't get any malicious vibe off him. I understood why he'd been angry with Bob. Anyone would have been upset in his situation. Being upset didn't make someone a cold-blooded killer. "Did Rita know about his philandering?"

"I'd assume so. If she didn't, she was deaf, dumb, and blind." He stared up at the flickering fluorescent lights. "She was agitated at the party. Circling Bob like a hawk. It didn't help any that there were a lot of single women at that party."

"Seems weird to want to be with someone you can't trust."

"Like I said, money and power talk."

"Yeah." He was right, of course. It was amazing how many people flocked to those with wealth and perceived power, even when it was detrimental to themselves. For some reason my thoughts drifted to

Maxwell. He'd been surrounded by rich and powerful men back in Los Angeles. Had he rubbed elbows with guys like Bob, drawn to their clout? Was I dreaming, thinking he'd be satisfied staying in Rainy Dale, dating a small-town cop?

I shook myself, embarrassed I'd allowed my thoughts to drift to personal things. Maybe it was because I'd done nothing for the last two and a half days but work this case. I missed spending time with Maxwell. I wasn't sure I should share that with him though. It might make him uncomfortable. He had trouble assimilating affection.

"I'm not kidding about Bob having a lot of enemies," Sal said, interrupting my thoughts.

"I'm looking at everything. Don't worry."

He glanced at his watch. "I hate to be a drag, but I have a meeting. Since I didn't get my preferred spot for my shop, I've had to try for a different location. I'm meeting Mrs. Numi in twenty minutes."

"Is that right?" Mrs. Numi was another local Realtor. Her reputation wasn't cutthroat like Bob's had been. She was of the silk scarves and finger sandwich ilk. Unlike Bob, she didn't rape and pillage in full view. She schmoozed her clients with well-bred charm, and if she fleeced them, they never knew it.

"Yeah." He smirked. "With Bob dying, her business is going to pick up a lot. Maybe you should look at her for the murder."

"She wasn't at the party."

"Maybe she hired someone to take Bob out."

I frowned. "Do you seriously think Mrs. Numi hired a killer?"

He laughed. "No."

"Yeah, me neither."

"So, can I take off?"

I hesitated, then gave a nod. "Yeah. Don't plan on leaving town for a while, Sal. And don't get paranoid. I'm telling everyone who was at the party the same thing."

"Okay." He stood, moving to the door.

I stayed seated, watching him go.

He stopped at the door and turned to me. "Sorry if I seemed hot under the collar earlier."

I gave a half-smile. "It's okay. I understand. This is a stressful situation for all of us. It's not like I'm looking forward to arresting someone I know."

He winced. "No. I guess that's probably true." He left, closing the door quietly behind him.

I studied the notepad in front of me. I hadn't made many notes because my gut said it wasn't Sal. The only other four people I didn't suspect were Maxwell, Girdy, Todd, and Penelope. Other than that, the killer could be anyone who'd been at the party.

I stood, feeling all of my forty years. I'd lived on nothing but coffee and beef jerky the last two days. I'd only gone home to feed and walk Grumpy. I also had a local girl, Tomasina, who watched Grumpy for me. Without Tomasina, I'd have been eaten alive with guilt leaving the pup alone so much.

I was tempted to call Maxwell to see if maybe he wanted to grab dinner and hang out tonight. I'd originally planned on working late again, but I couldn't interview the next witnesses until tomorrow. Plus, forensics had no fingerprint or DNA results for me yet, probably wouldn't get those until the end of the week, if we were lucky.

I hoped Maxwell wouldn't be insulted that I hadn't contacted him the last few days. I'd intended to call him about ten times, and every time I'd been distracted by something. When I finally would have a free moment, it would always be either too late or too early to call him. It was most likely wishful thinking that he'd missed me. It was hard to get a bead on how he felt about me, seeing as he wasn't terribly forthcoming with his emotions. I knew he enjoyed having sex with me, but then again, there weren't a lot of options for him here in town.

I fingered my phone, wrestling with the desire to see him and not wanting to seem needy. After a few minutes of trying to make up my mind, I decided to go for it. I dialed his number and was surprised when Girdy answered.

"Oh, hey, Girdy." I hesitated. "Did I call the wrong number? I was trying to get hold of Maxwell."

She gave a breathless laugh. "No, this is his phone. Uh… he's in the bathroom with a woman."

"Oh?"

"A patient woman." She grunted. "I mean a woman who's a patient."

"Okay." I frowned, not sure where to go next with the conversation.

"She had a bloody nose that just wouldn't stop. I mean, it was like Dracula exploded in here. It was insane."

Yikes.

"I… I guess just tell him I called?"

"Can you hang on the line? I think he's coming out of the bathroom now." She put her hand over the receiver, and I heard muffled voices.

"Royce?" Maxwell's breathless voice came over the line.

"Yeah. I'm here." My chest squeezed with pleasure at the sound of his husky voice. I stamped down my excitement though, since my intention was to sound casual. As if it had just occurred to me we hadn't spoken for days.

There was an awkward pause. "How's it going with the case?"

"I'm plodding along."

"Oh. Well, that's normal, I guess."

I cleared my throat, trying to drum up the nerve to ask him to dinner. I'd done it many times before; was it harder now because I was really starting to have feelings for him? "I'm taking the night off. Wondered if maybe you'd like to grab some grub with me." *Grab some grub?* Why was I talking like a cartoon cowboy?

"Tonight?"

"Yeah. I need to eat something not from a vending machine." Realizing that wasn't a very personal invitation, I added, "And I'd love some company."

"Grumpy has a date already?"

I grinned. "He's booked weeks in advance. He's a popular pup."

He gave a soft laugh. "Uh, yeah. I can have dinner with you, Royce."

Relief swamped me. "Great." I hesitated because I hadn't worked out the details before calling. "Do you care where we eat?"

"No."

"How about I pick you up in half an hour and we do Italian?"

"Sure. I love Italian food."

"I'm pretty certain Vinney's is open tonight. I'll call and make sure."

"Vinney's? Is that really the name of the restaurant?"

I frowned. "Yeah. Problem?"

"It sounds like a mobster's name." He seemed to catch himself and added quickly, "But I'm sure the food is delicious. Thank you for the invitation."

I chuckled, feeling a bit more relaxed now that he'd agreed to join me. "Nice save."

"I'm learning," he said dryly.

"You are. I'm proud of you." I heard voices in the background.

"I've got to go. See you tonight." He hung up.

Frowning, I stared down at my phone. Quirky as he was, I looked forward to seeing him tonight. I hoped we'd end up in my bed, but either way, at least I'd get to spend some time with him.

I exited the interview room and went to my office to make a few calls. Next time I glanced down at my watch, it was time to pick up Maxwell. I told my deputies I was heading out and left the station for the night. As I walked to my car, my thoughts once more drifted to Maxwell. He was such an odd duck. I wasn't quite sure why I liked him so much. We weren't anything alike, but I felt like I understood him. He could be moody and superior, but he also had a sort of vulnerability about him. He was often self-centered, much like a child. But I knew that was because he was a product of his unorthodox upbringing. Perhaps I felt a soft spot for him because he was trying to change.

I knew it was dumb to get attached to Maxwell. The odds of him staying in Rainy Dale permanently were slim to none. Whether I liked it or not, it was probably only a matter of time before he announced he was returning to Los Angeles. That thought depressed me, but I also accepted it. It was obvious Rainy Dale grated on Maxwell. A part of me was surprised he hadn't already bolted back to the big city.

Pushing those gloomy thoughts away, I parked in front of his house. I sauntered up the cobblestone pathway, skipping up the steps to the front door. My pulse skittered as I opened the door, but the only person I found was Girdy, standing near a filing cabinet with her back to me. The waiting room was empty and the door to Maxwell's examination room closed.

Girdy turned and jumped when she saw me. "Oh, wow. Sorry. I was so distracted I didn't hear you come in."

I smiled and pulled my Stetson off. "I'm having dinner with Maxwell."

"Are you?" She looked surprised. "He didn't mention it."

I frowned. "Hopefully he didn't forget."

"No. I'm sure he didn't. We were crazy busy today." She smiled brightly. "Where are you taking him?"

"Vinney's."

"Ooh." She nodded her approval. "I love their grilled salmon. It has this lemon garlic sauce that's insanely delicious."

"That does sound good."

"Damn. Now I want Italian food." She laughed. "Maybe I'll make Todd take me out to dinner."

It was on the tip of my tongue to suggest we should all four eat together, but then my selfishness took over. I wanted Maxwell all to myself tonight. Besides, Maxwell wasn't spontaneous. He'd loath suddenly having to dine with Girdy and Todd as well. No, best to leave things as they were.

The stairs creaked, and Maxwell appeared behind me. My heart picked up speed at the sight of him. He wore jeans and a fitted white dress shirt. His citrusy cologne wafted toward me, and it took resolve not to go to him and kiss him hello.

"There you are." I feigned a casualness I was far from feeling.

He pulled on a suit jacket as he approached. He eyed my clothing and hesitated. "Am I overdressed?"

"You look great." That heartfelt compliment sort of slipped out, and my face warmed. "There's no dress code at Vinney's, but some people dress up. What you're wearing is perfect."

He nodded. "Okay. Thank goodness I didn't wear a tie. I almost did."

Girdy laughed. "Don't worry so much about what you're wearing. It's dinner. Just go have some fun for once."

He wrinkled his brow. "I'm not worrying."

"Seem worried to me," she murmured, winking at me.

I didn't want to take sides, so I pretended not to notice the wink. Glancing down at my more casual attire, I said, "I probably should have worn a suit jacket."

"Want to borrow one?" Maxwell asked.

As finicky as he was, I was flattered he'd offer to loan me an article of his clothing. But I wasn't really a suit-wearing kind of guy. Not unless I had to go to court or church. "That's okay. I tend to get overheated inside restaurants."

Maxwell ran his gaze over me and then looked away. "I see."

There'd been definite heat in his glance, which gave me hope we truly would end up at my place. I moved to the door. "You have a good evening, Girdy. Say hi to Todd for me."

"Thanks, Sheriff. I will."

Maxwell said stiffly, "Uh, yeah, have a good night, Girdy."

Since I had my back to him, I allowed myself a smile at his obvious discomfort. Social graces weren't his thing, but I found it endearing he'd followed my lead. Once outside, I put my hand on the small of his back as we made our way to my car. I could feel tension in his spine. I really hoped he'd relax so we could enjoy our evening without too much awkwardness.

Of course, with Maxwell in the mix, there'd always be a smidge of awkwardness.

Chapter Three

Maxwell

Considering the name, I'd assumed Vinney's Italian Restaurant would have plastic chairs and disposable cutlery. But I was pleasantly surprised. The main dining room was painted a pale yellow, and a large mural of Venice adorned one wall. Each of the tables was bare, revealing smooth rosewood surfaces. There were candles flickering, and the warm light bounced merrily off the white china and blue cloth napkins. The word "elegant" came to mind, and that wasn't a word that usually married easily with Rainy Dale.

As the hostess led us to our table, I was exquisitely aware of Royce's warm hand pressing the small of my back. It was nice of him to take me out to dinner, but my baser side almost wished we'd skipped the meal and just gone back to his house to fuck. Seeing him after a two-day absence had me hungering for a little private time.

Once seated, he smiled at me, and my pulse fluttered. He really was strikingly handsome. The candles cast golden light over his angular features, and his brown eyes glittered warmly. I sometimes had to pinch myself that I'd been lucky enough to find a man like Royce in Rainy Dale. I shuddered to think what the past few months would have been like without him. Would I have run back to Los Angeles by now? Possibly.

I picked up my menu, and he did the same. We spent a few moments studying the pages, and then our waiter appeared. He was an older man, dressed in black pants, a white tuxedo shirt, and bow tie. His hair was silver and his face lined. He wore a practiced smile that didn't quite reach his eyes.

"I'm Roberto. May I bring you the wine list?" His expression was pleasant enough, but it slipped a bit when the busboy bumped into him while passing. He said something curtly in Italian, and the kid cringed.

Royce met my gaze. "Do you want wine?"

"I'm not sure." I didn't drink much, but the restaurant was so nice, ordering a club soda felt anticlimactic.

"It goes nicely with pasta," Royce nudged.

"We have an excellent house chianti, should you enjoy red wine." Roberto smiled at Royce. "Do you have any idea what entrée you'll be having? Perhaps then I could steer you more efficiently."

Squinting at the menu, Royce looked very serious. "I'm a pretty big meat eater. I kind of have my eyes on the lamb chops."

I shuddered, and Roberto noticed. He looked down his nose at me. "You don't eat meat?"

"I don't eat baby animals."

Grimacing, Royce said, "Now I feel awful. Maybe I'll just have the pumpkin ravioli."

Surprised he'd changed his order based solely off my comment, I felt guilty. "Royce, have whatever you want. I didn't mean to ruin your meal. If… if you enjoy consuming… baby things… that's none of my concern."

Looking queasy, Royce laughed. "'Baby things' sounds even worse. I'm definitely having the pumpkin ravioli."

"As you wish." Roberto scribbled on his order pad, giving me a scathing look under his brow.

I suspected his displeasure was probably because the lamb chops were fifty dollars and the pumpkin ravioli twenty-four. The more we spent, the bigger his tip. But he could glare at me all he wanted; I felt warm and fuzzy knowing Royce cared so much about what I thought.

Roberto turned to me. "And for you, sir? Perhaps the Italian nachos? Or mozzarella sticks?"

I frowned at his implication I had the palate of a toddler. "As delightful as that sounds, Roberto, I think I'll have the beet pappardelle."

Roberto arched one gray brow. "How wonderful. One of our very finest vegetarian delights." He returned his gaze to Royce. "Have you decided yet on the wine?"

Royce grinned at me. "Let's splurge a little, Max. What do you say?"

I couldn't deny him when he grinned at me like that, and I found myself nodding agreeably.

Handing his menu to Roberto, Royce said, "Bring us your best chianti."

"Very good, sir."

Roberto looked a bit happier as he wandered away, which made me worried about the price of the wine. But Royce was in such a good mood, I decided to go along with his happy energy. If the bill was too much, I'd pitch in. Not that Royce would want me to. He was very touchy about me inferring he didn't make much money. But of course he didn't. Rainy Dale was a tiny city, and there was no way he was making top dollar policing these loons.

"Thanks for the dinner invite." I fiddled with the cloth napkin in my lap. "I know you're very busy right now." Hopefully I didn't sound accusing. I wasn't trying to imply he owed me his time.

"Yeah, sorry I haven't called in a few days."

I winced. "No. It's fine. I understand. Your murder investigation has to come first."

"Unfortunately, that's true." He smiled at Roberto when the waiter returned with the wine. The older man went through the motions of opening the bottle, pouring a taste for Royce, and then filling our glasses. Once he'd left, Royce continued. "I don't think I've ever had a case with so many possible suspects present at the murder scene."

"Any good leads?"

He sipped his wine and then leaned back in his chair. His gaze was serious. "Too many."

"Better too many than too few."

"You'd think so." He laughed gruffly. "That reminds me, I need to bring you in for questioning."

"Okay. Whenever is fine."

"I should have brought you in already. My deputies keep suggesting your name, ever so politely."

I frowned. "I was with you. I couldn't have killed Bob unless you were in on it."

"They're not thinking it through. They just don't want me playing favorites."

"I'm sure there are other people you haven't spoken with yet. It's only been two days."

"There are plenty I haven't spoken with yet, but I have them scheduled."

"Oh." I shrugged. "Well, I'm at your disposal. Just tell me where and when."

His lips twitched. "Thank you for your cooperation, Dr. Thornton."

"But of course, Sheriff." I picked up my wine and took a sip. The tart flavor burst over my tongue, and I nodded. "Mmmm. This is a nice wine."

"It is."

I swirled the burgundy wine, examining it in the glass. "I've missed going out to nice restaurants. I hadn't really realized it until tonight." I glanced up in time to see worry flutter through his gaze.

"I can imagine," he said quietly.

"Not that I expect to be wined and dined all the time." Was he worried he couldn't afford me? I certainly didn't want to put that thought in his head. He was the one pleasant thing in this town. I'd go insane if he dumped me, simply because I'd said the wrong thing. "It's nice every now and then, but not something I'd want to do all the time."

"Yeah."

"I didn't go out that much in Los Angeles."

His gaze flickered. "Enough to miss doing it."

"I mostly worked. All the time." I laughed awkwardly. "To be honest, eating out is a hassle."

He frowned.

"I mean, I'm enjoying it *tonight*, of course." God, I was making it weird.

Thankfully, Roberto arrived with our salad and soup. "Cream of broccoli soup, and the dressing on the salad is our own homemade vinaigrette. Enjoy."

"Appreciate it." Royce smiled up at him.

"My pleasure," Roberto said, moving away to help another table.

Hoping I hadn't accidentally ruined the evening, I tried to think of a way to let Royce know how much I enjoyed his company. But everything I thought to say was too much or not enough. I was horrible at reassuring people and rarely bothered. But the idea of Royce giving up on me was too depressing not to at least try.

I cleared my throat. "I was… very… happy when you called me today."

He looked pleased. "Were you?"

"Most definitely."

His lips curved in a smile. "I'm glad. It had been way too long since we saw each other."

"I agree."

He studied me and then picked up his spoon. "This soup sure looks good."

Nodding, I tasted the soup. "It's delicious."

He dipped his spoon into the creamy soup and took a bite. "I've never enjoyed broccoli more."

From his warm smile, I gathered I hadn't destroyed the evening after all. I let out a sigh of relief, and we ate in comfortable silence for a while. I couldn't help casting glances toward Royce every few minutes. His serene demeanor was a great source of curiosity for me. Few things got him angry, and I admired that about him. Maybe it was the wine, but I felt relaxed and willing to be more open with him tonight.

"I like it here because of you. Not this restaurant, but I mean Rainy Dale."

He looked up, surprised. "Really?"

"Yes. I didn't think I would." I frowned. "In fact, the first month I had to try very hard not to purchase a one-way ticket back to Los Angeles."

His cheek twitched. "To be honest, that doesn't surprise me."

"No. I wouldn't think so. I'm not always… tactful when I don't like something."

He shrugged. "You're better these days."

I laughed stiffly. "Better perhaps, but still way off the mark of normal."

"Normal is overrated."

I studied him. "I've never had… friends before."

He wrinkled his brow. "Never?"

"No," I murmured. "I've had work colleagues, but no one who I felt actually… liked me."

"I like you," he said softly.

"I know." I frowned. "It's at once puzzling and amazing."

He tilted his head, his gaze assessing. "I'll admit you're prickly."

My face warmed. "I won't argue."

He grinned. "You're like an artichoke."

I raised my brows. "Am I?"

His smile widened. "Yeah. Hard to eat, but worth all the work. Once you get past all the sharp parts, there's a tender heart inside."

I couldn't help but laugh. "Can't say anyone has ever described me that way before."

"And probably never will again."

"We can only hope. I get what you were going for, Sheriff." I smirked. "But the imagery was a little clunky."

He chuckled. "I stand by my work."

I sighed and said quietly, "I… I suppose what I'm trying to say is, you might be my first real friend."

"Is that right?"

"I believe so." I appreciated that he didn't argue or try to say that was impossible. I suppose he knew me well enough by now to know it was entirely possible. Maybe even probable.

"That means the world to me, Max," he said softly.

"Does it?" I asked hopefully.

"Yep. Makes me happy."

I slumped. "Okay, good. That was my goal."

He laughed.

"Of course, I meant it too."

He bit his lower lip. "Just so you know, I'm really hoping you come home with me tonight."

A thrill shot through me at the heat in his eyes. "Is that right?"

"Yep. I don't want any awkwardness with you trying to figure out what I want, so I figured, I'd just flat out tell you what I want."

I swallowed hard. "The direct approach. I like it."

"So you're game?"

Happiness rippled through me, and I nodded. "I'm definitely game."

"Excellent." He lowered his gaze and went back to eating.

I watched him under my lashes, acknowledging Royce made me feel safe. He had a sturdiness about him. He was honorable and dependable. He didn't play games with people. If he told you something, it was the truth. You didn't have to guess or read between the lines. I'd never been involved with anyone like him. He was the very definition of a *good* man.

I had no idea why he seemed taken with me. But he was. The more I got to know him, the more I wanted him to respect me. I wasn't really sure what to do about him. I liked him a lot but had no idea where we were headed. On the one hand that was exciting, and on the other terrifying.

****

As feared, the meal was ridiculously expensive. I was sure it was all because of that damn bottle of wine.

But Royce refused to let me pitch in. I tried to convince him, but when he eventually got a certain ornery look in his eyes, I knew better than to keep pushing.

When we got to his house, we spent a little time playing with Grumpy and letting him outside to do his business. I was buzzed from the wine, and it seemed Royce was too. Every time he looked at me, I could almost feel the heat on my skin. We occasionally traded off who topped, but tonight, I *wanted* to bottom. I wanted to give up all my power to Royce.

Once Grumpy was snoring in his crate, Royce led me to his bedroom. He had the lamp on beside the bed, and we undressed wordlessly. I got on the bed, feeling breathless. His gaze never left me as he grabbed the condom and lube. The mattress bounced as he joined me, and I reached out to him. He smoothed his calloused hand over my stomach, and I sighed contentedly.

"Thought about you a lot the last few days," he drawled.

I liked the idea of that, although I wasn't sure how to respond. Royce was the kind of man who liked to form bonds with people. I still found that difficult. As much as I wanted to keep seeing Royce, I wasn't positive I had it in me to fully give myself to someone. Submitting my body to him was one thing, but my heart? I wasn't sure I had that kind of courage.

He didn't seem to need me to say anything though; he just kissed me. He slipped his tongue in my mouth, and the kisses became more demanding. Needy. I loved his lips; they were full but firm. His cologne was nice too, not super heavy like a lot of macho guys wore. The thing about Royce was, he was tough without having to announce it. To me, that was what a real man was like.

We hadn't discussed who'd be on top, but he seemed to read me right. He gently rolled me onto my back, and I parted my thighs in invitation. He held my gaze, his glittering with hunger. Then his weight was on me, pressing me into the mattress. We kissed more, writhing against each other, seeking friction. I tangled my fingers in his hair, enjoying the silky slide of the strands against my skin.

I hooked my leg around his hip, and we ground our erections together. I gasped when he suckled one of my nipples and arched into him. In Los Angeles, I'd been really selective about who I let inside me. I preferred to top, enjoying the control. Two guys fucking was different than a guy and a girl. Or so I'd been told. Often, when you had two aggressive males, they grappled for dominance. Royce wasn't like that. His calm energy made me eager to give myself to him. I knew he'd take care of me because he wasn't on a power trip. In bed or out.

He trailed hot kisses down my throat, moving back upward to claim my lips again. I moaned into his mouth, our kisses gradually increasing in desperation. He teased and suckled my tongue, flexing his hips and giving a chest-deep groan. He nudged my thighs apart and grabbed the lube. He slathered his fingers and slipped them between my legs, seeking that tender spot. With sure and gentle strokes, he relaxed the muscles of my entrance and coaxed my need.

"Yeah," I whispered.

"You like that?" His gaze was focused, his touch a mere caress.

I nodded, finding it difficult to speak. I didn't always like verbalizing what I wanted or needed in bed.

Especially when I bottomed. Luckily Royce seemed to know. When he slipped two slick fingers inside me, I cried out, holding his watchful gaze. As he slowly moved his fingers deeper and deeper, heat flushed all through me. No one had ever watched me during sex the way Royce did. It was as if he was fascinated with my every expression or sound.

"Fuck me," I whispered.

He lowered his head. "What'd you say, Max?"

Moaning, I rode his fingers. "Please," I whimpered.

His cheek curved in a smile, and he pulled his fingers from me. He sat up, slipped the condom on, and lowered himself on top of me again. I wound my arms around his waist, loving how holding him made me feel anchored.

What would it be like to belong to a man like Royce? He'd be protective, that was obvious. He was already that way, and what we had was so casual. If he believed you were his, there was probably nothing he wouldn't do for you. I'd never had that kind of love with anyone in my life. Not from lovers. Not from family. I hadn't been first for anyone ever, and I hadn't really even noticed until now.

He pushed inside me, and I hissed at the delicious pressure of being stretched and filled. The slow slide of his dick in me tugged groans from my tight chest. Somehow he invaded me and still set me free.

"Jesus," he rasped, thrusting forcefully. "*Fuck* that feels good."

Our mouths joined in hot, hungry kisses once more. As corny as it seemed, sex with Royce wasn't just a physical act. It was so much more. With every whisper and breath, it was as if we bonded tighter and tighter emotionally. I craved that intimacy with him, even as I dreaded it.

The bed creaked as our movements became more achingly frantic. His hands held my hips in place as he pounded into me, and whether he left bruises or not, I didn't care. I slipped my hand between our sliding bodies, squeezing my dick. His shoulders were bunched, and sweat gleamed on his forehead.

"I'm close," I wheezed, meeting his thrusts.

Our eyes met, his glittering salaciously. My balls tingled and swelled as I moved my hand faster. Any minute. Any minute I'd feel that delicious release I craved. It was obvious Royce was about to unravel too. His eyes were glazed, his movements becoming disjointed. I was teetering on the edge, and when he froze, all the muscles of his chest and neck distended, I knew he was a goner. His dick jerked inside me, and that was all it took to send me off the cliff too.

My body quaked around his shaft, and my cock spilled between us. He thrust through his climax, grunting and gritting his teeth. My body trembled with pleasure, the glide of his cock sending shock waves through me. Once he was satiated, he groaned, lowering his body onto me.

I loved the weight of him on top of me, but it did make breathing difficult. He must have noticed me struggling for air, because he pulled out and rolled off me. His stomach moved up and down as he lay on his back. I liked the way he kept one hand on my thigh, as if he wasn't done with me yet.

My muscles were warm and loose, and I sighed. "That was extra nice tonight."

"Very nice."

"I feel so relaxed. Who needs yoga when sex exists?"

He smirked. "Who needs yoga either way?"

I gave a gruff laugh. "You're not a fan?"

"I shouldn't put it down. I've never tried it." He grimaced. "We had a city girl move here once. She was gung ho to open a yoga studio. She only lasted two months."

"Really?"

"Yeah. I felt bad for her. But the folks of Rainy Dale just didn't take to it."

"What happened to the girl?"

"She moved back to Houston. I don't think small-town life agreed with her."

I didn't bother saying I felt her pain. "Maybe she should have tried teaching goat yoga. She might have had more luck with the people of Rainy Dale, if farm animals were involved." I chuffed.

He raised his head, squinting. "Come again?"

"Goat yoga. You've never heard of it?"

"You're yanking my chain, right?"

"No. It's a thing."

He sat up on one elbow, staring down at me. "How would you get a goat to do yoga?"

I rolled my eyes. "The goats don't do the yoga, the people do. The goats jump up on the backs of the people doing yoga."

"But… *why*?" Royce looked bewildered.

"Apparently it's very soothing."

He scowled. "It's soothing to have goats jump on you? In what world is that true?"

"Don't shoot the messenger."

"You LA people are screwy."

I scowled. "Hey, goat yoga was started in Oregon. Don't bash LA."

He laid down with a grunt. "Now I've heard everything."

He sounded so disconcerted, I had to squash my laugh. He handed me some tissues, and I cleaned off my stomach. Then I lay down and closed my eyes, enjoying how slack my muscles were. I wasn't sure if I should get up and go home or if he wanted me to spend the night. I didn't always spend the night after sex and didn't want to assume anything.

The mattress bounced when he rolled to face me. I opened my eyes and found him watching me. His expression was gentle. Affectionate. It made my heart tug with emotions I was afraid to examine.

"Would my new best friend want to spend the night with me?"

I blinked at him. "Is that what you want?"

"You know I do." He gave a sleepy smile. "I sure like waking up with you, Max."

"Probably because you don't do it very often."

A line appeared between his brows. "Nah. You know I like your company."

"If I want to go home, you won't hold a grudge?"

"Of course not."

"Even though you have to drive me?"

He sat up. "You want to go home, Max? I have no problem with that. Whatever makes you most comfortable."

I watched him closely, trying to see if there was any hint of resentment in his brown gaze, but there wasn't. He looked earnestly concerned for my feelings.

"Should I get dressed?" he asked. "You really want to go?"

I grimaced, feeling stupid for questioning him. He'd asked me to spend the night, not marry him. I was acting so weird, he probably regretted his offer. "I'll stay."

He smiled. "Good." He lay down again and patted his chest. "Come here."

I scooted toward him, resting my head on his smooth chest. His heart thumped steadily beneath my ear, and his strong arms wrapped around me. "Don't worry. I won't stay every time," I said.

"I'm not worried." His voice rumbled. After a few moments, he added, "I'm gonna say this because I feel like you need to hear it: I mean it when I say I like waking up with you, Max. You don't ever need to worry about overstaying your welcome, okay?"

I squeezed my eyes closed because he'd seen through me. I waited for the embarrassment to descend, but it didn't come. Maybe because he wasn't judging me? He was only concerned with reassuring me. "Okay."

"If I invite you home with me, just assume I expect you to stay. That way there won't be any awkwardness. But if you decide you want to go home, just tell me. It's no big deal."

"Except for when I make it one," I mumbled.

He sighed, his arms tightening. "Don't overthink things. Just go with the flow, Max."

Just go with the flow, Max.

Little did he know, those six words were the biggest challenge of all.

Chapter Four

Royce

I enjoyed my morning with Maxwell, especially the shower we took together. By the time I dropped Maxwell off at his office, I was in a great mood. Even Maxwell seemed cheerful. I hoped the things I'd said to him last night reassured him. I hated it when he got in his head too much, because he always tried to push me away.

When I arrived at the station, one of my deputies approached. "Larry Stephanopoulos is in interview room two," Deputy Juan said. He held a paper cup out to me. "Figured you'd need this."

I took the cup, nodding. "Yeah. Good call. Thank you."

"Of course." He gestured with his head toward the interview rooms. "You want me to sit in?"

"Nah. Could you go see if the lab has any fingerprint results for us yet?"

He frowned. "Kind of early, boss."

"I know, but maybe we'll get lucky."

"I'll check." His expression said he already knew it was a waste of time.

"What's Larry Stephanopoulos's attitude like?" I asked.

Juan grimaced. "Well, he's not happy about being here, but he was polite enough."

"That's something." I held the cup of coffee up. "Thanks again, Juan."

"Yep." He smiled and headed down the hallway in the opposite direction.

There was a small group of people I really needed to interview, and Larry was one of them. While Penelope had invited around fifty people to her birthday party, many of them had been outside or never came in contact with Bob. That helped narrow down who I had to focus on. Even so, anyone with a personal or business connection to Bob needed my attention.

I opened the interview room door and found an older man in a suit and tie. His hair was jet-black, obviously from a bottle, and his eyes brilliant green. His smile was brittle, but at least he tried.

He rose and held out his hand. "Larry Stephanopoulos. Pleasure to meet you."

I shook his hand. "Sheriff Callum." I smiled and tossed my notepad on the table. "Appreciate you coming in to talk to me."

"Did I have a choice?" He gave a laugh as he took his seat.

"I'm sure you want to figure out who killed Bob as much as we do." I studied him. "After all, you used to be business partners."

"Of course I want to find his killer. No one wants a murderer on the loose." He shrugged. "But I haven't been Bob's business partner for years."

"That's a kind of heartless response."

"Is it?"

"Did you two have a falling-out, or was it simply a mutual parting of ways?" Rumor was they'd quarreled, but I wanted to hear it from his lips. Gossip had no place in police work.

His gaze flickered. "I had no ill will toward Bob."

I smiled. "Not what I asked."

"When in business, there are many stresses."

"It feels like you're avoiding my question."

He sighed. "Our parting was a bit… acrimonious."

"On whose side?"

"Both."

I nodded and picked up my pen. "What was the problem?"

"We had a difference of opinion on how to run things. That happens more often than you'd think with business partners."

"I'm sure it does." Again, I got the sense he was doing his best to not actually give me any info. "What exactly made your split acrimonious?"

"I'm afraid I can't really discuss that. I signed an NDA with Bob."

I frowned. "Is that right?"

"Yep. Sorry. Can't divulge any details." He looked smug, and he clasped his fingers across his chest. "The law is the law. You of all people must get that."

I studied him. "Yeah, I do."

His smug expression remained, and he made no effort to elaborate.

I cleared my throat. "Did this NDA have a termination clause?"

His cheek twitched. "I'm sorry?"

I almost laughed. He'd obviously written me off as a dumb hick cop who wouldn't know anything about NDAs. He was wrong. I was no expert, but I knew some stuff. "Did your NDA with Bob have a termination clause? Because, if it did, that NDA terminated when he died."

His face flushed. "Um… no… I don't believe it did."

"You sure?"

He avoided my gaze, seeming to find the bland gray walls fascinating. "Pretty sure."

"We can get a copy of the NDA. There's no point in lying. In fact, it would look pretty bad if you were lying to me. I'd have to wonder why."

Rubbing his chin, he met my gaze. "I don't like speaking ill of the dead."

"Meaning what?"

He leaned forward. "Is what we discuss in here confidential?"

"Unless it's a confession, I can usually keep sensitive information private."

"I don't want Penelope getting wind of what I'm about to tell you, okay? She's already lost her dad. There's no point in her suffering any more than she already has. For whatever reason, she thinks her dad was a saint. I can assure you, he wasn't."

"So, there's something in this NDA that would hurt her?"

He sat back. "It would ruin her idea of who Bob was. She revered him. She doesn't need to know all the bad stuff."

I narrowed my eyes. "When you say 'bad stuff,' are we talking illegal stuff?"

A muscle worked in his cheek. "Yes."

"You do realize NDAs aren't designed to protect people from crimes?"

He sighed. "I didn't commit a crime."

"But Bob did?"

Raking a hand through his black hair, he groaned. "Does all this shit really matter?"

"It does. I didn't know Bob Cunningham well. I'm trying to get a sense of who he was. What sort of a man he was. Maybe you killed him because of who he was."

He bugged his eyes. "I didn't kill Bob."

"Then tell me why you had an NDA with him. What was it hiding?"

Gritting his teeth, he said, "Bob was a crook. A blackmailer. He was a total asshole who didn't care about anyone but himself."

I flinched a bit from the resentment in his voice. "Sounds like you really didn't like him."

Scowling, he laughed harshly. "Of course I didn't."

"Why?"

"That bastard embezzled millions of dollars from our company." Veins bulged in his neck. "And when I caught him, instead of falling on his knees, the son of a bitch threatened to tell my wife—"

"Tell your wife what?"

He exhaled roughly. "He threatened to tell her about an affair I had." His face twisted with pain. "I fucked up one time! Just one damn time, but that asshole knew about it."

"And he was going to tell your wife?" That sounded like a motive for murder to me.

"He said if I told anyone about the money, he'd go straight to Genie." He winced. "I love her. Yes, I screwed up. It was a moment of weakness, and we'd been fighting." He shook his head. "It doesn't even matter. The point is, she'd leave me if she knew. I know she would."

He sounded so distraught, it was hard not to feel pity for him. "So he made you sign an NDA about his theft?"

"Yeah. Not only that, the fucker forced me to sell my half of the company to him. Said he didn't want me around anymore because I couldn't be trusted. *I* couldn't be trusted?" His voice was thunderous. "I couldn't believe the nerve of the guy."

"But you went along with his demands?"

"I did." He slumped. "I went along with it because I love my wife. I couldn't lose her."

If he loved her so much, I wasn't sure why he'd fucked around on her, but that wasn't really my business. "So you dissolved your working relationship?"

"Yeah. Just as well. I couldn't look at the fucker. I wanted to kill him." He cringed. "I didn't though. I swear, I didn't kill him."

I studied him, not quite sure I believed him.

"Look, if I'd wanted him dead, I'd have done it ages ago, right? This all happened three years ago. I'd have just offed him back then. Why would I wait and then murder him at a party packed with eyewitnesses?"

He had a point. "Did you talk to him the day of the party?"

He shook his head. "No. I avoided him like the plague." He looked hopeful. "Ask Genie, she was with me. She can vouch for me that I didn't talk to Bob."

He seemed sincere, but I felt like he was hiding something. It was just something about the way he couldn't hold my gaze over a few seconds. "I will talk to her."

"I believe Penelope was there as well. If memory serves."

"Okay. I'll have a word with her too."

He nodded. "Okay, but promise you won't mention the affair to Genie?"

"I don't see any need to mention it. Not if you're being straight with me."

"I am. I'm telling you the God's honest truth about what went down with Bob and me."

I pushed my pad of paper and pen toward him. "Write down everything you just told me. Every detail. And sign it."

"Okay." He picked up the pen with trembling fingers and began writing.

I stood, scraping back my chair. "I'll be back in a minute." I moved to the door.

"Sheriff," he called out, sounding anxious.

Glancing back at him, I met his gaze.

"I swear I love my wife. People fuck up sometimes, right? Haven't you ever fucked up?"

I grimaced. "Of course." I'd never cheated on anyone, but I wasn't perfect. No point in pretending I was.

"I didn't kill Bob. I'm not a murderer. Maybe I'm not the best husband in the world, but I'm no killer."

Still not a hundred percent sure I believed him, I left the room. Juan was coming down the hallway as I exited the interview room. "Any news from the lab?" I asked.

He winced. "No. Sorry, boss. They said it would be a few more days at least."

"Damn." I realized the odds of finding a print on the hatpin were slim, but if by chance there was a useable print, I could solve this case quicker. I needed some type of DNA or something to tie someone to the murder. There were too many suspects right now, and I needed to narrow it down some. "We need to figure out where that hatpin came from. Penelope hadn't ever seen it before, so it wasn't hers."

"Huh."

"Why don't you make some copies of the photos forensics took of the pin? It's possible one of the shops around here sold it. It looked like an antique."

"I'll make those copies."

"If we can figure out whose pin it is, that would at least give us a trail to follow."

"Absolutely." He nodded. "By the way, Charity Bell and her husband are in interview room three." Juan glanced down the hall. "And they look nervous as hell."

"Yeah?" I perked up. "Can you keep an eye on Larry Stephanopoulos? He's filling out his statement. Let me know before he leaves. I want to read it over, make sure he didn't leave out any of the juicy details."

"You got it." Juan nodded and moved toward the room I'd left Larry in.

I finished my coffee and tossed the empty cup in the trash nearby. Then I made my way to the room Charity and Fred Bell were in. When I opened the door, they both seemed to jump guiltily. Juan was right—they looked ready to faint from nerves. I didn't know them well. I'd seen Charity perform around town at some of the bars and had a casual acquaintance with her. I'd spoken to Fred a few times as well, since he was never far away from Charity. He was known to be very protective of his young wife.

"Thanks for coming in," I said, pulling out the chair opposite them.

"Of course," Charity said. She was a very pretty woman in her thirties. Her hair was bleached blonde and cascaded down her shoulders. Her eyes were cornflower blue and her lips full. "This situation is just horrible. *Horrible*."

"That it is." I glanced at Fred Bell. "How are you, Fred?"

"Fine. Fine." Fred was much older than his wife and pushing sixty. His hair was white as snow, and he was a bit on the heavy side. He wore a blue-and-yellow Hawaiian shirt and a puka shell necklace. "I can't imagine why you need to talk to us, Sheriff. We didn't even talk to Bob the whole time we were at the party."

"I'm interviewing everyone who was there."

"Well, Charity was performing, and the stage was outside. No, we didn't talk to Bob the whole time." He shifted his gaze to his wife. "Did we, Sweet Pea?"

She swallowed. "Nope. I was performing, and the stage was outside."

They seemed a little rehearsed, and I decided to ask some questions to throw them off a bit. I'd already talked to Penelope about why she'd hired Charity, and I wanted to see if Charity would be honest about it. "So, Charity, any idea why Penelope hired you to perform at her party?"

She blinked at me. "Because I sing?"

I smiled. "Sure, but there are other bands in Rainy Dale. Why'd she hire you? From what I hear, you're pricier than some of the bands."

Fred scowled. "Penelope wanted her at the party because Charity is the best singer this side of the Rio Grande. Price wasn't a problem for Penelope."

I ignored him and addressed Charity. "Do you have a personal relationship with Penelope?"

"No." Her voice wobbled.

"People hire Charity all the time. She doesn't have to know them to be hired by them," Fred rumbled.

I gritted my teeth, hanging on to my patience. "It must have been exciting to be picked by the mayor of Rainy Dale to perform at her birthday party." I met Charity's gaze. "Especially if you had no personal connection with her."

"That's what hard work and talent will get you." Fred crossed his arms.

"Yeah. Hard work and talent," Charity repeated quietly.

"Did someone maybe put in a good word for you?" I asked. "Maybe you knew someone who knew Penelope? From what I hear, networking is the name of the game in the entertainment business."

Charity glanced at Fred, and he patted her leg. "No. Charity got that gig because she's one of the most popular singers in Rainy Dale."

"Is that right?"

"Yep." Fred's jaw clenched.

I cleared my throat. "Charity, I've spoken with Penelope about why she chose you. Did you know that?"

She shook her head, and the color seemed to drain from her cheeks.

"Now, I've heard you sing, and you sure do have a pretty voice." I smiled at her, but she still looked uneasy. "But we both know that it wasn't *just* talent that got you that gig, don't we?"

"What are you saying?" Fred bellowed. "Of course it was talent that got her hired."

I turned to Fred and gave him a hard look. "Fred, if you can't sit tight and let Charity answer the questions herself, I'm gonna have to ask you to leave."

"But," he sputtered. "You're confusing her."

"By asking her questions?" I frowned.

"Sure." He pulled a handkerchief from his back pocket, and he mopped his sweaty brow. "You're firing questions at her like a Gatling gun."

"I'm just doing what I always do. There's no other way to get the answers, Fred. Not unless I ask the questions."

"Well, I still say you're confusing her."

I turned to Charity. "Is he right? When I ask you to tell me the truth, does that confuse you?"

She glanced nervously at her husband. "It's okay, Fred. I think I should be honest with Sheriff Callum. I don't think he's trying to trick me."

"Now, honey. You don't know that."

"Of course she knows that," I rasped. "My job is to figure out why someone murdered Bob. I'm not looking to throw someone in jail if they're innocent."

Charity nodded, which I took as a good sign.

I blew out a breath, trying to let go of my irritation. "Now, let's try this again." I gave Fred a warning look. "Did someone put in a good word for you with Penelope and that's why she hired you?"

"Oh, God." Charity covered her face. "This is so humiliating."

Fred's face was flushed, and he looked a little nauseous.

"Bob put in a good word for you, didn't he, Charity? He asked his daughter to hire you for the party."

She dropped her hands, looking resigned. "Yes," she whispered.

"So, you had a personal relationship with Bob?"

Closing her eyes, she nodded.

Fred stood abruptly and glared at me. "Does this make you happy? Airing our marital troubles like this?"

I sighed. "No. Not in the least. But I have to know this stuff, Fred. I don't understand why you're having such a hard time grasping that. Again, if hearing this is too much for you, please step outside while I talk to your wife."

"Don't you have to interview me too?"

"I do. But I can do it separately, if that's easier on you."

He stared at me for a few moments, then slumped back down in the chair. "Go ahead and ask her your damn questions. The sooner we get this over with, the better."

Giving Fred a wary glance, I asked, "Just how close were you to Bob, Charity?"

"Not that close."

"Don't lie to me."

Her bottom lip trembled, and she clenched her fists. "He promised me he'd help me get my career going. All they want are kids these days, and it's hard to get noticed at my age."

"Okay. How exactly was he going to do that?"

"He said he knew people at Sony Music, in Nashville. He… he said he'd give them my demo."

"Why would he do that for you?" I figured I knew why, but I wanted her to tell me.

"He said… if I was real nice to him, then he'd be nice back."

My skin crawled at the picture of Bob propositioning her. "I see."

She looked up, her eyes glistening with tears. "I'm not a slut, Sheriff. I don't want you thinking I am. That was the only time I ever…" She winced.

"Damn lying bastard," hissed Fred. "He didn't know a soul at Sony Music. He was just trying to get my wife in bed."

Charity's face crumpled. "I just want to be famous, is that so bad?"

"Not at all." I grimaced.

"But Bob was lying. Once I… did stuff with him…" She looked like she had a bad taste in her mouth. "I asked him to follow through on his end of the bargain. That's when he told me the truth. He didn't have any connections at all over at Sony Music. Not even one."

Fred grunted, his eyes pinned on the table.

"I see."

"I couldn't believe my ears," she whispered. "He'd just made all that stuff up."

"I'm sorry he lied to you, Charity. Anyone who legitimately wants to help you wouldn't ask for... sexual favors in payment. I hope you know that now."

She nodded. "Yeah. But... he was a really good liar."

Whether he was a good liar or Charity was extremely gullible, I wasn't sure. Maybe a bit of both. "When you found out he'd lied, did you have an argument?"

"Well, of course," she said in a hushed voice. "I broke my... m... marriage vows just to get that chance, and the whole time he'd been lying to me." She started crying, and Fred patted her back.

"It's okay, honey. I forgave you long ago."

With a little hiccup of a sob, she moved to hug him. He wrapped his big arms around her and held her tight. I felt a bit embarrassed to be watching her meltdown, but we were in the middle of our interview. I couldn't very well call it quits because she was upset.

After a minute or two, Fred handed her his handkerchief, and she used it to wipe her face. Glancing up, she looked embarrassed. I smiled at her, hoping she'd understand I wasn't there to judge her. I just needed her statement of the facts.

Once she seemed calmer, I said, "Can you keep going? Or would you rather come back in tomorrow?"

She grimaced. "I'd rather get this over with."

"Yeah." Fred nodded. "Let's keep going."

I cleared my throat. "Okay, well, let's see, where were we?" I rubbed my chin. "If you and Bob argued, why did he put in a good word for you with Penelope?"

"Because I was so upset, I threatened to go to her about how he'd treated me." Charity scowled. "She's the mayor, after all; it doesn't look very good for her father to be seducing women with lies."

"No. I guess not." I turned my attention to Fred. He obviously knew about the affair. What better motive to murder someone than because they cheated with your spouse? "You must have been pretty angry with Bob."

His gaze flickered. "Of course I was."

Charity took his hand. "He didn't kill Bob. I know what you're trying to imply, but Fred isn't a violent man."

"Lots of nonviolent people turn that way when they catch their spouse sleeping around," I said quietly.

Fred curled his lip. "I didn't kill Bob, but I wish I had."

His cold voice sent a chill through me. "Is that right?"

"Yeah. He was a snake. I'm glad he's dead."

Charity gasped. "He doesn't mean that."

Yeah, he does.

"So were you lying when you said you didn't talk to Bob at the party?" I kept my voice even, making sure there was no accusation in my tone.

His face tensed. "I didn't talk to him."

I glanced at Charity. "How about you?"

She lifted one shoulder. "I just said hi. I had to act normal. Penelope would have thought it was weird that her dad put in a good word for me, but I was rude to him."

I doubted Penelope was paying that close of attention, but maybe I was wrong. "Did you speak to Bob where he was sitting most of the party? Or somewhere else?"

"Yes. On the patio."

"What time was that do you think?"

"I have no idea." She met Fred's gaze. "It was before my first set."

He nodded. "I remember, yeah. She went over to talk to him before you even got to the party, Sheriff. I saw you come in with that doctor fella. It caught my attention because I was surprised to see you with him."

His tone was derisive, and my face warmed. "Is that right?"

"Yeah. I thought you had better taste. The guy's a jerk."

Anger balled in my gut at his rude remark. I realized Maxwell had a contentious relationship with a lot of people in town, but I felt protective of him. "Feel free to keep your opinions to yourself."

"Why should I? He never does." Fred scowled.

Attempting to sound easygoing, I said, "Dr. Thornton isn't used to living in a small town. He's trying to adjust."

"And we're having to do the same. He's nothing like Dr. Pine. Dr. Pine was so accommodating, but Dr. Thornton, he's the opposite. Most people think he's an asshole." Fred smirked. "Since you were with him at the party, I guess you don't agree."

I gave a tense smile. "We're not here to talk about me."

"No." Fred's gaze was assessing. "I suppose that's true."

Charity watched us, looking uneasy. "Fred, leave Dr. Thornton alone. He's not so bad. I mean, not *all* the time."

Cringing inwardly, I said, "How about we get back to the reason you're here?"

"Sure." Charity nodded.

"Fine by me." Fred shrugged.

Leaning toward me, Charity's gaze was keen. "I was thinking, Sheriff, if I talked to Bob before my first set, well, he was alive when you got to the party, right? I… I couldn't have killed him."

"Yeah. Good point, Sweet Pea. See, Sheriff, she couldn't have done it." Fred frowned.

I didn't bother pointing out it was possible she'd spoken to Bob more than once. "What time was your first set? You never said."

"It was 1:00 p.m." Fred leaned back in his chair. "He was killed way after that."

Charity sighed. "I didn't even get to sing any of my new stuff because the party broke up."

I squinted at her heartless comment. "Neither one of you went anywhere near Bob, other than that one time?"

"Nope." Charity shook her head.

"Where were you both when Rita screamed?"

Fred pursed his lips. "I was working on the soundboard, and uh… Charity was behind the stage looking over her next set."

"That's right," she said, and they exchanged a glance.

I'd be sure to ask Penelope and anyone who'd been around Bob at the time of his death if they'd seen Charity talk to Bob more than once. I didn't get the feeling I could trust these two to tell me the whole truth.

I opened my folder that stored photos of the crime scene. Tugging out the photo of the hatpin, I held it out to them. "Have either of you ever seen this pin before?"

Charity inhaled sharply, and Fred gave her a stern look.

"No," Fred said quickly. "Never."

I focused on Charity because she looked sick. "What about you? Have you seen this pin?"

She swallowed hard. "It's just too horrible."

"Are you okay?" I asked softly. "You look upset, Charity."

"Of course she's upset, Sheriff." Fred's voice was harsh. "You're showing her the *murder* weapon." He put his arm around her. "That's why you're rattled, right, love?"

She stared at the photo as if it was a rattlesnake and nodded.

"You sure that's all it is?" I frowned.

Charity seemed to gather herself. "Sorry. It's just... seeing it up close, it's so awful."

"Hmmm." I studied her.

She forced a weak smile. "I'm sorry I'm being so dramatic. Please forgive me, Sheriff. I've never been a part of anything this ghastly. To think our little town could have some lunatic going around murdering people. Well, it just upsets me so much."

"Take a real good look, Charity. It's very important that if you have any information, you share it with me."

She glanced at Fred, and he turned to me. "Sorry we can't be more help. We've never seen that hatpin before."

Feeling frustrated, I set my pen down with a clatter. Charity winced, and Fred grunted. Charity's reaction to seeing the murder weapon could be good old-fashioned repulsion. But my instincts said it was more. However, I wasn't going to get anything more out of her today. Not with Fred hovering like a prison guard. So, I forced a smile and said calmly, "Okay, well, I think that's good enough for today."

Relief washed over both their faces.

"You mean, we can go?" she squeaked, looking wide-eyed.

"For now. I might call you back in though, if new information comes to light. Also, don't leave town."

Fred stood abruptly. "Come on, Charity. Let's go. You've got to get ready for your show at the Red Lantern tonight."

"Oh, that's right," she breathed, her eyes glittering with excitement.

It was obvious Fred had had enough of me for one day. He couldn't get out of there fast enough. I watched them move toward the door. There could be no denying Fred had hated Bob. He hadn't even tried to pretend he cared the other man was dead. Not that I blamed him for disliking Bob. What Bob had pulled with Charity had to be hard on his pride. I wondered how Charity had even found the time to sleep with Bob. I'd always thought Fred was attentive, to the point of smothering.

Charity paused at the door and glanced toward me. "Thank you for being patient with me, Sheriff."

"Of course. I'm not your enemy. I'm just trying to find Bob's killer."

"I know," she said softly.

Fred opened the door, and his wife slipped past him. I picked up my pad and just happened to glance up, meeting Fred's gaze. My stomach clenched as our eyes met because there was a hint of malice lurking there.

No doubt he resented me poking my nose in his marriage, but I was just doing my job. It was possible he had a more sinister reason for disliking my questions. If he had killed Bob, he wouldn't want me to figure that out. I didn't think Charity had killed Bob; she didn't seem the type to stab someone. But Fred... now he seemed the type to do whatever it took to protect what was his.

Chapter Five

Maxwell

The morning after my dinner with Royce, as I worked my way through appointments, there was a happy warmth nestled in my chest. Even though most of my patients were annoying as usual, I had a sense of serenity. It was all because of Royce, and there was no point in denying it. The way he'd looked at me this morning, when he'd kissed me goodbye, still stuck with me.

Unfortunately, he hadn't made plans to see me tonight, so I had to assume it might be another two days before we got together again. That was disappointing, but he was busy with his murder case. I needed to be understanding, difficult as it was.

I tried not to let the endless stream of annoying patients ruin my happy mood. But it was a definite struggle, and as the day wore on, my good humor began to slip. I was examining my last patient before the lunch break when things really careened downhill.

"I don't understand why your throat looks worse today than a week ago." I pulled the laryngeal mirror from Mrs. Miller's throat. "Did you get the prescription for amoxicillin filled?"

"Nah." Guilt fluttered through her eyes.

I blinked at her, trying to figure out if I'd heard her wrong. "No?"

"I didn't bother."

I blinked at her. "I'm sorry, you didn't bother?"

She shrugged.

"But… don't you want to get well?"

"Of course." She raised her unruly white brows. "Why wouldn't I want to get well?"

"If you do indeed want to heal, you must take the antibiotic I prescribed for you. It's not optional."

"The pills are too big."

"How would you know that if you didn't fill the prescription?"

"I've taken them in the past."

"Well, if you have an issue swallowing pills, I can prescribe you a liquid instead."

"I don't like taking medications, Doc." Mrs. Miller's chin had a stubborn jut. "That's the first thing all doctors suggest. The minute you say you have a little ol' sore throat, they try to pump you full of drugs."

"I'm not trying to pump you full of anything."

"You sure about that?" She narrowed her eyes. "You prescribed two things for me."

"One is a refill of your blood pressure medication. You requested that one." I scowled. "The other is the antibiotic to fight off the strep throat."

"Well, I must respectfully decline."

"But… you have strep throat." Her blank expression made me feel as if I was speaking into a black hole. "If left untreated, you could get kidney inflammation or rheumatic fever."

"I feel pretty good. I don't think I need that medicine."

"Mrs. Miller, I'm the doctor. I assure you, streptococcus is nothing to trifle with. Your throat looks much worse. It's very dangerous to let this go, especially at your advanced age."

She widened her eyes. "My *advanced* age?"

"Yes." I wrinkled my brow. "Surely you admit you're no spring chicken?"

Her mouth fell open, and she tugged her yellow knit sweater tighter. "Just how old do you think I am, Doc?"

Even as clueless as I was, I knew that was a very dangerous question. "I don't want to play guessing games with you, I'm simply trying to tell you that you must take the medicine. What's the point of coming here to see me if you have no intention of listening to my advice?"

"Never mind all that sidetracking. How old do you think I am?" Her gaze was piercing.

My face warmed. "I can just look at your chart. This is silly. Your age is irrelevant to the conversation."

"It wasn't a minute ago. You made a big point of my *advanced* age."

I swallowed hard. "You're taking me too literally." I tried to think of how to throw her off the scent. She was looking at me like a bloodhound who'd been given a whiff of an escaped convict's shoe.

She narrowed her eyes. "Tell you what, you guess how old you think I am, and I'll agree to take the amoxapine. Even if you're wrong."

I scowled. "*Amoxicillin*. Not amoxapine. That's an antidepressant." Although, seeing as amoxapine had some effects similar to those of major tranquilizers, maybe that wasn't such a bad idea.

"Do you think I'm a hundred or something?"

"Goodness, no."

She scowled. "Oh, I see, only ninety-nine and a half?"

I laughed awkwardly. "This is pointless." I moved to the sink and began to wash my hands. "I'm simply concerned about your health, like any doctor would be." Once I'd rinsed my hands, I grabbed a paper towel. I turned and almost fell over her because she'd crept up behind me. "What are you doing?"

"Trying to get a straight answer."

"No good will come of this."

She put her hands on her hips. "Are you saying that because you think I'm ancient?"

"No. I simply know that women are very touchy about their age."

"Well, you're the one who brought it up."

"Something I deeply, *deeply* regret." I tried to move around her, but she blocked my path.

"Come on, just take a wild guess." Her gaze was stubborn. "You must have a number in your head."

I sighed with frustration. Why couldn't she just drop it? "You really think this little game is a good idea?"

"The fact that you're so reticent to take a guess tells me you think I'm much older than I am."

Gritting my teeth, I said, "Fine. I'll take a guess." Everything in me said that was a horrible mistake, but it seemed the woman wouldn't let me move unless I capitulated to her demands. I'd simply use deductive reasoning and hopefully get close to the right number.

"You sure are taking a long time."

"I'm thinking." I studied her deeply lined face, taking in the thinning hair at her temples and crow's feet at the edges of her eyes. She had to be older than sixty, that was for sure. Her skin seemed rather dull, as if she'd never heard of using a facial mask to exfoliate dead skin cells away. I suspected I knew more about skin care than her.

"Well?" she growled. "How old do you think I am, Doc?"

"I'm narrowing in. Don't rush me." I was definitely wishing I'd paid more attention to her chart. "Um… let's see…"

Be smart. Aim low and then take ten years off.

Seeing as her hair was snow-white, and she had so many wrinkles, I felt safe guessing low eighties. But she didn't hobble around like someone that age might. She seemed rather spry. A number came to me, but just to be safe, I shaved off a chunk and settled on a lower number. "Seventy-eight?"

"*What*?" she screeched. "Are you insane?"

Since I'd been stupid enough to take a guess, I probably was. Wincing beneath her seething glare, I said, "I meant sixty-eight. I said the wrong number. Sixty-eight is what I meant to say."

Leaning toward me, she said through gritted teeth, "I'm fifty-nine!"

"Seriously?" I widened my eyes in obvious shock.

Her face was red as she sputtered, "You're the most horrible man I've ever met."

I'd sincerely thought my guess was generously low. But I'd screwed the pooch on that one. My heart sank because she looked on the verge of tears. As if people didn't dislike me enough in town, I'd now thrown fuel on the fire. She'd no doubt tell all of her friends and family what a monster I was. As worried as I was about my reputation taking more of a hit, I also felt horrible because she looked so wounded.

"This is why I didn't want to guess. I'm very bad at guessing ages." I searched my brain for someone who was older but still attractive. Problem was, I didn't really keep up with celebrities. But I'd seen a magazine in the waiting room this morning, touting older actresses. "You know… they say sixty is the new forty." I gave a weak smile.

"So what? You thought I was seventy-eight."

"No. Remember, that was the wrong number." I held out my hands. "I… I thought you were sixty-eight."

Her face twitched. "No wonder everyone hates you." She turned and strode toward the door, her little yellow sweater fluttering behind her.

Fuck.

As her hand touched the knob, I called out, "Mrs. Miller, wait!"

She glanced at me over her bony shoulder, and I hurried toward her.

When I reached her, I sighed. "Please take your medicine. I… I know you hate me and that I goofed up, okay? I didn't mean to hurt your feelings; I just do that a lot to people. All the time, really." I grimaced. "But I'm concerned for you. I don't want anything bad to happen to you."

Her gaze flickered.

"Please, I'm begging you. You can hate me all you want. But please, get that prescription filled. Your throat is really bad. Please start taking the pills *today*."

She blinked at me, looking a bit uneasy. "Fine."

"Really? You'll take the medicine?"

"I just said I would, didn't I?"

I slumped with relief. "Thank goodness."

"But I'm going to have my son drive me to Dallas from now on for my medical visits."

"I understand. I don't even blame you."

She left the room without another word. I leaned against the wall, staring up at the ceiling. I should never have been dumb enough to guess her age. What was wrong with me? Why had I given in to her? A normal person would have just ignored her nagging. Royce certainly would never have done something as stupid as guessing a woman's age.

I was a damn good doctor, but what good was that if I drove all my patients away? My private practice was going to fail if I didn't figure out a way to talk to people without alienating them. I couldn't get away with being a heartless clod in a little town like this. In Los Angeles, whether I was rude or not, my skills had been in demand because I'd been dealing with life-or-death surgeries. But here in Rainy Dale, I needed a completely different set of skills. Bedside manner, something I'd always scoffed at, was essential in a town this tiny. While I knew all of this logically, I didn't know how to magically fix my personality.

Feeling dejected, I opened the door and told Girdy I was ready for my next patient. Thankfully, the next three appointments were just routine exams. I did my best to seem attentive, but the whole time Mrs. Miller's wounded expression haunted me. When I'd first arrived in Rainy Dale, I hadn't ever felt bad about how I treated people. Mostly because I simply hadn't noticed their reaction to me. I noticed now though, and that was mostly Royce's and Girdy's fault.

When the lunch hour arrived, I sat behind my desk, feeling glum. I had no appetite. My cheerful mood from the morning had been snuffed out but good. When there was a knock on my office door, I groaned. Was it Girdy come to nag me about not eating?

"Come in," I said, grudgingly.

When Royce poked his head around the door, my mouth fell open. He grinned and came into the room, pulling off his hat. "I thought I'd surprise you with lunch." He had a bag of food in his other hand.

The joy I felt at seeing him was embarrassing. But I didn't have it in me to pretend I wasn't happy to see him. I stood and moved toward him. "Royce, you came to see me?"

He tossed his hat onto a chair behind me and slipped his arm around my waist. "Damn sure did, City Boy." Tugging me against him, he lowered his head and kissed me.

The comforting warmth of his mouth on mine did strange things to my heart. Royce was the one person in town who I knew liked me, just the way I was. I'd never thought twice about being accepted by someone. Probably because I never had been? But at the moment, after my disaster with Mrs. Miller, I craved acceptance.

He lifted his head, his eyes buzzing with hunger. "Food's gonna get cold if we're not careful."

I smoothed my hand down his shoulder, enjoying the hard bump of muscle. "I'm having the worst day."

He tossed the bag of food on my desk and frowned. "Yeah?"

I nodded.

"That's not good." He rested his arms on my shoulders and studied me. "What happened?"

I groaned. "I put my foot in my mouth."

His lips twitched. "So then, it's a day that ends in *Y*"?

I scowled. "It's not funny."

His smile faded. "You're really worked up. Tell me what happened, Max."

I leaned into him, pushing my forehead into his chest. "I hurt Mrs. Miller's feelings by telling her she's old."

"Uh-oh."

"I know."

"Why'd you go and do a thing like that?"

"She wanted me to guess her age."

When I glanced up, his expression was puzzled. "Seriously?"

"Yes." I winced. "It's a long story, but suffice to say, I blew it."

"*Is* she old?"

"Not as old as I thought." I sighed. "She doesn't even want me as her doctor anymore. She's going to have her son drive her to Dallas rather than ever see me again."

"Hmmm. She definitely sounds angry."

I frowned. "Why are you the only person who likes me? Is there something wrong with you?"

He laughed. "That comment is the kind of thing that gets you in trouble, Max."

Groaning, I pulled away. "I'm never going to make it in Rainy Dale. The way things are going, I'll be lucky if there are any people willing to see me."

I expected him to argue with me, but he didn't. Instead he perched on the edge of my desk and studied me. "Yeah, things can't go on the way they are."

"I know, but I have no idea what to do."

"The problem is, you have no filter, Max. You just say what you're thinking, and it gets you in hot water." He rubbed his jaw. "You need to figure out a way to listen but not necessarily respond."

"Huh?"

"Well, like if someone says something to you, before you respond, you should pause."

I held his gaze but didn't speak.

He frowned. "You don't agree?"

"I was pausing. You told me to pause."

He laughed. "Oh. I hadn't realized you were putting my advice in motion yet."

I sat in the chair usually reserved for the patients. "Why is it such a big deal to speak your mind? Shouldn't people want the truth?"

"Sometimes they do. Sometimes they don't."

"I must always get them on the 'don't' days."

He grabbed the bag of food he'd set on the desk. He pulled out a hamburger, a stack of napkins, and another sandwich. "I only have a half hour for lunch."

"Oh." I took the sandwich he handed me. Was he signaling he was bored with the conversation? Maybe he was tired of my problems. It was probably a strain dating me, seeing as everyone in town hated me.

"That's a mozzarella, tomato, and avocado sandwich." He bit into his burger, observing me.

"Thanks." I unwrapped the sandwich, my mouth watering at the scent of toasted bread and mozzarella. "I didn't mean to drag you into a therapy session for me." I took a bite of my food, sighing at how good it tasted.

"I have no problem talking with you, Max. I just need to eat while we do it." He took another big bite off his burger. His cheek bulged as he chewed, watching me with a thoughtful expression.

"I don't want to ruin your lunch, whining about my issues."

"You're not. I can multitask."

I laughed gruffly.

"Come on, talk to me," he coaxed.

I grimaced and pulled the chair closer to the desk. "I want to do better, but I feel pretty hopeless. I thought after three months I'd have less people angry with me. Lately, it feels like there are more." I sat again and put my feet up on the desk. I took small bites of my sandwich, impressed with how quickly he wolfed down his hamburger.

He wiped his face with a paper napkin and then went back to studying me with that same thoughtful expression. "Maybe it's no big deal whether you fit in or not."

I frowned. "How so?"

He shrugged. "I doubt you plan on staying here forever."

I wasn't sure how to respond, since I had no idea what the future held. I'd invested a lot of time and money into my private practice. Then there was the matter of my feelings for Royce. While I couldn't picture living in Rainy Dale until my last dying breath, I also didn't want to stop seeing Royce just yet.

A muscle worked in his cheek. "I notice you're not arguing."

"I told you last night, I like it here because of you."

"True. That was a nice surprise."

It seemed like he wanted some kind of reassurance, but I couldn't make him promises. I wasn't at that point. Not that he was asking for promises. "I… I don't have any plans to leave. I don't have any plans to stay."

His face tensed. "Right. Fair enough."

"Are you mad at me now too?"

He gave a gruff laugh. "No. I'm not mad."

"Disappointed in me?"

He gave a sad little smile. "Not even a little."

I took another bite of my sandwich, mostly so I'd have something to do other than stare at him. I wanted to tell him how much he meant to me but didn't want to lead him on. I didn't know exactly what Royce would expect from me were I to stay here for an extended period of time. Would he want to live together? That made my stomach churn. He'd probably want to murder me after a week.

He cleared his throat. "Sorry, I pulled you off into the weeds." He stood and came closer. He knelt down on his haunches in front of me, and my fingers itched with the desire to touch his golden tendrils. His eyes were warm, and he patted my thigh. "Try the thinking before you speak thing. Sometimes it's better to say nothing than to say the wrong thing."

I nodded. "I'll do that."

He licked his lower lip, gaze pinned on my mouth. "I'd love to spend tonight with you. But I have so much work, I don't think I can."

"It's okay. I didn't expect to see you at all today."

"I appreciate how understanding you are."

I shrugged. "You're a cop. I get it."

He brightened suddenly. "Hey, wait a minute. I still need to interview you."

"Yes."

"How about I do that tonight?"

"Oh, sure."

"My last interview of the night is with Rita Bayes."

"Bob's girlfriend?" I frowned.

"Yep. I should be done with her by seven thirty. Come in then. You can give me your statement, and then we can hang out a bit in my office."

Pleasure rolled through me. "Yeah?"

"Why not?" He grimaced. "I'll still have tons of paperwork to finish up, but I can do that after you leave."

Excited at the prospect of seeing Royce tonight after all, I smiled. "I'll do that."

"Great." He stood. "I should get going."

"Thanks for lunch. It was nice surprise." I moved up to him and lifted my face for his kiss. He didn't disappoint, and his mouth captured mine hungrily. I was embarrassed when a needy whimper escaped me, but he didn't seem to mind.

Once the kiss ended, he clenched his jaw and headed toward the door. "See you tonight, Max."

"Yep." I turned to my desk so I didn't wave like a lovesick schoolboy. I heard the door close, and when I glanced over, he was gone.

Chapter Six

Royce

Once I left Max, I decided to do a little on-foot investigating. I needed to get more information about the hatpin used as a murder weapon. I had a strong feeling it had been purchased locally. It didn't look mass-produced; it looked like a handcrafted piece of art. I visited several of the gift shops on Main Street and made the Squeaky Wheel antique shop my last stop because it was closest to the station.

As I entered the Squeaky Wheel, I felt a punch of sadness. The store had been owned by Hanna Montgomery and her husband, until they got involved in a murder and theft plot a few months ago. Hanna had really gotten herself into a mess, trying to find the legendary missing gold of the outlaw Sam Bass. In the end, all she'd found was jail time and a whole lot of heartache. She'd ended up selling her business to a local woman, Susan Hollister, to help with legal fees. Susan was a retired teacher who didn't enjoy being retired.

Susan was stocking shelves a few feet away, and she glanced over. "Evening, Sheriff." She straightened, puffing as if short of breath. "I was just trying to get all this inventory put away before closing time."

"Oh, well, this won't take long."

"Sure, what do you need?" she asked, smoothing a hand over her salt-and-pepper bob.

"I had a question for you." I wandered over to her and tugged a photo of the Cloisonné hatpin out of my pocket. "I don't suppose you sold this pin to someone recently?"

Susan took the photo from me. "Hmmm, I definitely recognize this pin."

"Yeah?" I perked up.

"It's got such a distinctive pattern and beautiful craftsmanship." She gave a gruff laugh. "I only remember it because I'd had my eye on it myself, when I was just a customer of this shop. When I bought the store from Hanna, I was disappointed to see it had sold before I took ownership."

"Any idea who bought it?" I tried to keep my excitement out of my voice. I'd struck out at the other shops and had begun to think I was out of luck.

"Not off the top of my head," she murmured. "But I'm sure Hanna kept a record. She was a meticulous record keeper. I can look through the books and let you know?"

"That'd be great." For the first time since the murder, I felt like maybe I'd have a lead. "Should I just wait here while you look in the back?"

She grimaced. "Oh, I don't have the books here at the shop. Might take me a couple of days to find them."

"Really?" I frowned.

"Well, this pin was sold before I took ownership of the shop. I only have my records here."

"Oh, I see." I stamped down my frustration. Sometimes the world moved slower than I liked, but that wasn't her fault.

"All of Hanna's books are stored in my garage. Her office here was so crowded, I couldn't move. But I can dig the most recent sales records out when I get home tonight and get them to you tomorrow."

"That would be much better than a couple of days."

She smiled. "I sensed you're a little eager to get your hands on them."

My face warmed. "Is it that obvious?"

"I taught school a long time. I know disappointment when I see it."

I laughed. "It's just, this might be my first solid lead. If I can figure out who this hatpin belongs to, I'll finally be moving forward in my murder investigation."

She frowned. "So, the pin is part of your murder case?"

I was surprised she didn't know that. Surely the rumor mill was buzzing with details of Bob's murder. It wasn't every day a person was offed with a hatpin. "Unfortunately, it *was* the murder weapon."

She pressed her hand to her chest. "Oh, good Lord."

"I know. Shocking as heck."

"I… I most definitely will get that information for you, Sheriff. To think that such a thing of beauty could be used for something so heinous. Well, it just makes me sick to my stomach." She hugged herself. "I was horrified to hear about Bob's murder, but no one told me any details."

"That's surprising, especially around here. Gossip usually spreads like wildfire."

"Oh, of course, I heard about the murder, but I just didn't know about the murder weapon. The day Bob was killed, I was here in my shop, just minding my own business, but then Amy Nelson came in. She was white as a ghost, and she blurted out that Mayor Granger's father had been murdered. I just about fell over."

"I can imagine."

"But it was so upsetting to me, I purposely avoided reading more about the murder in the newspaper. It's too distressing. Makes me uneasy to think a murderer is running around loose."

"That's why I need to catch them. With your help, I'll be one step closer."

She shivered. "If they used that hatpin, that means the killer has been in my shop." She widened her eyes.

"Now, don't panic, Susan. Bob's death was most likely a crime of passion. I don't see a hatpin being the weapon of choice for a premeditated murder."

"No telling with a psychopath." She swallowed hard. "Rainy Dale sure does seem to have its fair share of crime lately. First Hanna goes kooky, and now this person who murdered Bob."

"I'm sure it's just a fluke. Rainy Dale is still a very safe place to live." I wanted to change the subject because she was scanning the shadows, as if a murderer was lurking. "Speaking of Hanna, have you talked to her lately?"

"Not recently. They transferred her to Bryan Federal Prison Camp. It's minimum security. Just so you know, she credits you speaking up for her, for her good fortune."

I grimaced. "I don't know that my opinion held weight, but I'm glad she's ended up in a minimum-security prison."

Susan gave a weak smile. "You're always so modest, Sheriff."

"Nah." Heat returned to my cheeks, and I turned away. "Well, I'll let you get back to work. I'll stop by tomorrow to take a look at that ledger, if that works for you?"

"Yep. Sounds good."

I let myself out of the shop and strolled down the sidewalk, feeling optimistic. Tucking the photo of the hatpin back in my jacket, I couldn't deny I was excited to think Susan might help me figure out who'd purchased the murder weapon. I'd been yearning for a concrete lead of some sort so I could stop chasing my tail. Investigations were simply a matter of hunting down tendrils of information, but they often fizzled out. For the first time since Bob's murder, I felt hope I'd be able to solve this crime.

I glanced at my watch and quickened my pace. I was interviewing Bob's girlfriend, Rita, in about an hour and was running a little late. I wanted to have time to read over some of the notes I'd made from my other interviews. So far, the only person I'd talked to, who I could see actually murdering Bob, was Fred Bell. I had no proof of a connection with him and the hatpin though. And I couldn't arrest him on a hunch.

I entered the station through the back door and ran into one of my deputies on his way out. "Hey, Sam." I smiled.

"Sheriff." He nodded, looking tired. "I'm heading out to Tom Murphy's house. Someone broke into his toolshed again."

"Is that right?" I frowned.

"Second time this month." He sighed.

"Huh. Did they take anything either time?"

"He doesn't think so."

"Then why break in? That's odd."

Sam shrugged. "Truth is, Tom's shed is a pigsty. I don't think he'd know if anything was missing or not."

I laughed. "It's probably just kids causing mischief."

"Yeah." He nodded. "By the way, there's a girl waiting to talk to you. Sorry, her name slips my mind. She's pacing around in the lobby."

"I'll see what she wants."

"Catch you later, Sheriff." He headed out into the station parking lot.

Once inside the building, I headed straight to the coffee. I had a long night ahead of me, and the caffeine helped keep me sharp. Once I had a cup of joe, I wandered to the lobby area. There was indeed a young girl standing near the front desk, staring into space. She looked familiar, but I couldn't quite place her.

"Can I help you?" I asked, and she jumped.

Pressing her hand to her chest, she laughed. "Sorry. My nerves are shot."

I smiled. "I'm Sheriff Callum. You wanted to speak to me?"

She nodded, grimacing. "Yes. I'm Patrice O'Malley." She watched me, as if expecting me to know her name. "I was Bob Cunningham's secretary."

"Of course. Now I remember." I didn't get the feeling it was a social call; there was too much tension in her features. "I thought you were coming in tomorrow."

"I was." Her gaze flitted toward the officer behind the desk. "Is there somewhere private we could talk?"

"Sure. Follow me." I led her to one of the interview rooms and had her sit across from me. She fidgeted in her chair, looking uneasy. She was pretty in a girl-next-door way: a perfectly straight nose, symmetrical features, wide brown eyes. She wasn't stunning, but something about her was quite appealing. She had the sort of looks that snuck up on you. "What can I do for you?"

Her brows knitted with worry. "I'm sorry to jump the gun like this. I couldn't really wait until tomorrow to talk to you."

"I'm happy to talk now." I leaned back in my chair, wishing I'd brought a notepad and pen. I instead opened the note app on my phone. I was too tired to hold all the information she might share in my head.

"I wanted to come forward the day of the murder, but Larry didn't want me to."

I frowned. "Larry?"

"Yes. Larry Stephanopoulos. I… I worked for him."

"I thought you worked for Bob Cunningham?"

She grimaced. "I worked for both of them. I… I was Bob's secretary, but Larry hired me too."

"Okay."

"Larry hired me to spy on Bob."

I raised my brows. "Is that right?"

She nodded. "Yes."

"What exactly did Larry want you to find out?"

She hesitated. "He wanted me to dig up some dirt. He wanted to make Bob pay for being a thief and a shyster."

"Whoa. That's quite a task to ask of you."

"Yeah." She gave an uneasy laugh.

Now it made sense why I'd felt Larry had been hiding something from me. He had been. He'd done his best to pretend his animosity toward Bob was in the past. Obviously, he'd lied. "Did you… dig stuff up?"

"Kind of? But it wasn't as easy as Larry thought it would be." She scowled. "It wasn't like Bob kept files labeled *People I've Scammed*."

"No. I don't suppose he would." I studied her, taking in her pink cheeks and the way she avoided my gaze. She seemed embarrassed about her part in Larry's plan. "You don't seem comfortable with doing what you did. Why'd you go along with Larry's scheme?"

"I wanted to help Larry. I've known him all my life. He was best friends with my dad, before he passed. If I wasn't so close to Larry, I'd never have agreed to do what I did." She winced. "I'm not proud of my part. But it was impossible to say no to Larry."

I narrowed my eyes. "When I interviewed Larry, he implied he'd put his issues with Bob behind him."

"He had, until this year. Larry and Bob tangled over a piece of property, and Bob won out. Larry became obsessed. He kept saying Bob wasn't going to get away with it this time. I think he truly had been trying to put things behind him, but Bob got him all riled up again."

"Riled up how?"

"Larry was determined to take Bob down." She sighed. "But he couldn't let Bob know what he was up to. He was too scared Bob would go straight to Genie and tell her about Larry's… one… indiscretion."

"So, you know about the affair Larry had?" That was interesting. Larry had given me the impression no one but Bob knew about that. Maybe Larry lied about a lot of things.

"I didn't know about the affair at first. But when Larry came to me, trying to get me to take a job working for Bob, he confessed. I'd never seen him so desperate. It really worried me, and I started fearing he'd do something bad to Bob if I didn't help him."

"How bad?"

She swallowed. "Really bad."

I pursed my lips, taking in the sad tilt of her mouth, as if pained at her own candor. "How did he know Bob would hire you?"

She shivered. "Bob loved having young girls working for him. He was a very… hands-on employer, if you get my drift."

"You were willing to put up with that for Larry?"

Her gaze darkened. "I was trying to avoid Larry getting himself arrested."

"I see. You really care about Larry."

She lowered her head. "I… I do. He's been like a second father to me all my life. When my dad died, Larry looked out for me and Mom. He was always there with advice and money."

"That was honorable of him."

"Yeah. That's the kind of man Larry is." She frowned. "That's why it would have been a tragedy if Bob told Genie about his affair. Larry's a good man. He goofed up, and he's guilty about it too. But he truly loves Genie."

"Okay." I nodded. "So… you had trouble digging up dirt on Bob?"

"I'm sure I'd have found stuff, but I only worked for Bob a few weeks. Larry was getting super impatient. I kept telling him I just needed more time, but he seemed like he'd bust if he couldn't get stuff on Bob immediately. I was really worried about him."

"I'm sure you were in a difficult position." She certainly seemed to have a lot of affection for Larry. I didn't get the feeling she wasn't here to hurt him. It appeared she was here out of concern for him.

She sniffed and tugged a tissue from her purse. "I feel like such a traitor telling you what I'm about to tell you, but I don't know what else to do." Her voice broke, and a tear rolled down her cheek.

"I'm sorry you're so upset. This is obviously hard for you."

"It is." She dabbed at her eyes. "It's torture."

"Well, why don't you take a deep breath. When you feel ready, I'm here to listen."

She blew her nose and nodded. "Okay."

"Perhaps you'll feel better once you get it off your chest."

Guilt glimmered in her brown eyes when she met my gaze. "Or will I feel like the worst person ever?"

"I think you want what's best for Larry. It sounds like he was spiraling out of control. You tried to help him. You're still trying to help him."

She nodded. "Yes. I… I am. He may not think so, but I really am trying to do what I think is best for him."

"I'm sure you are."

She sucked in a shaky breath and said, "I… I think Larry killed Bob."

I grunted in surprise. After all her assurances that she adored Larry, I was shocked at her accusation. But if she really felt that way, I needed to hear why. "You do?"

Wincing, she said, "Yes."

"I see. And you think he did that because he was still angry about what happened all those years ago?"

"Yeah. I think when he butted heads again with Bob over that real estate deal, it brought up all his pent-up rage." She met my gaze. "I think he snapped. I was too slow getting him the information he wanted, and he took matters into his own hands."

"You really believe that?"

"I do," she whispered.

"From what I understand, Bob had a lot of enemies. You probably know that if you worked for him."

"Yes."

"Then why do you think Larry's the one who killed him?"

She winced. "Larry was just *so* angry." Another tear dribbled down her pink cheek. "I mean, Larry absolutely hated Bob by the end. I feel sick telling you this stuff, but I can't just go on as if nothing happened. I love Larry like a father, but I can't turn a blind eye to murder, right? If Larry did this, he needs help. I want him to get that help."

"Did you *see* Larry stab Bob?" I asked quietly. If she was an eyewitness to the murder, now that was a game changer. But I had a sneaking suspicion she hadn't seen the murder at all. She was here because she'd worked herself up out of concern for Larry.

"No." She wiped at her eyes, smearing mascara. "But I wasn't around Bob very much at the party. I didn't dare stay around him because Rita was shooting dagger eyes at me the whole time. She's crazy jealous of Bob… or she… she was."

I nodded. "I've heard that from several people."

She twisted the tissue in her hands. "I mean, I can't really blame her for worrying Bob would cheat on her. He cheated all the time. He even hit on me constantly. He'd make all kinds of promises, but I saw enough of how he bamboozled everyone to know he couldn't be trusted. I wasn't about to fall for his lies."

"I'm glad you saw through him."

She grimaced, looking guilty. "I could clearly see he was a cad. I had to cover for Bob all the time. I felt bad lying to Rita, but what could I do? I hated working for Bob, but I needed to keep the job because Larry wanted information. I was between a rock and a hard place."

"Sure sounds like it," I said sympathetically.

She sighed. "What will happen to Larry? Will you arrest him?"

I frowned. "I don't believe so."

"No?" She looked surprised. "Why not?"

"Well, now, Patrice, I've talked to Larry, and he says he didn't even talk to Bob the whole night. Genie substantiated his story too."

She raised her brows. "Really?"

"Yep."

She wrinkled her brow. "Can you trust what Genie says? I mean, Larry is her husband. She'd want to protect him."

"She probably would, that's very true. But I didn't just take her word for it."

"No?"

I shook my head. "No, I also asked around to make sure Larry was telling me the truth. People can tell me any version of the truth they want when they come in here, but I don't just swallow it whole."

"Oh." She nodded. "Yeah, I guess you can't do that."

"Nope. I interview everyone, and eventually the picture becomes clearer and clearer. Larry said he didn't talk to Bob at the party, and Genie agreed. But more importantly, Penelope agreed."

"She did?" She frowned. "Huh."

"Genie might try and protect Larry, but Penelope wouldn't. There's no way she'd lie about Larry not talking to her father, if she suspected he killed him."

"That's probably very true."

I scowled. "I don't appreciate Larry withholding all of the information you just shared. But I don't think he lied because he's the murderer. I suspect he lied because he knew it would look really bad that he sent you in to spy on Bob."

She widened her eyes. "You… you really think Larry is innocent?"

I shrugged. "I can't say that for sure, but so far my investigation isn't leaning toward Larry being the killer. Of course, as new evidence comes to light, that could change."

She slumped, covering her face. "Oh, my gosh. I'm so relieved." Her voice was muffled by her hands.

I cleared my throat. "Well, I'm glad I could set your mind at ease."

She lowered her hands, obvious relief in her gaze. "I thought I was doing the right thing coming in here, but I felt horrible about it."

"You did do the right thing, Patrice. Larry never should have hidden his plan to spy on Bob from the police. That's just the kind of thing that makes us suspicious. But Penelope affirming she never saw Larry anywhere near Bob goes a long way."

"Thank goodness." She wiped roughly at her eyes. "I've been losing my mind over whether or not to come talk to you, Sheriff."

"I hope you now know I'm just searching for the truth. It does me no good to put the wrong person behind bars."

"Of course not." She gave a weak smile. "I feel better. Thank you for taking the time to talk to me."

"That's why I'm here." I stood, and she did the same. "I say go home and put all of this out of your mind. Let me worry about who the killer is, okay?"

"I will. I feel better already just knowing we have a man like you as our sheriff." She shivered. "It is creepy though, knowing there's someone out there who killed Bob. They're simply walking around as if they've done nothing wrong."

I nodded. "I know, but we'll get them."

"I hope so. I just want Rainy Dale to go back to how it was. Way too much violence lately. I hate to think our little town is changing. We've lived in a happy bubble for so long."

"I don't think we're changing much. Rainy Dale is still a wonderful place."

"I'll just have to trust you on that, Sheriff." She sighed and left the small room.

Her words caused uneasiness to coil in my gut, but I pushed it away. This murder wasn't connected to what had happened with Hanna and Ned Tinkerson. I was aggrieved that we'd had another murder so soon, but two murders didn't mean our town was being overrun by psychopaths. We'd enjoyed many years of no violence; it was inevitable that streak would end eventually. I couldn't let this case shake me to the core. I simply needed to put my head down and find the culprit. That was the best way to bring peace and security back to Rainy Dale.

When I reached my office, I took a moment to ring up the lab and hound them. Without any lab results, I was dead in the water. I had no forensic info at all. No DNA. No fingerprint evidence. No autopsy results. I felt like I was wearing a blindfold while trying to solve this case.

I especially wanted to see my toxicology report. I strongly suspected Bob had been drugged before the murder. Stabbing someone wasn't a quiet affair, but Bob hadn't made a peep. Penelope had said her father had dozed off at one point during the party. However, even in sleep, a person would probably react to a hatpin being jabbed through their chest. The fact Bob hadn't uttered even a moan convinced me he'd been drugged.

I glanced at my watch, double-checking the time. Rita would be here soon for her interview. I grabbed the witness statements I'd accrued and began to slowly work my way through them. Once my interview with Rita was over, I had Maxwell's visit to look forward to.

I sighed contentedly at the thought of seeing Max and continued to leaf through the statements.

Chapter Seven

Maxwell

Girdy shut the front door on the last patient of the day and turned to me with a groan. "Is it my imagination, or was today the most annoying group of patients we've ever had?"

I sniffed. "They always seem annoying to me."

She moved to her desk, shaking her head. "I was counting the seconds until the last person left. I have a splitting headache."

"Maybe it's caffeine withdrawal," I murmured, clearing off empty paper cups left on the magazine table. "The new coffee maker isn't as good as the old one."

"No. It's not a caffeine headache. It's an asshole overload headache."

I laughed, and she grinned.

"Please tell me tomorrow isn't as busy?" I winced, waiting for her response.

"Thank the Lord, no. I booked you a half day because I knew today would be torture."

Girdy was good about things like that. She was always careful to stagger Hell days around half days. She was very young but also extremely conscientious.

Maybe you should compliment her on that?

That was probably what a normal nice person would do. I was trying to be a better person, right? I should probably start with Girdy. She was, after all, the only other person in town besides Royce who seemed to halfway tolerate me.

I cleared my throat. "Thank you for doing that, Girdy. It's very thoughtful of you."

She looked up from stacking files, her eyes wide. "Come again?"

My face warmed. "You do little things like that for me all the time. I never think to thank you."

She blinked at me. "Do you have a fever, Doc?"

I scowled. "No. I'm simply paying you a compliment."

"Exactly."

I rolled my eyes. "If you're going to be this annoying each time, I won't bother."

"No. Please keep telling me how wonderful I am. I'll be good." She smirked.

I stood with my hands on my hips, perusing the waiting room area. "That's better. I don't understand why people can't toss their own empty cups away."

"I know. Or why they leave cookie crumbs all over the couch. Does any of it get in their mouths?"

"Well, the cookies were your idea. I certainly wouldn't have fed these people."

She sighed. "It creates goodwill."

"Ha. We both know it will take more than cookies to make these cretins love me."

"The goal isn't to get them to *love* you. We'll settle for tolerating you."

"Yes." I nodded. "I'd be happy with that."

Girdy studied me as she tugged on her coat. "Mrs. Miller sure left in a hurry today."

I winced. After lunch, I'd taken Royce's advice and done a lot of listening to my patients. I'd kept my opinions mostly to myself. Not counting the one major faux pas with Mrs. Miller, I believed I'd managed not to insult anyone else.

"She also didn't want to book another appointment." Girdy's gaze was curious. "Can I assume you put your foot in it with her?"

"I'd rather not talk about it."

"I see."

She moved to the front door, and I followed. "Are you escorting me?" she asked, laughing.

"No. I'm waiting for you to leave."

"I'm going. I'm going. You're certainly in a hurry to get rid of me tonight."

"I need to take a shower, and I'm running late." I hovered my fingers over the security system keypad.

She frowned. "You're arming the system?"

"I always do when I'm here alone."

"Oh, yeah." She frowned. "I don't blame you after all that happened with Ned Tinkerson." She opened the door and skipped down the steps, heading toward her boyfriend Todd's car. "I'll see you tomorrow, Doc. Try not to alienate anyone tonight."

"No worries. I'm seeing Royce. He understands me," I called after her.

She laughed and climbed into Todd's car. I watched them pull away and was annoyed when another car parked in their place. I didn't recognize the car or the blonde woman who climbed out of it. She walked up the cobblestone path, her face tense.

I was tempted to shut the door and pretend I hadn't seen her. But I knew that would go against my attempt at redeeming my reputation as an asshole. Stifling my irritation, I waited for her to reach me.

As she came up the steps, she noticed me hovering in the doorway. "Hello, Dr. Thornton." She brushed long strands of blonde hair from her face, batting her eyes at me. She carried herself with confidence, and I got the impression she was used to men falling at her feet. "I'm Charity Bell."

Her name was familiar, but I couldn't really place her. "I'm afraid the office is closed." Seeing as I was trying to turn over a new leaf, I did my best to sound polite. Even so, some irritation did slip into my voice.

She grimaced, but her eyes were imploring. "I know, but I have a teensy-weensy favor to ask."

I gritted my teeth. I'd never met a person yet who said that who didn't actually want a massive favor. "You knew the office was closed, but you still came?"

"Yes." She glanced around uneasily. "Is it possible we could go inside and talk?"

What part of "the office is closed" aren't you grasping?

Managing to keep my temper intact, I stepped aside. She brushed past me, and I closed the door behind us. The office was silent as we stared at each other. Finally, she cleared her throat. "I need you to give me an examination."

"Of course. I'd be happy to, during business hours."

She swallowed hard. "No, you don't understand. It's a miracle I got away from him long enough to come today."

"Him?"

"My husband. He's a bit… controlling."

I frowned. "Are you in trouble?"

"I think I am."

"Are you a victim of domestic abuse?" I asked, feeling alarmed.

"Oh, gosh, no. Nothing like that." She sighed. "I'm pretty sure I'm pregnant. But… my husband can't know about this."

I narrowed my eyes. "Why? If he's your husband?"

Her face flushed a rosy pink. "Because if I am with child, it isn't his."

I raised my brows. "Oh. I see."

She pushed her lip out, looking on the verge of tears. "I just need to know for sure."

"What makes you think you're pregnant?"

She touched her stomach. "My breasts are sore, and I feel queasy a lot. I haven't got my period, and I'm three weeks late."

"Oh, dear." I grimaced because it didn't take a detective to see she wasn't happy about the possible pregnancy. "You could have used an at-home test."

"I did. I used two of them."

I frowned. "Did the tests show you were pregnant?"

"Yes."

I bit my tongue so my natural surly response didn't escape. "Well, those tests are very accurate."

"So I've heard. But I won't be able to rest until I get it confirmed by a real doctor."

"I see." Curiosity overrode my irritation momentarily. "If your husband isn't the father, who is?"

"I'd rather not say," she whispered.

"Hmmm." I tapped my finger against my chin. "I suppose I can spare you a few minutes of my time. But I have somewhere to go, so we'll have to hurry."

"Oh, thank you so much, Doctor," she breathed.

I went around Girdy's desk and opened the drawer where she kept new patient forms. "How about you fill this out while I prepare the examination table?"

She grimaced. "I'd rather there was no record of my visit. If you don't mind." She opened her purse and pulled out her wallet. "I'll just pay cash for the exam."

Wrinkling my brow, I said, "This is highly unusual."

"I know. But I'm in desperate straits, Doc," she wailed. "If I am pregnant, I'll need an abortion ASAP."

"I'm afraid you'll have to go into Dallas for that. It's not my area of expertise."

"Really?" She looked disappointed. "God, that's going to be almost impossible. How the hell am I going to go to Dallas without Fred knowing?"

She looked so crestfallen, I wasn't sure what to say. Even if terminating pregnancies had been in my wheelhouse, had she seriously assumed I'd perform an abortion right now? She was obviously in a bind, but there were procedures that needed to be followed. I did feel a twinge of sympathy for her, but there wasn't much I could do to fix her problem.

I cleared my throat. "How about we figure out whether or not you're pregnant, before we start worrying about the rest?"

"Okay." She opened her wallet. "How much do I owe you for the examination?"

I grimaced. "Honestly, I have no idea. Girdy handles all the billing."

"Oh." She frowned, looking uncertain.

"Just put fifty dollars on the desk. I'm sure it's more than that, but Girdy can refund you if I'm wrong."

She widened her eyes. "Oh, heck no. You guys just keep the change. I don't want anyone sending me anything from your office."

"Right. Of course." I studied her. "You're sure you're not being abused?"

She sighed. "Nope. But poor Fred would lose his mind if he knew. There's no telling what he'd do… or might have *already* done."

Her cryptic statement made me hesitate. "Perhaps it would be best if you sat down with… er… Fred and told him the truth. You might be surprised at his reaction. If he loves you, I'm sure he'd understand."

She shook her head vigorously. "No. No. No. Fred would go insane. He'd feel emasculated because well, he can't… you know… get it up anymore. We haven't had sex in over a year, and he already forgave me for the affair."

I was getting way more information than I needed or wanted. I held up my hand. "Let's just check you over, okay? We'll go from there." I moved toward the examination room. "Follow me."

Once inside my office, I had her disrobe behind a screen. I had her put on a paper gown while I gathered a speculum, lube, and gloves. She came out from behind the barricade, looking nervous.

"Up on the table, please," I said brusquely, raising the stirrups at the end of the table.

She obeyed and got into the position I requested. I went about my internal and external examination swiftly. I did observe a softening of her cervix and other telltale signs of pregnancy, and once I'd finished, I pulled off my gloves and had her sit up.

"I'll take blood to be sure, but I do believe you're with child." I kept my tone emotionless. I didn't want her to think I was judging her.

"Oh, God." Her face crumpled, and she started crying.

Since she'd told me she was pregnant to begin with, I was shocked by her reaction. I patted her shoulder awkwardly, unsure of what to do. "Let me take some blood to be sure. Okay?" I hurried to the cupboard over the sink and grabbed what I'd need to draw blood.

"I just can't believe this. I mean, what horrible luck. I can't have a baby. That would definitely put a nail in the coffin of my singing career." She sniffed, tears dripping down her face. "This is a nightmare."

"It's not the end of the world." I worked quickly, sanitizing the injection site and inserting the needle into her arm. I carefully filled two vials of blood and labeled them. "I'm sure all will be fine."

"You don't know my husband."

"No, I don't. But if you're afraid of him…"

"I'm not afraid of him hurting *me*." She sighed. "I just need this problem to go away. Then everything can go back to normal."

"I see." I nodded and pulled the tourniquet off her arm. "I should have the blood results by tomorrow evening. I'll call you and let you know."

"No!" She sounded panicked. "I told you, I don't want any connection between me and your office. I'll call you—do *not* call me." She slid off the table. "Besides, I'm sure I'm already screwed. From the tests I took at home, my missing period, and the physical exam you gave me, I'm sure I'm doomed. Can you give me a referral to a doctor in Dallas who handles abortions?"

"Uh… yes. You don't want to wait for the blood test results?"

"I said I'd call you, but I still want the referral. The less contact we have, the better." She rushed behind the screen, and I heard the rustling of her clothes as she dressed. When she came out, her jaw had a determined jut. "I'll handle it from here, Doc. Can I have that referral?"

Frowning, I went to my desk and logged on to my laptop. "Are you sure you don't want to think about this a little? No need to make a decision immediately. You have time."

"That's easy for you to say."

I held my tongue and wrote down the name of the doctor I usually referred patients to who wanted to terminate their pregnancies. I stood and held out the slip of paper. "Good luck to you, Charity."

"Thanks." She narrowed her eyes. "Remember, Doc, no one can know about this. *Absolutely no one.*" She snatched the paper from my hand and glanced at her watch. "Shit. I'm gonna be late for my show if I don't hurry."

I watched her race out of the room, scratching my head. "What a loon."

I heard the front door slam shut, and I hung my white coat on a hook near the door. Thanks to Charity, I too was now running late. I strode to the examination table, wiping it off with disinfectant and replacing the paper. At one point, I thought I heard the floorboards in the waiting room creak. I stopped what I was doing and listened. I hadn't locked the front door yet. Had Charity returned for some reason? God, I hoped not. I'd had more than enough of her.

Crossing the space to the door, I slowly opened it wider. "Hello?" I called out. "Charity?"

Silence.

The sun was setting behind the hills, and the waiting room was cast in shadow. The hairs on the back of my neck rose, but I told myself I was being paranoid. This was an old building. It creaked all the time and I never thought twice about it. I forced myself to leave my office and step into the waiting room. Glancing down the hallway that led to the kitchen, I shivered at the pitch-black room.

I'm acting like an idiot. There's no one here but me.

Forcing myself to stop cowering, I strode across the room to Girdy's desk. I flipped on her lamp and scanned the area. It was empty. Of course it was. Letting out a shaky breath, I gave a self-conscious laugh. Charity's cloak-and-dagger behavior had rattled me. That was all.

Glancing at the time, I grimaced. I still needed to shower, and thanks to Charity, I now only had twenty minutes to do that. I made myself check the kitchen, just to be sure the downstairs was empty. I locked all the doors and windows and armed the security system. Then I headed upstairs to shower.

Giving in to my insecurities, I checked under the bed and in the closet. Once I was assured there were no intruders lurking, I stripped and got in the shower. As the hot water spilled over my head, my mind returned to Charity Bell. She was definitely a girl who knew what she wanted.

Not once had she shown any remorse about terminating the pregnancy. Of course, that was her choice, and I didn't care one way or the other what her decision would be. It was just unusual that the actual baby itself had never once seemed to cross her mind. Her only concern had been her career or her husband finding out.

I wondered who the father of her baby was. Maybe some young musician she'd dragged into a coat closet after a show? She seemed driven, but I had no idea if she was talented. She was very pretty but slightly older than what I assumed music executives were looking for. I didn't keep up with the music industry, but the few music videos I'd seen the last few years seemed to be dominated by twenty-year-olds.

Once I'd was showered, I dressed quickly and grabbed my wallet and keys. Hurrying down the stairs, I deactivated the alarm, stepped outside, and rearmed the security system. I skipped down the porch steps, noticing it was an inky black night, with only a half-moon to light my way. Here and there filmy silver clouds streaked the sky.

The walk into town wasn't long, but it seemed longer than usual tonight. Charity had set my nerves on edge, and it didn't calm me knowing there was a killer still at large. Maybe it *would* be a good idea to invest in a car. I could definitely afford it, and it would come in handy when I grocery shopped.

Sand crunched beneath my feet, and in the distance the yelp of coyotes split the night. Even in LA I'd occasionally seen coyotes running down my cul-de-sac. Back then, they'd seemed out of place, but out here in the desert, this was their turf. I shivered and picked up the pace. The lights of Main Street beckoned, and I had to restrain myself from sprinting. I was a grown-ass man. There was no boogieman chasing me, and I needed to calm the hell down.

When I reached the outskirts of Rainy Dale, I breathed a sigh of relief. Passing Golden Goose Realty, the first building as you entered the town, I noticed there seemed to be someone inside with a flashlight. That struck me as odd, but I was in a hurry, so I just kept walking. When I reached the police station, I entered through the front. There was a young girl in uniform sitting behind the desk, reading. She glanced up when I came in, her expression curious.

"I'm here to give my statement to Sheriff Callum."

She nodded and glanced down at a clipboard on the counter. "Go ahead and sign in, Dr. Thornton. Rita Bayes's interview is ahead of yours." She gestured to a woman who sat behind me on the tan vinyl couch. "Hope you don't mind waiting."

"It's fine."

I hadn't noticed the woman as I walked in, but now I recognized her as Bob Cunningham's girlfriend. At the birthday party, she'd looked agitated even before Bob had been murdered. I gave her a polite smile and settled on the far end of the couch. I tried not to think about who might have sat on the vinyl monstrosity before me. God willing, no bodily fluids of any sort had desecrated the surface.

The girl behind the desk went back to reading, and I stared up at the water-stained ceiling. Rita grabbed a magazine off the coffee table and rifled through it. With a loud sigh, she tossed it down and turned to me.

"I keep meaning to make an appointment with you," she said.

I glanced over. "Is that right?" Did she think I had my appointment book with me?

"Yep." She bit her bottom lip, her gaze assessing. "I remember seeing you at Penelope's party. You and the sheriff are a thing, I guess?"

I frowned. "A thing?"

"Yeah. You're lovers? You do the nasty?"

My face warmed, but I decided to take the high road. "I believe you were dating Bob Cunningham before he passed?"

Her eyes flickered. "I was his official *girlfriend*."

"Okay."

"Why do you have that expression? What have you heard?"

I blinked at her, confused by her hostile tone. "I haven't heard anything. I didn't even know Bob."

Her mouth thinned. "Bob loved me. You can think what you want, but we were going to be married."

"It's really none of my business." I was tempted to pick up a magazine to bury my nose in but was too uneasy about all the bacteria that might be breeding on them. Instead, I pulled out my phone and pretended to scroll through messages.

She didn't take the hint and leaned toward me, so close I could see the little magnets on her false eyelashes. "Everyone fights. That's perfectly normal. Bob drove in from Dallas almost every weekend to see me. That's love. He came to Rainy Dale to see me because he loved me."

"I don't really know anything about love and stuff," I muttered, wishing I'd never sat down. "I'm sorry for your loss." I hoped tacking that last bit on would help smooth things over. The last thing I needed was Royce walking into the waiting room to find I'd already made a new enemy.

"So many women threw themselves at him." She clenched her hands into fists. "But he remained loyal to me."

I didn't know Bob from Adam, but I'd seen him at the party. He hadn't been particularly attentive to her. He also hadn't been terribly attractive, but what did I know? He'd been rich, and lots of people were drawn to that. Perhaps he'd been very charming. Who was I to judge? People certainly weren't throwing themselves at me.

The door that connected the lobby to the back opened, and Royce stood there. When his gaze fell on me, he winked. Warmth flushed through me, and I found myself smiling back at him. He looked so handsome and good-natured, and I just wanted to sneak off into the back with him. Unfortunately, he shifted his glance to Rita.

"Rita, I'm ready for you now." He smiled at her.

She stood, giving me an unfriendly glare. "It's about time. I've been waiting forever."

"I'm sorry. It couldn't be helped. I got stuck on the phone with forensics."

She moved past him, her nose in the air. He followed her, closing the door behind him without a backward glance.

The girl behind the counter snorted a laugh. "If Bob was faithful to her, I'll eat my badge."

Surprised she was addressing me, I met her gaze. "He cheated on her?"

"Yep." She glanced around and lowered her voice. "Bob was a complete dog. He didn't come to town to see her. He came here to check on his new office chippie." She shook her head.

"Oh. He had someone on the side?"

"He had several someone's on the side." She made a zipping motion in front of her lips and glanced at the door Royce had gone through. "I've already said too much. She just annoyed me the way she was glaring at you and insisting she was going to marry Bob. He wasn't going to marry anyone."

"Does Royce know all of that?"

"I assume so. The whole town knows." She frowned. "You won't tell him I told you that stuff, right? I don't want him thinking I'm gossiping. Sheriff Callum loathes gossips."

"My lips are sealed."

"Cool." She went back to reading her book.

Royce didn't talk about the case with me much, and I didn't ask for details. I knew there were some things he couldn't discuss, but there were plenty of things he could talk about. Perhaps I should have shown more interest? Was it weird that I never asked him if he was closing in on the killer?

Anytime I'd started to ask him about the case, I'd stopped myself. His job was stressful. I didn't want to remind him of work when he was trying to relax. Of course I was curious about the case. I'd been there when Bob was murdered, so naturally I wanted to know what Royce had learned so far. I'd been trying to be considerate.

I'd been trying to be considerate?

Me? Maxwell Thornton had put another person first? On purpose? Without anyone making me do it? I actually cared enough about Royce to put his needs above my own. That was definitely new for me. Was it possible I wasn't a lost cause after all?

Chapter Eight

Royce

As I led Rita to the interview room, I was glad to finally have a chance to sit down with her. I was a little frustrated with the forensic evidence I'd received right before her interview. The good news was the lab finally had some information for me; the bad news was it didn't help much as far as naming the killer.

The only print on the hatpin was a partial of Maxwell's. I remembered him touching the pin the day of the murder. His instincts had been to check if Bob was alive. He'd been thinking like a doctor, not a cop. It hadn't occurred to him by touching the pin, he'd possibly contaminated the crime scene.

The bloodwork was as I'd suspected: Bob had consumed a large amount of GHB right before his death. GHB, often referred to as a date rape drug, or circles, was a central nervous system depressant. I was hoping to find out from talking to Rita if Bob had possibly over self-medicated or if someone had slipped him the drugs.

Rita tapped her glossy red nail on the metal table, frowning up at the fluorescent lights. "Why are interrogation rooms so horribly grim?"

I frowned. Did she want frilly curtains and family photos hung on the walls? "Have you been in a lot of police interview rooms?"

She scowled. "No."

"You sure about that?" I opened a folder I had on the table. Rita didn't exactly have a rap sheet, but she'd had a few brushes with the law in her short twenty-four years. Mostly for things like animal protests. "You were arrested last year in front of City Hall."

"Those charges were dropped."

I squinted at her. "True."

"Someone has to speak up for the animals. It's not like they can do it themselves."

"I don't suppose they can." I read the report. "You really laid inside a wire dog cage for eight hours, covered in fake blood?"

She smirked. "You'd be surprised how effective that is. Pamphlets are great, but there's nothing like visuals to get your point across."

"I suppose so."

"When I was seventeen, I was arrested for shoplifting, but I've never been convicted of any crimes, Sheriff."

"I can see that." I glanced up, closing the folder. "How long were you and Bob dating?"

Her face flinched. "Seven months. By the way, it was way more serious than just dating."

I glanced at her fingers, taking in several costume jewelry rings but no engagement-type band. "Is that right?"

She noticed my glance, and her cheeks tinted pink. "It was only a matter of time before he proposed."

"Bob had quite a reputation for having a roving eye."

Her jaw clenched. "Rumors. That's all that was. He loved me and promised me many, *many* times he was going to marry me."

She was living in dreamland, and I couldn't help but feel sorry for her. If she really believed Bob had been on the verge of proposing, she was in for a rude awakening. "According to his daughter, Bob was just having fun with you. He wasn't serious."

Her lip curled. "Penelope never liked me. She was all butthurt because I'm younger than her. You can't pay any attention to what she says."

"It's not just her, Rita. There are a lot of women in town who claim they had relations with Bob, and I'm talking recently."

She leaned forward. "Why would you believe them?"

"Well, because there are so many of them. I can see one or two exaggerating things, but there must be five women I've talked to the last few days who claim to have slept with Bob."

"Liars," she hissed, clenching her hands into fists. "They're all lying."

"But why would they bother?" I frowned.

She avoided my gaze. "All I know is what Bob told me. If he said he loved me and was gonna marry me, then I believe that."

It was obvious she was digging her heels in, so I decided to change the subject. "I finally got a toxicology report back from the lab."

"Did you?"

"Yep. Was Bob on any medications that you're aware of?"

She bit her bottom lip, looking uneasy. "Why?"

"Because there were drugs in his system."

"What kind?"

I twisted my lips. "How about you tell me what you know first, then maybe I can be a bit more forthcoming."

She sighed. "He took drugs for his narcolepsy."

I raised my brows. "Bob had narcolepsy?"

"Yes. He didn't like people knowing." She grimaced. "That… that's why I didn't think anything of it when he fell asleep at Penelope's party. I thought he was just having one of his bouts."

"Did you know where he kept his drugs?"

She scowled. "What kind of a thing is that to ask?"

"It's just a simple question, Rita." I kept my voice even.

"Are you trying to imply I drugged him?" She widened her eyes. "I did no such thing."

"I'm not implying anything."

"What drug was in his system? Maybe I can confirm whether or not Bob was taking that particular one." She lifted her chin.

I figured if she was spending time with Bob, enough that he'd shared he had narcolepsy, she probably was already privy to what drugs he was taking. Probably no harm in telling her. "We found large amounts of GHB in his blood."

She blinked at me. "Really?"

"Yeah."

"Bob only took that at night. He took a stimulant during the day and then that GHB stuff at night to help him sleep."

"I find it weird a person suffering from narcolepsy would take any kind of depressant." I rubbed my chin. "Aren't they trying to stay awake?"

"People with his condition take it to help them get a deeper sleep. The theory is it will help reduce the sleepiness during the day." She sighed. "I was never sure it worked. Bob was constantly dozing off. He could have four cups of coffee and still nod off."

"Any idea how he'd have ingested a large amount of GHB at Penelope's party?"

"No." She shook her head.

"Did you serve him his drinks at the party?"

"Just what are you implying?"

I sighed. "Just asking routine questions, Rita. Did you serve him his drinks?"

"No. Penelope did. I think his secretary got him a few as well. She's another one always trying to ingratiate herself with Bob."

"Penelope must have known about his narcolepsy?"

"Yeah."

"Do you think his secretary did?"

"I don't know." She scowled. "Not sure why she would."

"They worked together."

"Yes, but Bob was wary of anyone knowing his condition. He was embarrassed about it."

"He couldn't help it."

"No, but you know, men can be prideful."

"I suppose so."

She frowned. "By the way, Bob didn't lock up his drugs. Anyone could have gotten to them. Not just me."

"But not everyone was as close to Bob as you, right?"

"Now wait just a minute, Sheriff."

"I'm just saying you spent a lot of time with him. You stayed the night at his apartment, I'd imagine."

She narrowed her eyes. "Bob had those pills everywhere. At his office, in his car. He didn't just keep them at home. He'd put them in vitamin bottles so no one knew what he was taking."

We'd searched Bob's car already, and he did indeed have several bottles of vitamins stashed in his glove compartment. I'd sent the pills in for testing but hadn't heard back yet. "Do you think it's possible he got them mixed up or took too many?" I asked, studying her.

"I doubt it. He was very careful." She slumped back in her chair, looking haggard. "Since you're looking at me so closely, simply because we were dating, I should mention there was one affair that was true."

"Oh, really?" After all her denials, it was surprising she'd admit that. Was she simply doing it to throw me off her scent?

"I know cops always assume it's the significant others, right?" Her face was pink. "Well, while most of the rumors were complete lies, there was *one* person who succeeded in seducing him."

"Can you tell me who this person was?"

She hesitated. "As close as I was to Bob, I knew stuff even when he didn't want me to." She shook her head, as if trying to push away dark thoughts. "This person was different. She wormed her way in where others failed."

"Did you confront Bob?"

"Yes. Bob always had an explanation handy." Her mouth was a grim line. "So I had to go snooping on my own."

"And you found stuff?"

"I did." She winced. "I don't see what was so special about that dumb bitch."

"Who was this woman?"

She sighed, looking annoyed. "You don't believe Bob was gonna marry me, do you? You think I'm making all of that up."

Grimacing, I said, "Who cares what I think, Rita? None of that matters anyway because Bob is gone.

Someone took him from you, and if you think you know something, you need to tell me."

"Oh, I know stuff all right," she muttered. "Lots of stuff."

I leaned forward on my elbows, fixing her with a stern look. "Tell me what you know. Stop beating around the bush."

Her bottom lip trembled. "He wasn't a perfect man by any means, but I loved him and he loved me."

I sighed. "Okay. If you really loved him, help me solve this case. Tell me something that can help me catch his killer. Who was this other woman?"

Her face distorted with pain. "I checked his phone bills, and there were so many calls to her. Then I found receipts for things that he'd bought her."

She was driving me nuts not just naming names, but I sensed if I pushed her, she might clam up. "What kind of things?"

"Oh, you know, little *special* gifts." Her voice was bitter.

"What kind of gifts?"

She swallowed. "He was killed with a hatpin, right?"

"That's right."

"Bob bought this woman a hatpin."

I widened my eyes. "He did?"

She nodded.

I'd planned on showing her a photo of the murder weapon later in the interview, like I had everyone else I'd questioned. But since she'd brought it up first, I pulled the photo of the hatpin out of the folder in front of me. "Have you ever seen this pin before?"

She winced, staring at the photo. "Oh, God."

"Do you recognize the pin, Rita?"

She shook her head. "No, but like I said, Bob bought an antique hatpin for this… person."

"But you never saw it?"

"No."

"Was this person at Penelope's party?"

She nodded.

Excitement hummed through me because now we were getting somewhere. "I need the name of this person, and I need it now."

She met my gaze. "Charity Bell." Her voice dripped venom. "She's the slut who was chasing after my man."

"Seriously?" Charity's version had been the other way around, although it was hard to sift through the lies with Charity and Fred. She'd admitted giving Bob what he wanted, to help her career. But who'd been the aggressor? That truth might have gone to the grave with Bob.

"And Charity was wearing a hat at the party too." She touched her own hair distractedly. "She was wearing her usual stupid pink cowboy hat. She's *thirty*. Why does she dress like a teenager?"

"You're sure he bought a hatpin for Charity?"

"Yes."

"How can you be so sure he didn't give it to someone else?"

She clenched her jaw. "I saw a text message from him to her, where he hinted at it."

"Really?"

"Yes. For a while there, she was texting him a lot."

"What did this particular text say?"

"Well, she was complaining how the wind always blew her hat off on stage, and Bob said he had a little special gift that would help her out."

"Hmmm."

"Then I found a receipt for lingerie and an antique hatpin. Since I'd read that text, it clicked in my brain right away what his *special* gift was."

I tapped my pen on the pad, studying her pinched face. "Charity probably wasn't the only person wearing a hat at Penelope's party."

"I believe she was the only woman there wearing a hat."

"This is Texas. People wear cowboy hats all the time."

"The men do. I don't see too many women wearing them to parties. No woman I know spends an hour on her hair, only to smash it down with a hat."

"Didn't you just say Charity did that?"

She leaned toward me, looking annoyed. "For the *stage*. She always wore her pink hat when she performed. It was like her signature look. You don't have to take my word for it—her website has tons of photos of her performing. I'd lay odds they all have her in that *stupid* pink hat. I have no doubt at all Bob bought that pin for Charity Bell."

If Rita was correct, that could explain why Charity had looked so upset at the photo of the hatpin I'd shown her. The pin was a potential link to her. Fred had been quick to distance her from the pin, but it was clear to me now he'd probably lied.

"Why would Charity kill Bob?"

She dropped her head. "I made an ultimatum. Either he stopped seeing her, or I'd leave him."

"And he chose you?"

She glanced up, her eyes angry. "Of course he picked me. How many times do I have to tell you he loved me!" Her voice went up an octave. "We had our problems, but he promised me he'd marry me. He *promised.*"

I held out a calming hand. "I'm not arguing with you about that, Rita. I'm just trying to figure out what Charity's motive for murder would be."

"Well… he dumped her. She was angry."

I grimaced. "I'd need more than that to arrest her. Being angry isn't a crime." I gave her a pointed look. "You yourself argued with Bob the day of the party."

Her face tensed. "Yes. But we… we worked it out."

My memory of the party was Rita sulking in the corner while Bob held court. I hadn't noticed him being affectionate with her at all. I suspected they hadn't worked anything out. Maybe they would have, but they never got the chance.

"Sal Brenner had a big fight with Bob." She widened her eyes. "Have you talked to him yet?"

"Yes. Of course. Sal was with Penelope around the time we believe Bob was murdered."

She squinted at me. "You sure about that?"

"I am."

"Well, what about Charity's psycho husband? Maybe he found out about the affair, and he killed Bob in a fit of jealous rage."

I exhaled a tired breath. "Now, don't just start naming off everyone in town, Rita. For goodness' sake. You gave me some good information about the hatpin and what Bob was up to. Let's stick with what you know, not conspiracy theories."

She slumped, her mouth drooping. "Okay."

"All right, then." I smoothed my hand over the folder. "Now, how was it you discovered that Bob was dead?"

"I brought him a plate of food." She had a faraway look in her eyes. "At first, I just thought he was asleep. But he was just so… still." She covered her face.

"I'm sorry."

Lowering her hands, she met my gaze. There was real pain there. Maybe Bob had been a lying, cheating bastard, but she did seem to have loved him. "Then I saw blood, dripping down his arm. I… I couldn't believe what I was seeing, and I just screamed."

"I'm sure it was a horrible shock."

"Of course it was." She wiped at her eyes with the back of her hand. "Then you and the doctor came over, and everyone started yelling."

"Did you move anything when you found Bob?"

"Move anything?"

"Like his glass?"

She shook her head. "No. I didn't touch anything. I was too distracted by… Bob."

"But he was drinking at the party?"

"Yes. He loved a good stiff drink."

"Hmmm." There hadn't been any glass or bottle anywhere near Bob at the time of his death. Had it been moved during the chaotic scene by one of the party guests or the murderer? "But you brought him food?"

Her bottom lip trembled. "I did. But of course he didn't eat any of it because…" She lowered her head. "I… I was trying to make him happy. We'd had that stupid fight, and I wanted to make him happy by bringing him some of his favorite foods."

"I truly am sorry, Rita."

She nodded, sniffing. "Nobody believes he loved me," she whispered, looking up, her eyes glittered with tears. "He did, I swear."

I didn't know what to say. Maybe he had loved her. Who was I to say that when they'd been alone together, Bob hadn't been a completely different person? I myself saw a very different Maxwell than most people. Sometimes people held parts of themselves back and only shared it with those they trusted most. Perhaps Bob had felt that trust with Rita.

I reached over and patted her hand. "Like I said, it doesn't matter what anyone else thinks or doesn't think. You know how Bob felt. Hold on to that, Rita. Don't let anyone take it away from you."

For the first time since I'd met her, her face softened and she gave me a real smile. "Thanks, Sheriff."

I sat back in my chair. "Is there anything else you want to tell me?"

She shook her head. "I don't think so. Are you going to arrest Charity?"

"No."

"Why not?" She scowled.

"I need to follow all the leads before making an arrest. We'll dump Bob's phone and check out who he talked to. I'll definitely have another chat with Charity and Fred."

"I see."

"I need evidence to make things stick, Rita. That's how the law works."

"I understand." She bit her bottom lip. "You should at least see if she can produce the hatpin Bob gave her. If not, that's pretty suspicious, right?"

"I'm running down leads on the hatpin, Rita. Don't you worry about it."

"I guess it's all in your capable hands," she murmured.

I stood. "I'm telling everyone the same thing: don't leave town just yet. Not until this case is wrapped up."

"All right." She sighed. "I don't really have anywhere to go anyway."

I studied her, fighting the urge to write her off as a suspect. I couldn't allow myself to be blinded by empathy. It was true that, even in a fit of rage, I couldn't see Rita murdering Bob. But until the case was closed and I had the murderer behind bars, I'd keep her on the back burner with the other possible suspects.

Chapter Nine

Maxwell

After an hour of waiting for Royce to finish up his interview with Rita, my stomach began to growl with hunger. I glanced at the officer behind the desk, hoping she couldn't hear my gastrointestinal issues. Royce and I hadn't made dinner plans, and I'd fully intended to stuff down some food before heading over here. But because of Charity's impulsive visit to my office, I'd barely had time to shower.

When the door to the back opened, Rita strolled through the lobby without a backward glance and left the building. I watched her go, wondering what all she'd been able to tell Royce.

"Dr. Thornton, I'm ready for you now." Royce's amused voice came to me from the doorway.

I glanced over and then stood. "So soon?" I asked sardonically.

He grinned as I approached. "Sorry. I'm trying to solve a murder, in case you didn't know."

"Oh, are you a cop?" I smirked, slipping past him.

"I can show you my cuffs later to prove it."

"Pfft. Please, you can get those anywhere."

He chuckled, and I followed him to his office. Once inside, he closed the door and immediately kissed me. Pressing my back against the door, he explored my mouth with his skilled tongue. I slid my arms around his neck and sighed happily. He deepened the kiss, and

I responded. Everything was going great, until my stomach gurgled alarmingly.

He laughed against my lips and lifted his head. "Holy shit. Is there an alien inside you?"

"No. I'm too empty for that."

He frowned. "Didn't you eat dinner?"

I sighed. "I planned on it, but I had a last-minute visit from Charity Bell."

He squinted, releasing me. "Really?"

"Yep." I wasn't at liberty to discuss her personal business with Royce, so I just said, "She had a space open in her busy schedule."

He smiled, but his gaze was keen. "Did she bring her husband along? If so, that must have been an interesting examination."

I laughed. "No. She left him at home."

"I thought she had a show tonight." He wrinkled his brow.

"I believe you're correct. She was in a big hurry to get out of my office."

He tilted his head. "Why didn't she just make an appointment like a normal person?"

"You know how flighty celebrities can be," I said, avoiding his gaze.

"Yeah, I don't think Rainy Dale has any of those." I could tell he wanted to push for more info, but he seemed to catch himself. "How about we go grab some food? I could eat a little something myself. All I had today was that burger at your office."

"What? Why didn't you eat more?"

He laughed sheepishly. "I got busy and just kind of forgot to eat."

I sighed. "We're a real pair, eh?"

An affectionate smile lit his face, and he tugged me close again. "Yeah we are." He kissed me a few more times, working my lips gently, and then he let go of me. "Okay. Let's eat."

"Is anything open? It's almost 9:00 p.m."

Frowning, he grabbed his jacket off the back of his chair. "I believe the falafel place is open until 9:30 p.m. If we hurry, we can get there in time."

"Go. Go. Go, soldier!" I did my best drill sergeant impression.

He grinned. "I've never seen you this animated."

"I'm starving, so I'm not myself."

We left the station and got in his car. He backed skillfully out of the small parking lot, pulling onto Main Street. The street was quiet, probably because most of the businesses in town were closed for the night.

"It's not far, and usually I'd walk. But this is an emergency." His cheek curved in a smile, illuminated by the dashboard. "We need sustenance, stat."

"Worse comes to worst, I can just make us some eggs at my place."

"Or mine."

"Yeah, but if we go to your place, Grumpy will think you're home for the night. He'll be brokenhearted when you leave him again," I murmured.

He glanced over. "Wait, did you just show empathy for my puppy?"

I shrugged. "I like dogs. It's people I can't stand."

"Oh yeah." He parked on the street in front of the Falafel Palace. "Good, the open sign is still on." He shut the engine off, and we climbed from the vehicle.

I was pleased when he nonchalantly slipped his arm around my waist. Back in LA, I'd never gotten to know anyone well enough to receive that kind of treatment in public. Dating hadn't been like it was with Royce. He actually liked hanging out with me. The guys I'd slept with back in LA had merely been bodies. My life had been too busy to bother with getting to know people. When lusty need had visited, I'd called whoever, and if they were in the mood, they'd obliged. There hadn't been any affection involved.

When we entered the shop, there was a young boy behind the counter mopping. He glanced up as we approached the register, and while frustration fluttered through his gaze, he was nice enough to hide it immediately.

"Hey, Sheriff," the kid said, smiling. When his gaze shifted to me, the smile vanished. "Dr. Thornton, how are you?"

"Good." I vaguely remembered his mother had brought him in for an examination a few weeks ago. I didn't recall actually insulting either of them, but I obviously must not have left a great impression.

"I know you're about to close. We don't want to hold you up too long." Royce perused the menu board on the wall.

"It's no problem." The kid shrugged.

"I'll have the number six." Royce turned to me. "I think you'd like that one too."

I squinted at the menu. "It sounds good." I met the boy's gaze. "Is it possible to have it minus the radishes?"

"Of course."

"I'll do that, then. A number six, no radishes." Royce reached for his wallet, but I grabbed his arm. "Uh, no, this is on me." I pulled my wallet out of my back pocket and offered my card to the kid.

"What? Why?" Royce scowled, trying to knock my card away.

"I'm buying." I gave the boy a stern glance. "Take my card. Ignore him."

Grimacing, the kid looked conflicted about what to do.

"Max, let me pay." Royce also held out his credit card.

Leaning toward the kid, I said tersely, "I said *I'm* paying."

With a sheepish expression, the boy took my card. He swiped it quickly, shooting Royce an apologetic glance, and handed it back to me. "Would you like a receipt?"

"No, thank you." Feeling proud of myself for managing to pay, I tucked my wallet away.

Royce shook his head. "Getting food was my idea."

"Only because my stomach made demonic sounds."

He laughed and led me to one of the brightly colored tables. "It was pretty scary."

"Besides, you bought me an expensive dinner the other night, and you brought me a sandwich today. You're not made of money, Royce."

"I can certainly afford to buy us a few meals."

"Okay, but you can't buy them *all*," I grumbled. "I know you're touchy about money around me, but don't forget, I'm a grown man. I like to pay for things too."

"I'm not touchy about money."

I snorted a laugh. "Yes. You most certainly are. Ever since Jennie Grafton let slip in front of me how much you make a year, you've been grabbing for your wallet like a gunslinger anytime we eat out."

His face flushed. "I'm not embarrassed by how much I make, Max."

"Then stop overcompensating."

Silence followed my comment, and when I glanced over, Royce's jaw was hard. A muscle worked in his cheek, and I could see the wheels turning in his head. I frowned, catching on he was angry. My stomach dropped because I hadn't intended to insult him. What had I said that was so bad?

The boy behind the counter said, "Here are your drink cups, guys. Just fill them up at the machine, and grab a bag of chips each from the rack near the door. Your falafels will be up in minute."

I was glad of the interruption because it gave me time to think. Royce was sensitive about how much money he made. Or more to the point, he was sensitive about how much *more* money I made. I wasn't with Royce for the monetary perks, so I wasn't sure why money mattered at all. But he had a lot of pride, and he'd admitted to me he'd never dated anyone who made more money than him before. Was it so bad that I knew that? Or that I'd addressed it?

We rose and got our cups from the counter, then made our way to the big soda machine. As Royce filled his cup with ice and Pepsi, I studied him out of the corner of my eye. His jaw was definitely clamped more than usual. The last thing I wanted was to fight with him. He was my one true ally in this town.

"If I insulted you, I'm sorry," I said quietly. "That wasn't my intention. To be honest, I'm not even sure what I did wrong."

He glanced over. "Then why apologize?"

"I can tell something is bothering you. I assume it's my fault," I admitted.

Giving a grudging smile, he sighed. "I'm tired. I'm being too sensitive."

I put my cup under the spigot, pushing the lever so that soda filled my cup. "You've been very generous with me, but I like to buy you meals too. That's really all I meant."

"Fair enough."

Happy he seemed less annoyed, I breathed a sigh of relief.

"Food is ready." The kid behind the counter pushed a bag toward us.

"Thanks." Royce grabbed the bag. The kid looked relieved when we walked to the door instead of sitting at a table.

"Have a good evening," he called after us. "And thanks a falafel lot for giving us your business."

I stifled a groan, but Royce just laughed.

"Do you suppose his boss makes him say that?" I whispered.

"I highly doubt he came up with that on his own."

Royce held the door for me, and the kid hurried around the counter and locked it behind us. We headed to the car, and once inside, Royce handed me my food.

"Mind having a picnic in the car?" he asked.

"Not at all."

"It's just nice to get out of the station for a while. I feel like I live there lately."

"Probably because you do."

Parked where we were, there was an unobstructed view down Main Street, in the direction of my house. The shops and restaurants were dark, but little white lights were hung through the trees that lined the main road. Royce had once said he wanted me to stay in Rainy Dale at least until Christmas. He'd said the little town was pretty all covered in a blanket of snow. I could see that. The place had a rustic charm, and snow made everything prettier.

I carefully peeled the orange sandwich paper from my falafel and took a bite. The Middle Eastern spices of coriander and cumin bathed my tongue, and I gave an approving nod. The crispy little fritters inside the pita were delicious, with just the right crunch. I'd only had a falafel once in LA, and it hadn't been nearly as good.

We ate in companionable silence, watching the quiet street. Once I'd consumed most of my falafel and half of my chips, I tucked the rest away in the bag. I didn't want to overeat before bedtime. Royce, however, ate every bite of his falafel and chips. His situation was different though; while I'd soon be tucked away in bed, he'd be working most of the night.

"Did your interview with Rita go well?" I asked.

He nodded. "It did. She had a lot of information."

"Can you see her as the killer?"

He scrunched his face. "Not sure. Probably not, but never say never."

"The little interaction I had with her was uncomfortable. She was very defensive." I frowned. "And I don't think it was because of anything I did."

For once.

"She was touchy. I think she really loved Bob though," he said softly.

"Love or not, she could still be the killer."

"True." He laughed gruffly. "Maybe even more likely."

I glanced at him, frowning. "Why do you say that?"

He shrugged. "Love can drive people nuts."

I'd never been in love, so I had no real insight. "Do you think Bob's murder was premeditated?"

"I'm not sure. Probably?"

"What makes you think it maybe wasn't?"

"The murder weapon seems so random." He sighed. "But then, he was drugged, which makes me think that the murder was planned."

"I see what you mean. Any luck figuring out who the hatpin belonged to?"

He hesitated. "I think I'm on the cusp of getting that nailed down."

"Really?"

"Yep. I talked to Susan at the Squeaky Wheel antique shop, and she's digging up the record of sale for me." He glanced over, his expression optimistic. "And Rita was actually very helpful as well. She pointed me toward the possible owner of the pin."

"That's wonderful. I'm glad you're finally making some progress."

"Me too."

I gazed out the windshield. "I can't say I'm surprised that Bob was drugged. He didn't make a sound from what I can tell, and getting stabbed through the heart… well… I'd probably scream bloody murder."

"As would anyone not drugged." He sighed. "I still can't believe someone used a hatpin. I didn't even know people used those anymore."

"The only woman I've ever known who used hatpins was my grandmother." I shivered. "She was a terrifying woman."

He laughed. "Was she?"

"Oh, yes. She made my mother seem warm and fuzzy, and my mother was about as warm and fuzzy as the Babadook."

"Good Lord." He widened his eyes.

I laughed. "Okay, I'm exaggerating. I'm simply saying, my mother wasn't warm, and my grandmother was even worse."

He studied me, but I couldn't really read his expression because it was dark in the car. "I'm sorry your childhood was difficult."

I grimaced. "Water under the bridge."

"Sure."

"Perhaps my parents weren't very affectionate, but they did praise me a good deal when I did well in school. I have them to credit for my drive to succeed. Without them pushing me, I probably wouldn't have done as well in my profession as I did."

"You're a very skilled doctor, Max. No one can fault you on your medical knowledge, that's for sure." He seemed to choose his words carefully.

"I never put much stock in the idea of perfecting a good bedside manner. It just wasn't necessary as a surgeon, or at least, not the way it is with a small-town practice. But I think if I put my mind to it, I'll be able to get a handle on it."

"I'm sure you're right."

"You don't sound convinced."

He lifted one shoulder. "I think you're the sort of man who sets his mind to a task and accomplishes it."

"You still have that tone."

He laughed gruffly. "What tone?"

"Like you're being very polite, trying not to offend me. But I don't buy that you believe what you're saying."

He sighed. "I suppose to me the issue isn't that you can't white-knuckle it and improve your bedside manner. The real problem is to be a caring doctor… you have to actually… *care.*"

I raised my brows. "You don't think I care about my patients?"

"I think you really care about the medical part. You want them healed. You want to do a good job."

"Well, just because I don't want to have lunch with them doesn't mean I don't care about them as… you know… people." I felt flustered, having to defend myself. Did Royce truly believe I didn't have *any* empathy at all for my patients? "If I was indifferent to my patients, I wouldn't have felt so awful about hurting Mrs. Miller's feelings the other day."

"Okay, that's a good point."

Happy I'd scored any point at all, I said, "Life is full of irony."

"How so?"

"Well, in my job, empathy would be useful, yet it's not natural for me. However, you're loaded with compassion, and it's actually a negative in your profession. The last thing you need is to feel sorry for the people you might have to arrest."

"I do struggle with that."

"Of course you do. You're a real softie."

He frowned. "I'm not a softie for *everyone.* It's just sometimes good people get themselves into bad situations. It's not that they're evil, although evil definitely exists. It's the people who stumble into crime I feel sorry for. I wish I could go easy on them, but I can't. Not once they break the law."

He was so obviously speaking from the heart, without thinking I said, "You're such a good man, Royce."

I think I was as surprised as him when those words spilled out of my mouth. He laughed gruffly, and my face flushed with heat.

"Thanks. That means a lot coming from you, Max."

"Don't mention it." I laughed awkwardly.

He chuckled and leaned over the center console. "Come closer, Doc. I want to kiss you."

Excitement rippled through me, and I inched over. "Beware, I have cabbage and onion breath from the falafel."

"So do I," he whispered, right before he claimed my mouth.

I was always amazed at how much I enjoyed simply kissing Royce. His lips were firm yet soft. His tongue was salaciously insistent as it pushed between my lips. It was impossible to not get lost in the heat of his mouth on mine. I slipped my hand down his stubbled cheek, slanting into him more.

Necking in a car was a new experience for me. Unlike so many people, I'd never made out in the back seat as a teenager. Growing up a Thornton, I'd missed a lot of things other kids took for granted. There'd been no prom for me. No parties. No frivolity. I'd spent all of my time with my books. I'd strived to get the best grades possible so that my father would say something nice to me.

Why am I thinking about that asshole?

I focused instead on Royce. I inhaled his clean scent and slipped my hand around the back of his neck. Royce somehow managed to be gentle, without any hint of weakness. The more time I spent with him, the more

I was willing to accept that affection didn't make you weak. It couldn't, because Royce was one of the kindest, warmest, most affectionate men I'd ever known, and he was the farthest thing from weak.

When Royce pulled his mouth from mine, it took me a minute to snap out of my lusty haze. He peered through the windshield, his body suddenly rigid with tension. I followed his gaze, noticing he seemed fixed on the Golden Goose Realty building.

"What's wrong?" I asked, sitting up.

"I… I'm not sure, but I think I see someone inside that building."

I nodded. "Yeah, I thought I saw a person there when I walked past on my way to the station."

He frowned. "Why didn't you say anything?"

I blinked at him. "Because I didn't think much of it. People work late sometimes, right?"

He started the engine, and the car jerked forward. "Not when they're dead."

"*What?*"

"Bob Cunningham was the owner of Golden Goose Realty," he growled. "And dead men don't work overtime."

Chapter Ten

Royce

"Stay in the car," I barked, climbing from the vehicle. "I'm going to check things out." I'd parked on the street instead of the parking lot, hoping whoever was inside the building wouldn't see my car.

"Wouldn't a burglar alarm have been tripped if someone broke in?" Maxwell asked, right before I closed the door.

He had a point. I knew for a fact Golden Goose Realty did have an alarm. So if someone was inside, either they knew how to hack a security system, or they had the alarm code. But if they knew the code and had a right to be inside, why were they creeping around with a flashlight?

Keeping low to the ground, I hurried across the parking lot to the long brick building. My heart pumped fast as I inched along, closing in on the back door. When I reached it, I carefully tried the handle. The knob turned freely, indicating it wasn't locked. It also didn't feel damaged. That led me to believe whoever was inside had a key, and since the alarm wasn't blaring, probably the code to the alarm too.

I pulled my gun, slowly opening the door. I cringed when it squeaked, and assuming my presence was now known, I yelled, "Rainy Dale Sheriff Department, come out where I can see you."

The sound of a file cabinet slamming shut and muted cursing echoed through the silent space. Unfortunately, whoever it was didn't immediately surrender. Instead they stopped moving, probably trying to hide.

I felt along the wall for the light switch, and when I found it, flicked it on. The room was illuminated in stark fluorescent lighting, revealing a room strewn with papers. I scowled at the mess and crept along the wall, searching out all the best places to hide.

"I know you're in here. You're not getting past me, so you might as well reveal yourself." I kept my gun level, the hairs on the back of my neck prickling. I had no idea if this person was armed or not and prayed they didn't have a weapon trained on me. If they were carrying, the fact they hadn't fired a shot off yet was promising. "Come on now, so far all you're guilty of is breaking and entering. Don't do anything stupid, okay?"

I crept toward the front, crouching as low as possible. I could hear someone breathing on the other side of the room and adjusted my direction. I didn't think it was kids because they'd have most likely made a run for the door by now. No, from the wheezing sounds, I surmised it was a single intruder. One distressed, very out of shape prowler.

"This will be better for you if you just give yourself up. We don't want anybody to get hurt, now do we?" I tried to sound reasonable. Cajoling.

"O… okay," a nervous male voice called out. "I'm… I'm coming out. Don't shoot me." A tall man climbed out from under a big desk. He was dressed head to toe in black, and he had his hands in the air. "Please don't shoot."

I moved toward him, keeping my gun trained on his chest. "Do you have a weapon?"

"God no," he rasped.

His voice was familiar, and I frowned. "Do I know you?"

Slumping, the man groaned. "Now I've fucked everything up even more."

"Take your mask off."

With a sigh, he reached up and tugged off the mask. Gerald Granger, Penelope's husband, stood there, his salt-and-pepper hair sticking up in sweaty clumps. His fleshy cheeks were red, and his eyes glittered with embarrassment.

"What the hell are you doing in here, Gerald?"

"It's a long story, Sheriff." He grimaced.

"How did you get in?"

"I borrowed Penelope's key."

"And the alarm?"

"She keeps all her passwords in a notebook by the bed." He hung his head. "God, she's going to kill me."

Scowling, I holstered my weapon. "Did you make this mess?"

He winced. "Yes."

"For goodness' sake, Gerald. I'd think you're above this kind of nonsense."

"You don't understand."

"No. I definitely do not."

The sound of footsteps behind me had me spinning around, my hand instinctively seeking the butt of my gun. But it was only Maxwell, standing in the doorway, looking puzzled.

"Is that Mayor Granger's husband?" he asked, staring at Gerald.

"Yes." I narrowed my eyes. "I told you to stay in the car."

He shrugged. "You were taking too long. Besides, I could see you two through the windows. When you holstered your gun, I knew it was safe."

"Sheriff, this isn't what you think." Gerald's voice wobbled. "I know this looks really bad, but I swear, it has nothing to do with Bob's death."

Obviously, I couldn't just take his word for it. Exhaling, I tugged my cuffs off my utility belt. "I'm sorry, but I'm going to cuff you and take you to the station. Maybe then you can tell me why you're dressed like a damn ninja."

"Do you really need to cuff me? I'll go with you peacefully."

I hesitated. "Will you let me pat you down? I need to make sure you're not a threat, Gerald."

"Sheriff, you know me. I'm not a violent man."

I narrowed my eyes. "I wouldn't have pegged you as a burglar either."

He winced. "I told you, this isn't what it looks like."

"Can I pat you down or not?"

He nodded, appearing resigned. "Okay."

I strode over to him and did a quick search. It was surreal to be frisking the mayor's husband, but lately things were out of control in Rainy Dale. I didn't find any weapons on Gerald but did find a single key in his front pocket.

"That's the key to this building," he said.

"Great. I don't want to leave this place unlocked."

"No. Of course not." He grimaced. "I'll rearm the security system too."

"Sounds good." I led him toward the door. While I didn't have him cuffed, I did keep hold of him. Just in case he decided to make a run for it.

Maxwell followed us. "What's the code for the alarm? I'll punch it in for you guys."

Gerald studied him warily. "I'm not sure I should just tell you the code."

Maxwell rolled his eyes. "I'm not the one being detained by the cops."

Gerald's face flushed red. "I'm not a crook."

"Fine. Neither am I," Maxwell said.

"Just give him the damn code, Gerald," I growled.

"Fine." With a scowl, Gerald said, "24840."

"Thanks," Maxwell said curtly.

I steered Gerald out of the building and heard some high-pitched beeps as Maxwell rearmed the alarm system. He came outside, closing the door firmly behind us. I marched Gerald to my car, helping him carefully into the back. I closed the door and met Maxwell's emotionless gaze.

"I think I'll have to postpone your interview until tomorrow."

"That's fine," he said quietly.

Sighing, I said, "I'm sorry this interrupted our evening."

"I appreciate you saying that, but I realize you couldn't just let him burgle the place without investigating."

"No." I was frustrated because I'd really been looking forward to spending some time with Max. Now I'd get the dubious pleasure of questioning Gerald instead. "When we get back to the station, I'll have one of my deputies drive you home."

"Don't bother. I'll walk."

I shook my head. "No. Things are too weird around here right now. I'd feel better if you'd let me set up a ride for you."

He looked like he was going to argue, but then he nodded. "Okay."

Relieved he'd relented, I moved around the car to the driver's side, and he slid into the passenger seat. Gerald didn't say a word on the drive to the station. Granted, it wasn't a long ride. Once parked, I led Gerald into the back of the building and straight to one of the interview rooms. I went ahead and read him his rights, just to cover all the bases.

"Am I under arrest?" Gerald asked. His eyes were bloodshot, and sweat slicked his ruddy face.

I hesitated. "Not yet." I wanted to ask him questions but wasn't sure I needed to arrest him yet. Technically, he hadn't broken into Golden Goose Realty, and because he was Bob's son-in-law, he'd probably say he had the right to be there. Ransacking the place didn't bode well for him though. He'd obviously been looking for something, and I very much wanted to know what.

"So then, I can leave and not talk to you, if I want?"

"You can." I gave him a hard stare. "But I'd have to wonder why you don't want to talk to me."

"I have reasons. Personal ones."

Sighing, I said, "Gerald, if you'd prefer, I can arrest you. Right now, I just want to talk, but if you want to push it, I can oblige you by escalating things."

His swallow was loud enough to hear. "I guess we can talk."

"Okay, good. I'll be back in a minute. Would you like a soda or water?"

"Either would be great." He slumped.

I left the room and met Maxwell in the hallway. "Let me go grab Deputy Juan. He's still here, I believe."

"Sure." Maxwell seemed unusually docile, which I considered a gift.

I found Juan in the breakroom, making a fresh pot of coffee. "Can I ask you to do me a favor, Deputy?"

He glanced over, his dark brows arched. "Of course."

"Would you mind driving Dr. Thornton home? I need to question Gerald Granger. I just found him ransacking Golden Goose Realty."

"What the hell?" He scowled. "The mayor's husband?"

"Yep."

He gave a disbelieving laugh. "Uh… sure. I'll drive the doc home."

"He's waiting in the hallway. Thanks, Juan."

"You bet."

I left him and approached Maxwell. "It's all set." I gave him a tired smile. "I'll call you tomorrow."

"Sure." He studied me, a line between his smooth brows. "When you're done talking to Gerald, please tell me you're going to get some sleep. You look thrashed, Royce. Even superheroes need sleep."

"That's funny. I'm the furthest thing from a superhero."

"Promise me," he said gruffly. "Lack of sleep is very unhealthy."

I couldn't help but smile at his concerned tone. It felt nice to have him worrying about me. Maybe that meant he cared more than he showed. "I promise I'll get some sleep tonight, okay?"

He gave a curt nod.

Deputy Juan came out of the breakroom behind me, so I wasn't able to give Maxwell the goodbye I'd have liked. Instead, I just said, "Have a good night, Max."

"You too."

"Thanks again, Juan." I gave my deputy a grateful smile and headed toward the room Gerald was in. It was annoying my night with Maxwell had been ruined, but stumbling on Gerald looting his dead father-in-law's office was an intriguing development. I stopped at my office to get my notepad and a pen. Then I visited the vending machine and grabbed a couple of sodas. I made sure mine had caffeine.

When I entered the room where Gerald was, he sat up straighter. "Does Penelope need to know about this?"

I slid his soda toward him, frowning. "I guess that depends on what you tell me."

"God, she'll murder me," he groaned.

I clicked my pen and popped open my soda. Taking a few long pulls of the sweet soda, I set the can down. "I'm awfully curious to know what you were up to tonight, Gerald."

He rubbed his face roughly. "I'm sure you are."

"How about you tell me exactly why you were in Bob's office and what you were looking for."

He gritted his teeth, avoiding my gaze. "This is humiliating."

"It's definitely surprising." I studied him. "You're the chief loan officer at Rainy Dale Mortgage and Loan. I wouldn't expect his kind of thing from you."

Seeming to wilt, he distractedly spun the soda can I'd given him in a circle. "I've been under an enormous amount of stress lately."

"You mean because of your father-in-law's murder?"

"No. I mean, that didn't help any. Penelope hasn't gotten out of bed in three days. All she does is cry." He sighed. "But this stress began way before Bob died."

"Care to elaborate?"

He scrunched his cheek. "Let's just say, Bob wasn't a very pleasant father-in-law."

"Did you two have a falling-out?"

He glanced up, resentment glimmering in his gaze. "A falling-out implies we were once close. He never approved of me. I've spent my entire marriage to Penelope trying to prove my worthiness, but nothing worked with that asshole."

I frowned. "Sounds like you really disliked Bob."

"Most people in Rainy Dale did, Sheriff. If you don't already know that, you aren't paying attention."

"I've noticed he rubbed a lot of people the wrong way."

He chuffed. "What a nice way to put it."

"Bob lived in Dallas. How come he has so many enemies here?"

"Because he did a lot of business here. There's a reason he called his company Golden Goose Realty. That's how he saw this town. He couldn't wait to chop Rainy Dale up into little pieces so he could sell it off and make a killing."

I frowned. "You really think that was his plan?"

"I know it was." He laughed humorlessly. "He had lunch with the planning commission every week. He's been trying to change the zoning laws for years. He was making headway too."

"How so?"

"Well, his daughter is mayor, so he already had an in there."

"Penelope has always fought to keep this town small. I don't believe she'd sell everybody out like that."

He smirked. "No, but Bob would sell *her* out like that. Or he would have. He was a master manipulator."

I wrinkled my brow. "You really believe that?"

"Hell, yeah." He shook his head. "Bob didn't care about anyone but Bob. I mean, he loved Penelope. But he'd have figured he was doing her a favor by making her richer. Money was what mattered to him. If you don't believe me, go look through his office yourself."

"We already looked through his office."

"Yeah, but you weren't looking for things like building plans. He has schematics for a huge development to the west of Rainy Dale. The water table slowed him down some, but he found a few council members willing to grant him emergency permits to get around that."

Shocked at what he was telling me, I leaned forward. "Are you implying someone knocked him off because he was planning on building a housing track?"

He sighed. "Not exactly. I'm saying he had a lot of enemies, and that's just one more reason someone might have wanted him dead."

I studied him. "You work for a bank. I'd think you would be all in favor of developing Rainy Dale."

"I never said I wasn't. I'm simply saying, Bob was greedy, and there are a lot of other people who don't want Rainy Dale to change. My wife is one of them."

I gave a gruff laugh. "Surely you're not implying Penelope wanted her dad dead?"

He widened his eyes. "God no. She adored him. She'll be brokenhearted if she finds out about his plans to rape and pillage Rainy Dale. No, she'd never have harmed Bob. She's fucking devastated."

It felt like he was bouncing all over the place. What I really wanted to know was why he'd snooped through Bob's office. "It's disappointing to hear Bob was conniving behind Penelope's back. But, how about we focus on you and what you were up to tonight?"

He exhaled and leaned back in his chair. "Fine. I guess there's no hiding it now."

"What is it you were trying to keep secret?"

His mouth thinned, and he kept his gaze pinned on the table. "I have a little problem, and it gave Bob an opportunity to blackmail me."

"Blackmail?" I raised my brows. "You're saying Bob was blackmailing his own son-in-law?"

"He'd have blackmailed his mother if he thought it would serve him somehow," he said derisively.

I sipped my soda, trying to decide what to ask him. I set the can down and decided the direct approach was best. "What did he have on you?"

He didn't respond immediately, but then he met my gaze. "I have a bit of a gambling problem."

"Gambling?" I frowned. "The only casino I'm aware of is the Kickapoo Lucky Eagle casino, and that's six hours away."

"I didn't go to the Eagle casino." He shrugged and popped open his soda can. "I got hooked going on these things called 'cruises to nowhere' years ago."

"Never heard of 'em."

He sighed. "No. I wouldn't suppose you have. They were these casino boats on the Gulf Coast."

"Seriously?"

He nodded. "They'd take players out into international waters, where there were no gambling laws."

"Huh. And you did that a lot?"

"Yeah. I did it for years. But then in 2016, they shut them down and no longer allowed them in American ports."

"Something tells me you didn't stop gambling?"

He gritted his teeth. "No. I started taking 'business trips' to Vegas every few months instead."

"And Penelope didn't mind?"

"She didn't know I was going to Vegas."

I narrowed my eyes. "You lied to her?"

"Like I said, I have a problem." His face flushed. "So long as I used the excuse of business trips, Penelope didn't question it. I guess she liked to believe I was so important, my bosses sent me all over the country."

"Jesus, Gerald."

"I know. But gambling is fucking addicting. I got in deep with those damn cruises, and then I was going to Vegas to try and dig my way out. Unfortunately, I just got deeper in debt."

I blinked at him, baffled that a seemingly upstanding guy like Gerald Granger had a gambling problem. "So Penelope has no idea?"

"Hell no." He sighed. "I juggled everything as long as I could, but eventually I got so deep in debt, I had to go to Bob for help. That was the worst decision I ever made."

I'd have given that honor to getting involved in gambling period, but maybe that was just me. "So, Bob helped you get out of debt?"

"Yes. But then I was just in debt to *him*." He scowled. "He was after me constantly to pay him back, or he'd go to Penelope and tell her."

"How much did you owe Bob?"

He looked ill as he said, "A little over three hundred thousand dollars."

I bugged my eyes. "From gambling?"

He cringed. "You'd be surprised how easy it is to go down that rabbit hole. I put up my house as collateral at one point, and thank God Bob paid that off for me. If I'd lost our house, Penelope would have divorced me for sure."

And who would blame her?

"So Bob saved your ass."

"Yes." He glanced up, looking angry. "Of course, he never let me forget it. He kept telling me what a worthless piece of shit I was and how I didn't deserve Penelope."

I was kind of on Bob's side with this one, but I kept that to myself. "I'm sure you were very angry with Bob. Maybe you felt a little desperate even."

"Of course." He narrowed his eyes. "But I didn't kill him. I'm sure that's what you're getting at, right?"

"Blackmail is a dangerous game. He threatened you, and maybe you felt you had no choice."

"I didn't kill Bob."

"You wouldn't be the first person to crack under that kind of pressure."

"Sheriff," he growled. "I didn't *kill* my father-in-law."

I didn't respond. I'd never particularly liked Gerald, but I certainly hadn't suspected he was capable of the level of lying and deceit he was admitting to. He'd seemed very bland, maybe even boring. Offshore gambling and breaking and entering were not things I'd ever pictured Gerald getting involved in.

He leaned forward, his face tense. "When you caught me, I was searching Bob's office for any record of the money he loaned me. I just wanted that to go away. Bob's dead, and there's no reason Penelope needs to know about our transaction."

I sighed. "Problem is, Gerald, blackmail is an age-old reason to murder someone."

He scowled. "I told you ten times I didn't do it."

"I'm not sure you'd tell me if you had."

His gaze flickered. "Okay, probably not. But while I loathed Bob, and I can't say I'll miss him, I'd never have harmed him. I wouldn't hurt Penelope that way. You might think I'm a jerk, Sheriff, but I love my wife. I'd never have put up with Bob all these years if I didn't." He closed his eyes, wincing. "It's torture watching Penelope suffer. As much as I hated Bob, if I could bring him back, I'd do it for her." He opened his eyes. "I swear on my life, I'd never have hurt Bob because it would hurt *her*."

His impassioned speech seemed sincere, but so far, out of all the suspects I had, his motive was the most compelling. What I didn't know was if he'd had the opportunity. "Did you spend any time with Bob at the party?"

"Hell no. You kidding me?"

"Where were you when Rita screamed?"

"I was with Herman Todd. He works at the bank with me. We were bitching about work, along with Patrice, Bob's secretary." He squinted. "Patrice wandered off to get another drink, and then after a bit, Rita screamed."

"I think I know Herman."

"He's a good guy. I'm sure he'll remember our conversation." He ran a finger under his collar. "I swear, I didn't kill Bob."

"You still broke into Bob's office."

"But I didn't break in, Sheriff. Remember, I had a key. I've been in Bob's office tons of times."

I frowned. "When he wasn't there?"

He looked embarrassed. "No."

I could probably scrape up probable cause to arrest him, if needed. Problem was, I wasn't convinced he was my killer. He'd had motive, but if he was talking to Herman, he probably hadn't had opportunity. I was still waiting on approximate time of death from the ME. Until I had that, it was hard to make a real timeline. Max wasn't a coroner, but he'd noticed certain things, while checking for signs of life from Bob. He'd remarked that the body temperature was still almost normal. He'd also mentioned there were zero signs of rigor mortis, which could set in as soon as fifteen minutes. Whether or not the ME would agree with Max, remained to be seen.

"I'll verify your story with Herman."

He nodded. "Okay."

"Don't call Herman to coach him either, and don't you go near Bob's office again."

"I won't."

I gave him a hard look. "You should come clean with your wife about the gambling. It would be better coming from you."

He looked horrified. "God, no. I… I can't tell her. Are you going to tell Penelope?"

"Not at this time. But the truth has a way of bubbling to the surface, Gerald. It would be way worse if Penelope finds out about your gambling from someone other than you."

"She can never find out," he rasped, looking apprehensive. "I'll take that secret to my grave."

I felt he was being foolish, but from the stubborn set of his jaw, he wouldn't be swayed. "Suit yourself."

"Can I go? I answered all your questions."

I sighed. "Yeah. You can go."

"Thank God." He stood, his chair dragging noisily on the tile floor.

I watched him shuffle to the door. "Hey, Gerald."

"Yeah." He froze, his hand on the knob.

"If I find out you're gambling again, I'm going straight to Penelope."

He winced. "Okay."

"I mean it."

"I know."

"If I was you, I'd get professional help. You could end up losing everything if you slip up again."

He nodded, but I doubted he'd take my advice. He struck me as the type of person who thought he knew best. He left the room, and I pinched the skin between my eyes. I was beat. I had way too much information from the case buzzing around in my head, and it was all blurring together.

Technically, anyone at the party could have killed Bob. There were a few standouts like Charity and Fred Bell and Gerald. But until I knew the time of death, or whether the antique pin used to kill Bob was the same one he'd gifted Charity, I was grasping at straws. At least tomorrow Susan would have the sales record for me of the hatpin used in the murder. Hopefully that would give me a firm direction.

Bob's narcolepsy muddled things even further. Penelope and Rita had both assumed he was just sleeping as usual. It was possible Bob had been dead way before Rita discovered him. Because this murder had taken place in a private home, there were no surveillance videos for me to look at. I just had the witness statements to go by. Cross-referencing everything was tedious and time-consuming work. Eventually I'd make my way through all the half-truths and smokescreens and catch the discrepancies, but at this point, I felt like I was tied up in a big ball of yarn.

I stood and headed toward my office. My intention was to scour all the statements again, just in case I'd missed anything. I was bone-tired and longed for bed, but I owed it to Bob to track down his killer. Right? Pushing open the door to my office, I sat behind my desk with a grunt. It seemed like every time I looked at the work piled on my desk, it multiplied tenfold.

Groaning, I tugged the files stacked on my desk forward. I had a mild headache, and my limbs felt leaden. I stared at the manila folders, fighting my more selfish side. I desperately needed to solve this case. But what I really *wanted* to do was head over to Max's place and spend the night. I didn't even mean that I wanted sex. I just needed to be with him. Near him. Would he like that? Or would that kind of spontaneity make him uncomfortable?

Once more, I eyed the pile of folders in front of me. My eyes were almost crossing from exhaustion. I'd never get through all of those tonight, and even if I did, I'd probably miss tons of stuff. I glanced at my watch, observing it wasn't even midnight yet. Maxwell wasn't exactly a night owl, but if I hurried over to his place right this minute, maybe I could catch him before he went to bed. But if he was already in bed, would he be pissed that I woke him or happy to see me?

Anxiety nipped me as I pushed the files away and stood. I wasn't really an impulsive kind of guy, so this was way out of my comfort zone. But at the moment, my desire to see Max outweighed my fear of rejection. Grabbing my jacket off the back of my chair, I hurried out of my office.

There was no doubt Maxwell would be astonished to see me. But maybe he'd have the same happy reaction to my surprise visit tonight he'd had when I'd dropped in on him today for lunch. He'd definitely been pleased to see me earlier. It had been one of the rare times he'd shown that to me.

With a little luck, this spontaneous decision wouldn't backfire on me.

Chapter Eleven

Maxwell

It turned out Deputy Juan had a few things he needed to finish up before he could drive me home, so I waited in the lobby. The night had definitely been a letdown. I'd hoped for more alone time with Royce than we'd had, but who could have known Gerald Granger would turn into a cat burglar before our very eyes?

Naturally, I'd done my best to hide my disappointment when Royce had suggested Deputy Juan drive me home. I'd have been willing to wait as long as it took in his office, but he hadn't offered that option. So I'd meekly accepted the offered ride home, hoping Royce would be pleased with my easygoing attitude. I wondered if perhaps Royce had sent me home because he was annoyed with me for not waiting in the car as instructed. This was the second time I'd done that, so perhaps he was trying to punish me for not obeying his direct order?

Deputy Juan came into the lobby, giving me an apologetic smile. "I'm sorry, Dr. Thornton. My computer was freezing, and it took me forever to finish my reports."

"No problem." I stood. "You're doing me a favor by driving me home."

He shrugged and headed for the door. "I don't blame Sheriff for not wanting you to walk home late at night. Not with the crazy stuff happening around here lately."

"I suppose." I followed him to his patrol car.

Once we were inside the vehicle, he started the engine and pulled out onto the deserted road. "I'm trying to help where I can, but Sheriff Callum likes to do everything himself. I wish he'd delegate more. Sometimes I worry he'll get burned out and not want to be sheriff anymore."

I frowned. "Really?"

"Well, no man is an island."

"I can't see Royce quitting. He cares too much about Rainy Dale. He's not the sort of man who shirks responsibility. He's the kind who rises to the occasion. I think it's in his DNA."

Deputy Juan glanced over at me, and I could feel his surprise. "I'm amazed you know that about him."

"You are?"

"Well, if you don't mind my saying so, people don't seem to be your thing. I wouldn't have figured you'd be able to read him so well."

"*Most* people aren't my thing." I hesitated. "I like Royce. He's worth trying to understand."

"I see." His cheek curved in a smile. "So it's like a selective thing that you employ when needed."

"I suppose so." I was relieved Deputy Juan seemed easygoing. I'd had a few conversations with Deputy Sam in the past, and he'd seemed more judgmental. He hadn't liked me much, and he hadn't cared if I knew that. But Deputy Juan had a similar energy to Royce.

We were quiet for a few moments, and then he said, "People sure are surprised you and Sheriff Callum hit it off."

My cheeks warmed because I knew I was the odd part of the equation. "Royce is easy to be around."

"Agreed."

"The town should relax. What I have with Royce is casual." Mostly I was telling him what I thought he wanted to hear. I realized no one in town understood what Royce saw in me. Half the time I didn't either.

He hesitated. "Are you sure Sheriff Callum knows it's casual?"

I frowned. "Why do you ask?"

"Well, he's not the kind of man who plays the field."

"No?"

"Not really. I mean, that's not to say he's never done that, but if he starts seeing someone on a regular basis, he's probably thinking of the future."

The future.

I stiffened at that word and what it represented. I knew Royce liked me, and it was mutual. It was obvious he didn't want me to return to LA too. But Royce seemed content with things the way they were. Was that an act? Was Deputy Juan merely guessing at what Royce wanted, or did he have inside knowledge?

"Has he had many… serious relationships?" I knew Royce would murder me for gossiping with his deputy. Frankly, I couldn't believe I was allowing myself to be drawn into this conversation. But it was rare I found anyone so easy to talk to who actually had knowledge of Royce's personal life. And I was uncharacteristically interested in Royce's romantic past. I refused to ask Girdy stuff because she always got this annoyingly knowing gleam in her eyes.

"Not many." He cleared his throat. "He's not looking to settle. He's holding out for the real deal."

Was he trying to tell me I wasn't worthy? Or was it an innocent remark? I couldn't tell because Deputy Juan had such a happy-go-lucky demeanor, I got the feeling he could tell you your dog had died and you'd be okay with it.

Just in case he was warning me off, I said, "I don't think Royce wants anything serious with me." I gave a humorless laugh. "I'm sure that's a huge relief to you."

He slowed the car as my home came into view. "Not at all. If Sheriff Callum is happy, I'm happy."

His response surprised me. "You sure about that?"

"Yep."

I studied his sharp profile, not sure what to make of him. "You don't disapprove of me?"

"Oh, I don't know you well enough to do something like that, Doc."

Was he for real?

"You're a rarity in this town," I murmured. "Most people seem to dislike me, whether they've met me or not."

"Don't pay people any mind. They're bored, and they make up stuff. It's just how they are."

"I guess." It was hard not to take it personally when you were the one they hated.

"Hey, Doc?"

"Yes?"

"Would you do me a favor and not mention we had this conversation?" He gave a sheepish laugh. "Sheriff would skin me alive if he knew I was talking about his love life."

"I won't say a word." Mostly that was self-preservation. Royce would skin me alive too.

"Home sweet home," Deputy Juan said as he parked in front of my house.

The headlights of his patrol car illuminated the white porch and the steps leading up to the front door.

The house looked rather eerie in the dark, the windows black and unwelcoming. I should have left a light on, but I'd been in a hurry to get to Royce. I shivered, remembering my earlier uneasiness after Charity bell's visit. I'd felt on edge ever since.

I turned to the deputy. "Thanks for the ride. I could have walked, but Royce insisted."

Juan shrugged. "I don't mind at all. It's nice to get out of the station. We've all been doing overtime since Bob's murder."

"Hopefully you guys can close the case soon and go back to a normal routine."

"That sure would be swell." Juan smiled.

I opened the door and got out of the car. Since my goal was to be more like a normal person, and one thank-you was never enough for most people, I leaned down and said, "Thanks again."

"You bet."

I closed the door, feeling pleased with myself. Juan slowly pulled away, made a U-turn in the road, and headed back toward town. Sighing, I walked up the path to my house, feeling a bit let down. I hadn't expected to be coming home so soon. Gerald Granger had certainly fucked up my night. Scowling, I pulled my keys from my back pocket. A moth flapped around the corner of the porch roof, dive-bombing the yellow bug light every few seconds.

Unlocking the door, I stepped inside. The alarm beeped loudly, and I hurriedly entered the security code. As I turned to close the door, a dark bulky shape detached from the shadows of the porch and barreled toward me. Taken completely off guard, I had no time to react. The person slammed into me with the force of an angry rhino, and I went down with a surprised yelp.

Gloved hands encircled my throat and tightened. Still in shock at the sudden violent attack, I punched at the person's head. They far outweighed me, and while I struggled valiantly to get them off, it was like a butterfly trying to fend off Mothra. I gasped for air, and my fists did connect a few times with my assailant's face. But it soon became clear hitting at this thug wasn't going to save me. With him restricting my air, I was already dangerously close to passing out.

Calm the hell down and think.

I'd taken a few years of tae kwon do in the past but never thought I'd actually have to use it. With my heart thumping wildly, I tried to remember the techniques I'd learned to throw someone off when pinned on the ground. We'd done the drills hundreds of times, but putting it into action in the real world was completely different. Since my brain wasn't helping much, I gritted my teeth and moved instinctively.

Pushing up with the balls of my feet, I threw him off-balance so that he fell forward. Next I thrust my pelvis upward, further causing him to lose his equilibrium. Twisting my body, I rolled us until I was on top of him. From there, I forgot everything I knew. I vaguely recalled that I was supposed to switch to offense now but couldn't recall the exact moves. Also, I'd managed to dislodge his grip from my windpipe, and now all I could think about was sucking air into my oxygen-starved lungs.

"Asshole," he growled, trying to throw me off.

Self-preservation kicked in, and I crawled off him, scrambling in terror for the still-open door. I wasn't going to be able to fight him off with hand-to-hand combat. He was too big, and I was no match. Even if I'd been an expert in martial arts, because of his size, he'd have been a challenge, and I was far from an expert. I bolted out of the door, aware of his big feet thudding behind me. I had no idea of how to save myself. Even if I made it to the road, was I supposed to run all the way into town? I'd never make it.

Fuck.

I didn't even get down the steps before he caught me. He grabbed my arm, and I swung around to face him. I tried a few kicks, hoping to catch him off guard again, but he avoided them. I turned and half ran, half fell down the stairs, trying desperately to get away. He caught hold of my shoulders and shoved me forward hard. Unable to keep my balance, I smashed down on the ground, my face slamming into the grass. Groaning, I lay where I was, literally seeing stars.

"You like it rough, buddy?" he snarled, hauling me to my knees.

"Stop," I rasped, bewildered by what was happening.

He slipped his arm around my throat and put me in a choke hold. The pressure of his bulging bicep was powerful, and all I could do was uselessly claw at his beefy arm. My back was pressed to his front, and I had no leverage to fight him. I tried punching backward toward his groin but just landed on his thick thighs. Who was this guy? Why was he so fucking angry?

Gasping like a fish out of water, I began to lose consciousness. In desperation, I did a backward head butt. He screamed in pain and loosened his grip, but not enough for me to escape. Within seconds, his arm was tight around my throat again. My head pounded, and I was once again on the verge of passing out. I clawed at his face and dug my fingers into whatever skin I could connect with. My grasping fingers tangled in something around his neck: dog tags maybe? I pulled hard, and it snapped free.

"Will you just fucking *die* already?" he hissed, punching the side of my head with his free hand.

I really had no interest in obliging him by dying, but I was running out of steam fast. Without oxygen my brain was shutting down, which meant my body was too. I tried the head butt again, but he avoided it. My muscles began to shake, and my eyes rolled up in my head.

I'd always heard that at the moment of death, you thought about your life and your loved ones. But as I slipped away, the only thought in my mind was the agonizing burning of my lungs. I'd never experienced anything so painful and couldn't help but think maybe death would be a relief.

When he suddenly released me, I slumped face-first into the grass again. My body's reflexive inhale of air was so violent, I sucked particles of grass and dirt into my mouth. My head throbbed from head-butting him, and my limbs were like lead. Wheezing, I panted on the ground, uselessly. I thought I heard shouting, but all I could do was lie like a rag doll, eyes closed, body aching.

I knew I should get up, because if he came back, I'd die. But my muscles were mush, and there was no hope of getting to my feet yet. Someone knelt beside me, and groaning, I braced for the hands to return to my throat. But instead, gentle hands turned me over onto my back. I vaguely heard the words "Ambulance" and "Emergency" sprinkled in with a string of curse words.

I tried to open my eyes, but only one seemed to work. The other felt swollen shut, and even the good eye was blurry. My entire face throbbed, and when the person touched my throat, I cried out in pain. I'd never been beaten before, and it was odd to be on this end of things. The inability to speak and tell this person what I needed was terrifying.

"Max, can you hear me?" A familiar voice spoke near my ear.

It was Royce.

I moaned, wanting to tell him to be vigilant. Maybe that fucking psychopath was still around. But my lips wouldn't move easily, and all I could manage was "*Careful.*"

"Shhh. It's okay. Don't move. I've got you."

In the distance I heard sirens. Medical professionals would be here soon to help me. Royce continued to talk to me while we waited for help to arrive. He couldn't do much for me other than to reassure me I'd be fine. His voice was low and soothing, but of course I knew more about my chances of recovery than he did. There were some very real dangers associated with facial trauma. The brain, along with the origin of the airway, was contained within the bounds of the face. Additionally, any strong force to the face could potentially disrupt the cervical spine, leading to disabilities. From what I could feel, the bruising and injury felt superficial, but until a professional examined me, I couldn't relax. I knew I'd be terrifying to look at for a while because of the contusions, but I didn't think I was in mortal danger.

Will you just fucking die already?

I shivered, remembering the thug's words. I still couldn't believe I'd been attacked. He hadn't just come to beat me up either. He'd come to kill me. Not knowing who my assailant was made it ten times more frightening. My attacker could be someone I knew, and he could easily come after me again.

Eventually the ambulance arrived, and it was a blur of flurried activity. I groaned in pain as they lifted me onto a gurney and then into the emergency vehicle. Still feeling stunned by the attack, I wanted to ask Royce to come with me. At the moment, he was the only person I trusted. In the end, it wasn't necessary because Royce climbed up into the back of the ambulance anyway.

As the EMTs tended to me, Royce's hand slipped into mine. It was a surprisingly comforting gesture. That simple touch let me know he was here and watching over me. I assumed they'd take me to the Dallas Medical Center since that was usually where people in Rainy Dale were transported. By the time we arrived at the hospital, my pain had begun to dull a bit. I deduced the EMT techs had given me something to take the edge off.

I was examined by a young-sounding ER doctor, whose name I didn't catch. She explained to Royce that most of my damage was from the chest up. She ascertained that I had no broken bones but needed treatment for severe bruising of the face and throat.

They put me in a room for the night, for observation, just in case I had a concussion. They put ice packs on my throat and face, but I didn't remember much after that because I fell asleep. I woke several times with nightmares but always went back to sleep again. Eventually it was morning, and I was relieved that I could open both of my eyes. There was a cloth-covered ice pack resting on the side of my face. It was no longer cold but cool, and it slipped off when I lifted my head. My left eye still felt puffy and painful, but my right eye almost seemed normal.

Royce was a few feet away in a chair. His head was tilted back and his lips parted in sleep. His lashes were thick and dark against his angular cheeks, and my heart squeezed with affection. I was grateful I hadn't died last night and that I'd have a chance to talk to him again.

When his eyes opened suddenly, he seemed to jerk awake. He appeared disoriented, and then our eyes met. He got up swiftly and came to the side of my bed. As he studied me, his dark brows were knitted and his mouth a grim line. "You're awake."

"Yes," I croaked.

"You gave me a real scare, Max." His voice was husky, and he took my hand.

I opened my mouth to speak again, but just a hoarse squawk came out. Grimacing, I gingerly touched my throat. I was lucky my assailant hadn't crushed my windpipe. He'd been big and strong, but he hadn't had great technique. If he'd been better at assault, I'd probably have died.

It was exhausting to try and force words from my swollen throat, so I made a writing motion, indicating I'd rather write what I had to say. Royce pulled a small pad and pen from his shirt pocket and handed them to me. I scribbled the question that was burning in my soul.

Did you get him?

Shaking his head, Royce said, "No. He ran, and I went to you."

Scowling, I winced. I guess I understood why he hadn't just left me lying on the ground like a hooked trout. But I really wished he'd grabbed the asshole.

You should have chased after that guy, instead of letting him go.

He sighed, looking uneasy. "You were in bad shape. I… I wanted to make sure you kept breathing. I wasn't sure if you'd need CPR or what."

I exhaled with frustration.

"Was there anything about him that seemed familiar?" Royce asked. "Maybe his cologne or something about his build or voice?"

No.

"Nothing at all?"

I thought back over the fight, straining to remember details. Outside, on the lawn, I recalled the snapping of a cord beneath my grasping fingers. **I ripped off his necklace.** At the time, I'd been starved for oxygen, and when the strand had snapped, I'd hallucinated little white teeth sprinkling down onto my shoulders and chest.

"My guys are searching the scene now. Hopefully they'll find something to help identify him." He squeezed my hand, studying my face. I assumed I looked pretty horrific because every time he scanned my face, his jaw clenched with anger.

When can I go home?

"The doctor is coming by this morning to check you over. If you're showing no signs of concussion, then she said you could go home today." He hesitated. "You're staying with me though, Max. No way in hell are you going back to your place."

If he thought I'd argue, he was wrong. I suppose I could have stayed in a hotel, but the idea of being in Royce's home was comforting.

Does Girdy know what happened?

"Yeah. I called her. She's cancelling all your appointments and rescheduling for a few weeks from now."

I slumped with relief. Girdy truly was a godsend. She was efficient and pleasant, and she put up with me with little complaint. I needed to be sure she knew how much I appreciated her. In fact, she deserved a raise.

The door opened, and a nurse walked in. She wore a pink smock and carried two ice packs. "Good morning, boys." She smiled and stopped near the bed. "I'm Nurse Rhen."

"Hello, Nurse Rhen." Royce nodded. "Thank you for taking care of… my friend."

His hesitation wasn't lost on me. I supposed I too wouldn't have known exactly how to title Royce if our positions were reversed.

"It's our pleasure." She flicked her gaze to me. "Mr. Thornton, I've been informed you're a doctor?"

"He is," Royce responded for me.

"You're not going to be difficult, I hope?" She lifted one brow. "Right now, you're simply a patient. We know what we're doing, so don't feel the need to boss us around."

I wasn't sure how to respond.

"It's time to replace your cold packs, Doctor. Lie flat, please." I complied, and she gently removed the used pack on my neck and replaced it with a fresh one. I was grateful for the new cool pack but winced because touching the skin around my neck, even lightly, was extremely painful. She placed the other pack on the side of my face that still felt swollen. "You look much better this morning," she said brightly.

"He does." Royce nodded.

She grimaced. "You won't be doing any liver rounds anytime soon, Doc, but I'm guessing you should be up and around in a week. You'll still be bruised as heck, naturally."

I grunted.

Royce frowned. "Liver rounds?"

She laughed. "It's hospital slang."

Royce continued to look confused.

"Sorry. It's slang for happy hour."

"Oh."

"In layman's terms, I just mean he won't be partying anytime soon." She grabbed a water container on a tray near my bed. "I'll get you fresh H2O. It tastes stale when it sits overnight. Be back in a second."

Once she'd left the room, I scribbled, **Do I look scary?**

He gritted his teeth in response.

Before I could reply, a young Asian woman strode into the room. She wore her hair in a severe ponytail, and she was talking on a phone. "I'd like a Dacron swab of her posterior nasopharynx for bordatella PCR and culture, and if it's positive, I'd like a course of azithromycin." She hung up and tucked her phone into the pocket of her white coat. Her smile was forced, but rather than being insulted, I sympathized. I recognized an overworked physician when I saw one. "Hello, Dr. Thornton, I'm Dr. Zhao. How are you feeling today?" Without waiting for a response, she grabbed the clipboard on the foot of the bed and scanned it.

"He definitely seems more alert today," Royce said.

She glanced up, and I got the impression she was so focused, she hadn't noticed Royce was even in the room. "That's great." She narrowed her eyes. "Did you spend the night in here?"

Royce's cheeks seemed flushed as he shrugged.

"That's sweet," she murmured. She moved closer, tugging a small light from her pocket. She examined my eyes, nodding. "Pupils are responsive. Any headache or nausea?"

"Mild headache," I squawked. Something about her authoritative demeanor made me hesitant to write out my responses. I think I was subconsciously worried she'd critique my penmanship.

"Excellent. A mild headache is to be expected." She straightened and glanced at Royce. "I assume you'll be driving him back to Rainy Dale?"

"Yes."

"Okay. Well, I don't see any obvious signs of concussion. Of course, if you experience any nausea or dizziness, I expect you to return immediately. I'm sure you know the spiel, Doctor?"

"I do," I whispered.

"In that case, I'll sign your release." She pulled her dark brows together. "I expect you to take it easy for at least a week. As you well know, rest will help you heal faster. None of your patients will want to see you anyway. You're extremely scary-looking."

I grunted, and Royce laughed.

She smirked and headed for the door. "Let's not meet again, okay?" And she was gone.

"Whoa. I never thought it would happen." Royce grinned down at me. "I think I just met a doctor with an even worse bedside manner than you, Max."

Since scowling and speaking hurt too much, I let him know my feelings about his rude comment the good old-fashioned way: I flipped him the bird.

Chapter Twelve

Royce

During the night, while Maxwell slept at the hospital, I'd had Deputy Sam come get me and take me back to get my car. In his condition, I'd figured it was kinder to drive Maxwell home in my car rather than make him ride in a taxi. I didn't want anybody gawking at him and making him feel worse.

Maxwell dozed off the minute we got in my car for our trip back to Rainy Dale. I was glad too because I didn't have it in me to make superficial conversation. The events of last night churned in my brain, and over and over again, I relived the horror of driving up on Max being choked to death. At first, I'd assumed I had to be imagining what I was seeing, but then I'd blared the horn and jumped out of my car before it even came to a full stop.

The guy had taken off across Max's property, disappearing into the night. I'd started to chase after him, but Max's body had gone so still, I was terrified he'd stopped breathing. I'd made the decision to tend to him instead, and maybe it had been the wrong call. I wasn't sure. Perhaps it would have been smarter to try and catch the guy who'd attacked him, but running past Max's crumpled body had been impossible. When I'd first reached his limp figure, for one gut-wrenching second, I'd thought he was dead.

I swallowed hard and glanced over at Max. Bruised and battered, he looked defenseless as he slept. His usually stern jaw was slack and his cool blue eyes hidden. In sleep, he looked like a different person. He appeared gentle. Vulnerable. I didn't even want to think about how close he'd come to dying. It made me sick to my stomach and enraged.

What I didn't understand was why someone had attacked him at all. He wasn't the most popular person in Rainy Dale, but I found it hard to believe one of his patients had come after him like that. Of course, after what had happened to Bob Cunningham, it was possible we simply had a murderous psychopath on our hands, someone who killed for the sheer pleasure of killing. Perhaps the same fucker who'd murdered Bob had tried to kill Max. But what possible connection did Max have to Bob? None that I could see.

I felt powerless because without knowing the motive for attacking Max or Bob, I didn't know the enemy. If I didn't know the enemy, how was I supposed to protect Max? At least he hadn't squabbled about staying with me. I'd feel much more in control of things with him in my home. My house was within the town limits, instead of on the outskirts like his. Hopefully that alone would make him safer.

Bob Cunningham was killed in the middle of a party full of people.

Negative thoughts like that wouldn't help anything. Once Max felt better, I'd question him in depth about his assault. It was very possible he'd seen or heard things he didn't even realize. As soon as I had Max safely tucked away at my house, I intended to run over to his place. I wanted to see what my guys had found while I was in Dallas. Hopefully they'd found something.

I also needed to visit Susan at the Squeaky Wheel today. She'd promised to have the sales record of the antique hatpin available to me. Perhaps that would provide me with a good solid lead. I didn't see how Max's assault and Bob's murder connected, but my gut told me there had to be one. Just because I didn't see it didn't mean it wasn't there.

Max groaned and jerked, punching the door. He slowly lifted his head, looking confused.

"It's okay, Max. You're in my car. We're going home now." I spoke quietly so as not to startle him.

He closed his eyes and swallowed hard. "Sorry. Nightmare," he rasped.

"You don't have to apologize."

Rubbing his knuckles, he sighed. Overnight, the swelling had gone way down on his face, although he had a lot of contusions, and the bruising was beginning to set in. One entire side of his face was red with a hint of blue. He had a cut over his left eye, and the eye socket itself was still quite puffy. The left corner of his mouth was swollen, but somehow his nose had escaped unscathed.

With trembling fingers, he reached for the water bottle I'd bought him at the hospital. He undid the lid and lifted it to his swollen mouth. Some of the liquid dribbled down his chin, and he wiped it away impatiently. Something told me he was going to be a difficult patient. I knew enough about Max to know depending on others was his greatest nightmare.

"Are you hungry?" I asked. Not that he could really chew. But I figured maybe I could get him a shake or something. He'd checked out of the hospital before lunchtime and had slept through breakfast. I knew he must be hungry.

"No."

"You need to eat."

"Later, Royce," he mumbled hoarsely.

I pursed my lips and dropped it. I'd make sure I got some food in him later, once we were at my place. I'd make chicken soup or something.

He closed his eyes again, and soon he was asleep. They'd given him a lot of pain medication to help him with the trip home. I dreaded when it wore off because I knew he'd be hurting. They'd offered him a pain prescription to take home, but he'd declined. I wasn't sure why. Maybe he thought suffering was good for him or something.

When we finally neared Rainy Dale, I breathed a sigh of relief. We had to drive past Max's house on the way to mine. As we passed, I observed my guys still processing the scene. I was happy to see my deputies had taken this assault seriously, even with me not here to supervise. It reassured me I had a good team.

I pulled into my driveway and shut the car off. Max roused, once again looking confused. "We're here." I opened my door and hurried around to his side.

He had the door open by the time I got there. Grunting, he let me help him out of the vehicle. He moved stiffly, but he could walk fine. His lower half hadn't been hugely injured in the fight. He'd be bruised, but he could move around okay, so long as he took it slow.

I watched him closely as he made his way up the steps to the porch. I didn't want to help him if he didn't need it. I knew he'd resent it. Once he was safely up the stairs, I unlocked my front door. Grumpy howled from the kitchen, and I heard him scratching at the gate to be let out.

"Hold on, pup. I want to get Max to bed first."

"It's fine," Max grumbled. "Let him out."

I frowned. "You sure?"

"Yes."

Shrugging, I moved to the kitchen. Max walked slowly down the hallway toward the guest room. He'd stayed with me before, so he knew his way around the place. I was actually happy he seemed relaxed enough to just head to his room. I wouldn't have minded if he'd wanted to bunk with me, but I also suspected he'd want his space. I wasn't surprised he'd headed straight for the guest room.

I opened the gate that kept Grumpy in the kitchen, and he jumped up on me, whining. "It's okay. Come on, let's go outside." I headed to the glass door, and the puppy ran after me. I went out in the backyard with him, and once he'd done his business, threw the ball a bit for him. I figured if he burned off some energy, he'd be less likely to make a nuisance of himself when he discovered Max was in the house.

Once I felt the pup was sufficiently worn-out, we went back inside. The second Grumpy entered the house, he seemed to catch Max's scent. He scampered down the hallway and ran into Max's room. As I followed down the hallway, I heard the puppy whining and Max grumbling under his breath. I stopped at my room and grabbed a pair of pajamas for Max.

When I came into the guest room, Max was sitting on the bed with Grumpy in the curve of his arm. I hadn't been sure if the puppy would be thrown off by Max's appearance. But I guess he'd seen past the bruising and swelling and recognized a friend. The puppy's tail was swirling in a fast circle, and he wiggled against Max.

Max glanced up as I entered the room. His gaze dropped to the pajamas, and relief flickered through his eyes. I set them next to him on the bed and crossed my arms. "I thought you might want to change into something clean and loose."

"Thanks."

"Looks like Grumpy is happy to see you." I smiled.

Nodding slowly, Max winced. "Didn't think he'd recognize me," he whispered.

"He sure did." I smiled. "Can I help you get undressed? Might go faster."

He hesitated. "Okay." He toed off his shoes as he spoke.

Knowing how independent he was, he had to really be hurting to accept my assistance. I helped him stand, and I slowly unbuttoned his shirt. He kept his eyes on my chest, and I could feel tension radiating off him. I knew he was self-conscious of his looks at the moment, which seemed pretty silly to me. Why be worried about something so unimportant? Didn't he know I was just beyond happy that he was alive and in my care?

Grumpy waddled to the corner of the bed and lay down sleepily. I smiled at the puppy and turned to Max. I carefully peeled his shirt off his shoulders, and he shivered. There were bruises on his chest and arms, and anger swam through me. I tossed his shirt on a chair and turned back to him. Slowly, I undid his belt and then the clasp of his jeans. His breathing was raspy and quick. It occurred to me he seemed almost aroused, which got me kind of turned on. I wasn't about to make a move on him. He needed sleep, and my only goal was to get him into bed. Alone.

I unzipped his jeans, and he helped me push them down. He had on white briefs, and I could see he definitely had a semi-erection. I did my best to ignore that fact, fully aware my dick was pressing against my zipper painfully. I reminded myself that what he needed right now was nurturing, not sex. His body was simply responding to being touched.

"Why don't you go ahead and sit." My voice was gruff.

He obeyed, and I tugged his jeans off all the way. He sat there in just his underwear, looking dejected.

"Hey," I said softly.

He flicked his gaze to mine.

"It doesn't matter."

He blinked at me.

"None of the outside stuff makes any difference. You're still you, Max. Bruises fade. Thank God you're alive, that's all I'm thinking."

"I'm hideous."

I laughed. "No."

"Liar."

"I ain't lying." I crouched down in front of him and ran my hands up his bare thighs. "If I weren't a gentleman, I'd prove to you just how much I still like you."

He shivered again.

I sighed. "But I am a gentleman, and we don't take advantage of guys who have loads of pain medication in their bloodstream." I grabbed the pajama pants folded next to him. "Now, I'm going to be a good boy and put these on you. Don't try any funny business."

He chuffed.

I slipped the pajama bottoms up over his feet and calves. When it came to sliding them over his thighs, he aided me by lifting his rear end. Unable to help myself, I leaned in and kissed his flat stomach, inhaling his familiar scent. When I straightened, I gave a sheepish grin. "I'm only human."

"Tease." His tongue darted out, sweeping over his swollen lower lip.

Gritting my teeth, I grabbed the pajama top. "Put your arms above your head, please."

He obeyed, watching me as I slipped the silky top over his head. He helped by inserting his arms into the sleeves. Once his top was on, I smiled at him. "Now get under the covers."

Without a word, he slowly did as I instructed. Grumpy got up and wandered over to settle next to him. He lay on his back, holding the covers up to his chin. "Thanks," he whispered.

"Of course." I studied him. "I have to go out for a while, but when I get back I'm going to make some chicken soup. Get some sleep, okay? We don't want Dr. Zhao making a house call."

He grunted.

"Sleep. I mean it." I picked up his jeans from the floor as I spoke and grabbed his shirt. I moved to the doorway.

"Royce," he croaked.

I turned to face him, "Yeah?"

"Be safe."

"Always am."

****

I parked in front of Maxwell's house and climbed from my car. Deputy Sam met me on the porch, looking way more alert than I felt. He'd probably pulled an all-nighter too, but I guess that was youth for you.

"Find anything interesting?" I asked, pushing my hands in my coat pockets. It was a nippy day; a cool October breeze blew, and the sweet scent of milkweed infused the air.

"Collected some fresh cigarette butts on the end of the porch. We're thinking maybe whoever attacked Dr. Thornton was waiting a while for him to come home. I highly doubt the doctor smokes."

"No." I frowned. "The butts could be from one of his patients though."

"Maybe. Although I don't believe Girdy would allow that. I think she'd reprimand someone who lit up anywhere near the office."

I smiled. "That's probably true."

"The forensics team found some little beads or something in the grass. I took a photo for you." He pulled his phone from his pocket and scrolled through a few menus. He held it out to me. "I thought they were teeth at first. I wondered if maybe the doc didn't lose a few pearly whites during the assault."

I squinted at the photo of the bag. "What are those? Shells?"

"I think so."

"Huh. We're a long way from the ocean."

He nodded. "I was thinking the same thing."

I studied the photo, some vague memory gnawing at me. "I feel like I've seen something like this recently."

"Yeah?"

"God, my brain is tired. It'll come to me."

"Forensics will figure out what they are." He tucked the phone back in his pocket. "How is the doctor, by the way?"

I grimaced. "Bruised and battered."

"Did he get a look at the guy?"

"Doesn't seem so. I haven't really had a chance to talk to him much about the attack. He was out of it.

I'll try tomorrow. I think he'll be more alert once the pain meds are out of his system."

"Sure." He hesitated. "Is he coming back here?"

"God no."

He looked surprised at my passionate response.

I laughed gruffly. "Not right away… He's, uh… staying with me for the moment."

I had to hand it to him, he cloaked his emotions well. "Makes sense."

Deputy Juan came out of the house. "Hey, Sheriff. You're back."

"I am."

"I think the scene is processed. There wasn't much to find, honestly." He sighed. "I feel awful he got attacked right after I dropped him off. The perp was probably waiting on the porch for him, and I just drove away."

"You couldn't have known, Juan." I frowned.

"Still." He sighed.

"Oh." Deputy Sam snapped his fingers. "I have a couple of messages for you, Sheriff. Let's see, Larry Stephanopoulos said he can't come in to talk today for a second interview, but tomorrow will be fine. Also, Susan from the Squeaky Wheel called for you. She said she lost your number, so she called the station. She said to tell you she has the book, and she'll be at her shop all day."

Excitement jolted through me at the news of Susan's call. "Yeah?" I moved down the steps. "That's good news. I'll see you guys back at the station."

"Sure thing, boss," Deputy Juan called after me.

I got in my car and drove back into town, feeling optimistic. Larry's interview could wait, that was fine. I was mostly just going to chastise him for withholding the fact he'd hired Patrice to spy on Bob. But Susan at the Squeaky Wheel I definitely wanted to talk to. I longed for one solid lead to ground me; maybe Susan would provide that lead. I parked in front of the Squeaky Wheel and went into the shop. Susan wasn't out front like last time, and as I made my way toward the counter, I saw Patrice O'Malley perusing a display of cufflinks.

She glanced over and looked a bit surprised to see me. "Oh, hello, Sheriff."

I really just wanted to get to Susan so I could find out who'd purchased the hatpin that killed Bob. But I didn't want to be rude, so I changed direction and went to say hi. "Fancy meeting you here." I smiled.

She laughed. "Best place in town for unique gifts."

"That it is."

She cleared her throat. "I'm just looking for a birthday gift for Larry. It's his birthday today. Genie is having a small get-together."

"It's nice how close you all are."

"Larry's been so good to me and Mom. How could I not love him, right?" Her cheeks were pink, and she avoided my gaze. "I still feel awful for coming to you and telling you I thought he'd killed Bob."

"You did what you thought was right."

"Yes."

"Hey, since I have you here, Patrice, do you mind if I ask a few things?"

Her face tensed. "Not at all." She was saying the right thing, but she looked like she wanted to hide behind the cufflinks.

"It's nothing bad." I smiled. "I just wanted to verify something Gerald Granger told me in his statement, and something Rita Bayes said."

"Oh, really?" She frowned. "I don't know Rita or Gerald that well."

"I'm just cross-referencing things they said. It's no big deal."

"Okay."

"Let's see, Gerald said at Bob's party, you, him, and Herman Todd were talking right before Bob's murder was discovered." I studied her. "Do you remember that?"

"Umm…"

"He said you three were complaining about work."

She looked relieved. "Oh, yeah. Now I recall. Yeah, we were venting."

"Okay, good."

She laughed. "Mostly I just listened though. The two of them were really irritated at their boss." Her gaze flickered. "But of course, Bob was my boss. I didn't say much."

"It's okay if you did, Patrice. You were at a party. You're allowed to let off steam."

"Yeah?" She sighed. "I'm glad to hear you say that. With you being a cop and all, I always feel like you're examining every word out of my mouth."

I frowned. "Not exactly *examining*."

She put her hand on my arm. "Sorry. I don't mean to insult you. I just mean, well, men in power make me nervous." She gave a breathy laugh.

"I see." I smiled.

She removed her hand and went back to looking at the cufflinks. "Was that all you wanted to ask me?"

"Just one more thing. Rita Bayes said you and Penelope were serving Bob his drinks at the party. Is that true?"

She frowned. "I don't remember serving Bob any drinks."

"No?"

She shook her head. "No. Remember, I avoided Bob because Rita was looking at me so hatefully?"

"Yeah, I do remember you saying that, now that I think about it." Why would Rita have lied? Had she simply been trying to throw suspicion off herself? Or was Patrice lying? I'd have to double-check who was telling the truth with Penelope.

"Maybe Rita got me mixed up with someone else." Patrice frowned.

"That could be it."

She glanced at me. "Was there… anything else?"

"Let me think…"

Keeping her eyes on the display rack, she said, "I left Gerald and Herman to go get another drink for myself. Did Gerald tell you that?"

"Uh, yeah, he did."

She flicked her gaze to me and said in a conspiratorial tone, "I didn't really need another drink. I was already pretty tipsy. But I'd had about as much ranting as I could take. I mean, complaining will only get you so far, right?"

"That is true."

"They were both so full of resentment. I hate negativity. It depresses me," she said quietly. "I prefer positive people."

I smiled. "Me too."

"Do you?"

"Absolutely."

She sighed. "You really are so nice, Sheriff. You're not scary at all. I'll try not to get nervous around you anymore."

I laughed. "I'm glad you don't find me scary."

I heard Susan coming out of the back room. "Well, have fun at Larry's birthday party."

"Thanks." She smiled.

I headed toward the cash register and found Susan slicing open a carton with a box cutter. She glanced up and smiled. "Hello, Sheriff. You'll be happy to know I found that sales record you wanted."

"Excellent." I was filled with anticipation but trying to play it cool.

She reached beneath the counter and tugged a small ledger from the shelf. She set it on the counter and rifled through the pages. She pressed her finger to the page. "Here it is. Hanna kept such detailed records. I aspire to be as thorough as her. She also had such lovely handwriting. So clear and easy to read."

Clamping my jaw, I held on to my patience. "Can I see the book?"

"Oh." She laughed. "Sorry." She pushed the book toward me. "See, he bought my Cloisonné hatpin before I could."

I studied the ledger, seeing the sale of one red-and-blue Cloisonné hatpin written neatly, along with a vintage lace garter belt and stocking set. Both purchased by Bob Cunningham. So Bob had bought the item that killed him, and according to Rita, Charity Bell had been the one who'd received the pin as a gift.

So the Bells had lied to me about that. If they'd lied about that, what else had they lied about? I met Susan's gaze, excitement building in my gut. "This is great, Susan. Do you mind if I borrow this book? I'd like to enter it into evidence."

"Uh, sure. Whatever you need."

"Appreciate it." I closed the ledger and strode toward the door, tugging my cell from my pocket. I dialed Deputy Juan. As soon as he picked up, I said, "I need you to bring Fred and Charity Bell in for questioning, now."

"Sure, boss." Deputy Juan sounded surprised. "Did something happen?"

"Can't talk right now. Just please call them and get them down to the station."

"You got it."

I hung up and hurried to my car. Once I reached the station, I copied the page that showed Bob's purchase and bagged the ledger for evidence. I went to the breakroom for a cup of coffee and was happy to find a fresh pot. It felt like things were finally going my way, until Deputy Juan came into the room.

"Bad news, Sheriff." He grimaced.

"What?" I scowled, stirring cream into my coffee.

"Charity and Fred drove to Cactus Springs early this morning. She has a gig at a private party."

"Seriously?"

"I'm afraid so."

"I told those two not to leave town," I grumbled.

"Looks like they didn't listen."

I sighed. "Well, isn't that convenient?"

"Fred said the gig was booked months ago. He said they'd be happy to talk to you first thing tomorrow morning. They're staying the night in Cactus Springs."

Fucking fantastic.

"I can go haul them back if you want?" He raised his brows.

"Hmmm." Cactus Springs was only about three hours away to the east. While I hated making my deputies drive there, I also resented the Bells for ignoring me about leaving town.

"What do you say?" Deputy Juan asked. "I don't mind going after them."

I was torn. Receiving a gift from a dead person didn't instantly incriminate you. But they'd lied straight to my face many times, which made them look pretty bad. What I didn't know was had they lied because they were guilty of murder or because they were just afraid of looking guilty of murder? "You sure they're actually in Cactus Springs and not just making a run for the border?"

"Not really."

Wrestling with what to do, I scowled. "Go get 'em, and take Sam with you."

He nodded and headed for the door. He paused and glanced back at me. "Am I arresting them or just bringing them in to talk?"

"Use your judgment. If they give you trouble, arrest their asses for obstruction of justice. I believe I have probable cause to arrest them anyway. Apparently, the hatpin used in the murder was a gift to Charity from Bob."

He raised his brows. "No shit?"

"No shit."

"Wow."

"Yep. Yet they both acted like they'd never seen it before."

He grinned and rubbed his hands together. "I kind of hope they give me trouble so I can arrest them."

I frowned. "Keep it professional, Deputy."

"I know. I know." He left the room.

I headed to my office, and just as I sat down, my cell rang. "Hello?"

"Hey, Sheriff, it's Julie from the lab. I'm about to send over some photos from the crime scene at Dr. Thornton's office. There weren't too many. Just some cigarette butts and the broken puka shell necklace. The crime scene was pretty Spartan."

"Wait, did you say puka shells?" My heart began to pound.

"Yeah. We collected them from the grass. Like I said, there wasn't much to photograph."

"Uh… thanks, Julie. That's very helpful." There was only one guy I knew who wore a puka shell necklace, and that was Fred Bell. Feeling breathless, I said, "I appreciate you taking the time to call."

"You bet." She hung up.

Fred Bell wasn't *necessarily* the only person in town who wore a puka shell necklace. They weren't exactly in style, but it still could be a coincidence that Maxwell's attacker had worn a puka shell necklace, same as Fred Bell. I needed to calm down and not get ahead of myself. Did it look damning for the Bells that I kept catching them in lies? Hell, yes. But people lied to the cops all the time, and not only when they were guilty.

I glanced at my watch, anxiety eating at me. It would take my deputies six hours round trip to fetch the Bells. Six long torturous hours before I could question the Bells again. Since Charity and Fred had lied to me about the hatpin, I couldn't help but wonder what other lies they'd told me, just to throw me off their trail. As a cop, I realized it was important that I not jump to conclusions, but they definitely had some explaining to do when they got back into town.

But for now, I had six hours to kill. Maybe that was a good thing because Maxwell was at my house, and he needed me to take care of him. I'd go home and check on Maxwell. I'd make him some dinner and spend a little time with him, and in the process, take my mind off the Bells.

Chapter Thirteen

Maxwell

I guess I felt safe tucked away at Royce's place, because I slept like a log. I didn't wake up until I heard him moving around in the kitchen, hours later. Grumpy must have gone to be with his master because I was alone in the bedroom.

Needing to pee, I slowly got out of the bed. I braced myself on the wall, feeling woozy. My muscles were sore from the hand-to-hand combat I'd been involved in, and my head pounded painfully. I'd turned down the pain medication but was second-guessing that decision now. I'd refused it because I hated the feeling of being drugged. But I was beginning to realize, I equally loathed being in pain.

Blowing out a shaky breath, I padded to the restroom. Once I'd taken care of business, I wandered into the kitchen. My heart squeezed oddly at the sight of Royce stirring a big pot on the stove. He wore a floral apron he'd told me his mother had left behind one holiday. I'd never had another man take care of me before, but Royce seemed to enjoy doing it. Oddly enough, his tending to me wasn't as annoying as I'd thought it would.

He must have sensed my presence because he glanced over his shoulder. "What are you doing out of bed?"

"I'm not an invalid," I mumbled, sitting quickly at the kitchen table because I felt light-headed. It would be embarrassing to faint at his feet after my grouchy declaration.

He set the wooden spoon he held on a ceramic spoon rest. "How's your throat?"

I touched it lightly. "Tender, but better."

"And your head?"

"Throbbing. Back of my head hurts." At least I found it easier to speak now. My voice was hoarse, and probably would be for a while. But it was no longer impossible to force the words out. "I head-butted the asshole. I hope his head feels worse."

He bugged his eyes and approached. "You head-butted him?"

"I've told you before I know some tae kwon do."

"Didn't know head-butting was a tae kwon do move."

"I'm sure there's a head butt in all forms of martial art." I leaned back in the chair, sighing. "Do you have an ice pack by any chance? The cold feels good on my face."

He grimaced. "Yes. God, I should have thought of that." He hurried out of the kitchen and returned with a blue cloth ice bag. He went to the refrigerator and scooped ice into the bag. "I kind of forgot I had this thing."

"If you have any Advil, that would be appreciated as well."

"You got it." He returned to me, holding out the ice bag. "I'll get the Advil. Be back in a second."

I pressed the bag to the side of my face and groaned. The ice hurt and simultaneously felt good. Grumpy was lying in a little bed in the corner, and he lifted his head, ears pricked. "It's fine," I told the puppy. "I'll live."

Royce returned, and he got me a glass of water. He held out two small pills, and I took them from his palm. I was slightly nervous swallowing would be a challenge, but I managed to get the pills down fairly easily. It seemed the majority of the swelling was now external.

Studying me, Royce crossed his arms. "Mind talking a little about the attack?"

"That's fine."

"I'm wondering if any details are coming back to you. Maybe some physical details of your assailant?"

I took my time answering, then said, "The guy was big. Taller than me by a few inches."

"Thin? Fat? In between?"

I thought about when I'd been straddling my attacker. "He seemed to be a mixture of flab and muscle. His arms and thighs were muscular, but he had fat around the middle."

"Okay, good. Could you see his hair?"

"No. He wore a mask, and his whole head was covered."

"Any tattoos?"

My throat was dry, so I drank some more water before responding. "There really wasn't much skin showing." I winced. "And to be honest, I was fighting for my life. I… I wasn't really *looking* at him."

He nodded. "Yeah. I get it."

I shivered and tried to push away the panic that wanted to bubble up. Not knowing why I'd been attacked was twice as terrifying. "Wish I knew why he picked me."

"There may not be any real reason. It could have been random."

I didn't agree. The attack had felt very personal. "He was waiting for me."

The way his face tensed showed he already knew that. "Maybe he was just camping on your porch, and you happened to come home."

"Don't think so."

"Did you smell alcohol on his breath or anything?"

"No."

He exhaled as if frustrated. "Did you hear his voice?"

"He did speak. Twice."

Royce perked up. "Yeah? What did he sound like? Did he have an accent? A twang? A high voice, or low?"

"He sounded angry." I swallowed hard. "Deep voice. Mature."

"What did he say?"

"I don't remember his exact words." I lowered the ice bag to my throat, wincing as it rubbed my tender skin. "He didn't like it when I fought back." I met Royce's curious gaze. "He seemed upset that I wouldn't just… die."

His face flushed, and anger glittered in his brown eyes. "Fucker."

"Amen."

He moved to sit next to me at the table. His expression was gentle, and he said quietly, "Now, don't take this the wrong way, but can you think of anyone that you've upset recently. I mean, really upset."

"No more than usual."

"What about that woman you called old?"

I frowned. "Mrs. Miller?"

"Yeah. Do you think maybe her husband or son came after you?"

Was that possible? She'd been very upset. "I don't think so? I hurt her feelings, but I can't picture someone murdering me for that."

He tilted his head back, looking frustrated. "Yeah, me neither. I can't shake the feeling this is connected to Bob's death."

"But why? I didn't even know Bob." I sipped more water, feeling bone-tired.

Royce studied me, his brow wrinkled. "I found something out today. I probably shouldn't share this with you, but I feel like you're somehow in the middle of this damn case already."

"I don't know why I would be," I whispered.

"Me neither, but I can't imagine why someone would come after you, unless you're somehow connected."

I stared at him, feeling at a loss. "So then, you really don't just think it was a random attack?"

"Of course, I'm not sure. But my gut says it wasn't."

Maybe in the long run that was better. I wanted there to be a real reason why someone would try to kill me. Simply being at the wrong place at the wrong time felt so… anticlimactic. "What did you find out?"

"Bob Cunningham purchased the hatpin that was used to kill him."

I widened my eyes. "What?"

He nodded. "His girlfriend, Rita Bayes, says he gifted it to Charity Bell."

"Do you believe her?"

"I kind of do. Rita is wacky and delusional about Bob's feelings for her. But I think she's right about this." He frowned. "She made some good points. She said

Charity Bell was the only woman at the party wearing a hat."

"I didn't see Charity at the party."

"I didn't either. But I did check her professional website, and she does always wear a signature pink cowboy hat. It's like her thing."

"Huh."

"Rita supposedly saw a text from Charity to Bob, complaining her hat always blew off on stage, and he said he had something for her that would help. A 'special gift.'" Royce's eyes buzzed with excitement. "I found out for a fact that Bob bought the hatpin, and I believe he gifted it to Charity."

"Okay."

"But what I don't get is why Charity would turn around and kill him, or how you figure into any of this."

Remembering Charity's spontaneous visit to me last night, I frowned. Her pregnancy was her business. I wasn't at liberty to just tell everyone her personal information. But if she was a suspect in Bob's murder, did that change things? Should I mention her pregnancy to Royce?

"You have a funny look on your face, Max." Royce's tone was curious.

I avoided his gaze. "I'm thinking."

He didn't speak for a moment, and then he said, "I need to question Charity again about the hatpin. She and Fred both told me they'd never seen it before. But if Bob gave her that pin, then she and Fred lied to my face."

"I wasn't aware of the personal connection between Charity and Bob." My heart began to beat faster as all sorts of scenarios swirled in my head. Charity had been adamant that her husband couldn't know about the pregnancy. Her concern hadn't been for herself though. Had she been afraid of what he might do to the father of the baby?

"I wasn't either at first." Royce said softly, "Now I know that Charity had an affair with Bob."

I froze, holding his gaze. "Really?"

"Yes."

"When?"

He shrugged. "I don't know the exact dates, but I got the feeling it was recent."

I wasn't sure what to do. I wanted to tell Royce about Charity's pregnancy, but a patient's privacy was a big deal. But knowing now that she'd slept with Bob put a new spin on things. Had Bob been the father of her baby? That would be a good motive for murder, perhaps. "Could… could she have stabbed him with the pin?"

Royce shook his head. "It doesn't seem likely. She was outside onstage."

"Maybe her husband?"

"Supposedly, he was with her working the sound. Of course, it's possible one of them did talk to Bob right before he was killed, but no one noticed. There were a lot of people there."

"Right." I clenched my fists, struggling with my decision. I wanted to do the right thing. Keeping pertinent information from Royce felt wrong. It felt like I was blocking him from solving his case.

"I haven't got the autopsy results or time of death yet, but you didn't think Bob had been dead long before being discovered. Right?"

I murmured, "No. I suspect it had just happened. His skin was way too warm and his muscles flexible."

"Of course, I have to wait for the official report from the ME."

"Sure." I took the ice pack from my neck and stared at it in a daze.

Royce touched my arm. "You look exhausted. Go lie down. I'll bring the soup to you when it's ready."

I *was* exhausted. My entire head and throat ached, and my lids were heavy. I didn't feel equipped to handle a heavy conversation with Royce, but I also felt he needed to know about Charity's pregnancy.

"I shouldn't have told you about the hatpin and Charity. I can see you're all stressed out now. I'm sorry," Royce said quietly.

"It's not that." I met his confused gaze.

"No?"

I sighed. "I'm not privy to all the details of your case. I really didn't know much about Charity's involvement until just now."

He frowned. "Okay."

I grimaced. "I need to tell you something, but in doing so, I'm breaking patient-doctor confidentiality."

"So, you must really feel I need to know... whatever this is?"

"It could point to motive for killing Bob."

"I see." He rubbed his jaw. "Who's the patient we're talking about?"

I studied his face, taking in the alert gleam in his eyes. "Charity Bell."

Raising his brows, he leaned forward. "Really?"

"Yes."

"Well, in a murder case, I don't think patient confidentiality holds. Not if this person may pose a threat."

I winced. "That's where it gets tricky. I have no idea if Charity is dangerous. I have no idea if she's actually involved in Bob's murder. I only know that… something has come to light that might give her, and potentially her husband, a motive for killing Bob."

He didn't push me; he stayed silent and waited. I appreciated that because it let me come to terms with my decision. Charity had been adamant that no one, especially her husband, could learn about the baby. But the more I thought about it, the more her pregnancy seemed like a really great reason to kill Bob.

I frowned. "I wouldn't even think about telling you this, except I find the timing of my attack odd."

"So you think this secret of Charity's was the motive for your assault?" He looked uneasy.

I nodded. "It's possible. After I examined her, I swear there was someone else in the building." I shivered. "I could just feel their presence. They might have overheard my discussion with Charity."

"What is it you need to tell me about Charity, Max? I'm still in the dark."

"Right." I hesitated. "She's pregnant."

His face tensed. "Shit."

"Yeah." I met his gaze. "And the baby isn't her husband's."

"She told you that?"

"Yes. Apparently Fred has ED. She was positive it wasn't his. Said they hadn't had sex in over a year."

He leaned back in his chair, raking a hand through his hair. "Holy shit."

"She was adamant Fred couldn't know about the baby. She wanted to terminate right on the spot." I gave a humorless laugh. "I explained it doesn't work like that."

"You think maybe Fred followed her to your place?"

"It's just a hunch. She said he was hard to get away from. That she'd had to sneak over to see me. Now I wonder if she wasn't actually able to shake him. She just thought she had."

He scowled. "But why go after you?"

"I'm not sure he did." I shrugged and rubbed my sore shoulder. "I'm just trying to think of who would want me… dead. Charity was convinced Fred would be humiliated if people found out she was pregnant by Bob. I don't know Fred, but you do. Is he a violent guy?"

Royce narrowed his eyes, looking deep in thought. "He's the kind of guy who protects what is his. He's extremely possessive of Charity."

I shivered. "Okay."

Standing, Royce paced back and forth. "Everything sure is pointing toward the two of them. Doesn't make it a fact, but I'm beginning to see a lot of reasons why Fred Bell might have gone after Bob and then potentially you."

"If it was Fred who attacked me, that was dumb. We probably wouldn't be having this discussion right now. I wouldn't have known that Charity slept with Bob, and probably wouldn't have felt the need to tell you about Charity's pregnancy. I had no idea she had a connection to Bob until right now."

"That's very true." He nodded.

"Then again, maybe it wasn't Fred who attacked me. Perhaps it was just a random psycho."

"It's possible."

I sighed. "Do you realize I've almost died *twice* in three months since moving here? I was never once attacked in LA."

He didn't speak; he simply watched me, looking a little apprehensive.

"Those are horrible odds," I murmured.

He cleared his throat. "We've had an unusual rash of violence in Rainy Dale, I'll give you that. But I don't believe that will continue."

"But you can't guarantee it won't either." I frowned.

"No, I can't guarantee that."

I swallowed hard. "I suppose that's something to think about."

"Meaning what?"

I avoided his gaze. "I may not be so lucky next time."

"There won't be a next time. We were due a few hiccups. Rainy Dale hasn't had any crime until now. Two murders in three months—it's a fluke."

"Perhaps."

I suddenly felt overwhelmed with depression and exhaustion. I knew most of it was because of the assault. But there was more to it as well. I felt weak. Vulnerable. Two of my least favorite things in life. Being attacked for a second time had been a sort of wake-up call. It reminded me how out of place I was in Rainy Dale. It was as if the universe was trying to tell me to go back to LA.

I stood, holding on to the back of the chair. "I think I'll rest."

"Of course." He watched me, looking deflated. He was good at reading me and could probably see I was, once again, questioning staying in Rainy Dale. "I'll bring you some soup when it's ready."

"Thank you, Royce." I left the kitchen and moved down the hallway to my room.

I hated that I'd put that dejected expression on his face. I really, really liked Royce, otherwise I'd have sold my practice and gone back to LA ages ago. But if I was realistic, what did the future hold for us? Even if no psychopaths came after me ever again, did I actually believe that Royce and I would spend the rest of our lives together? I didn't even think that was an attainable goal. Certainly not a goal I'd ever envisioned for myself.

What I'd started with Royce had been casual, but it had grown into more without even trying. Opposites though we were, we meshed well. But if I was logical and not emotional, we'd probably have a year of fun, and then he'd tire of me. Maybe I'd tire of him. Then what? Were we supposed to live in this small town together, watching each other move on with other people? Odds were Royce would be the one moving on too. I didn't imagine there would be many options for me in Rainy Dale. It had been a miracle I clicked with Royce.

I threw back the covers and crawled into the bed. My head was pounding again, and I didn't want to think about the future. I pulled the covers up and closed my eyes. At the moment, I couldn't imagine having the strength to leave Rainy Dale, and most importantly, Royce, behind. But I also realized that *real* strength was needed to stay in a relationship. I'd never once even tried. Mostly because I'd never found anyone worth the effort, but also because I'd suspected I lacked the stamina. The courage.

I sighed, trying to ignore the aching of my face and throat. Why was I putting all of this unneeded pressure on myself? I didn't have to make this decision right this second. For now, I'd enjoy Royce and what we had. Once I was healed and feeling stronger, I'd revisit things. I'd put logic ahead of emotion, like I'd always done. If ultimately I decided to go back to LA, Royce would understand. Even if he didn't, in the long run, my leaving would be best for him. He deserved a normal relationship. He deserved someone who could give themselves fully to him. He had so much love to give, and he had every right to receive that in return.

Painful as it was, I had to face the fact that I probably wasn't Royce's person. I was broken. Emotionally stunted. I'd do more harm than good, and even he possibly knew that. But he wasn't a man who gave up easily. No doubt he thought he could fix me. He thought with enough time and loving kindness, he'd rehabilitate me. Turn me into something I could never be: a stable, emotionally giving partner.

Maybe the real problem was that I was a coward. I didn't want to stick around and see him fail. I didn't want to witness the moment he realized I was a lost cause. It was easier leaving before he caught on, that I'd always let him down.

Chapter Fourteen

Royce

Cop or not, I wanted to murder whoever had attacked Maxwell. They'd given him the push he needed to question his place in Rainy Dale. I knew how bullheaded Max was too. Once he got it in his head he didn't belong here, he'd begin to pull back. I'd finally made some progress breaking down his walls, and now he'd probably build even bigger ones.

While Maxwell slept, I sat out on the back patio with Grumpy. The sun felt warm and comforting on my face, helping to soothe away a bit of the depression I felt. I couldn't imagine the moment Maxwell left Rainy Dale. I'd always known that day would come, but that didn't make it any easier. Selfishly, I wanted more time with him. Even if he could never give me all of himself, I liked what we had. Didn't he realize part of him was enough for me?

My mom always said I gave more in relationships so the other person didn't have to work too hard. So they didn't quit on me. I wasn't sure if that was true or not, but it probably was with Maxwell. I tried to make things smooth sailing for him so he didn't have an excuse to bolt. But he'd found one anyway.

Not that I blamed him for being rattled about having been assaulted twice. He had every right to question whether or not staying here was a good idea. But we both knew he'd been looking for a reason. He'd probably even admit that, and maybe give me some speech about how his leaving was better for me. He might even convince himself of that lie.

Glancing at my watch, I saw Deputy Sam and Deputy Juan would be arriving back in town within the hour. I scooped Grumpy off my lap, and he gave a groan of disapproval. "Need to feed Max, little fella." I kissed the pup's fuzzy head before setting him on the ground. "Come on, you can supervise."

I entered the house, Grumpy close on my heels. I went into the kitchen and lifted the lid on the pot. The fragrance of chicken, carrots, celery, and potatoes filled my nostrils. I made a mean chicken soup, family recipe, courtesy of my grandmother on my late father's side. I scooped a small serving for Maxwell into a china bowl and grabbed a spoon and napkin. I found an old bed tray in the kitchen pantry and put the bowl of soup and utensils on that. I carried the tray to Maxwell's room, finding him sitting up already.

It was always an unwelcome shock seeing his bruised face. It made me furious to think someone had tried to harm him, but I tried to hide my anger from him. It just made him more self-conscious about his injuries.

"Are you hungry?" I asked cheerfully, setting the tray over his lap.

"Not really."

"Do you want more Advil?"

He sighed, staring forlornly at the soup. "Not until I get food in my stomach. I don't need stomach bleeding on top of everything else."

"There's a bottle in the bathroom. Help yourself when you're ready."

"Okay." He picked up the spoon, eyeing the food. "It smells good."

"It is good. Family recipe."

He nodded. "I don't think my family had any recipes to pass down. We had a personal chef, so I'm not even sure my mom knew how to cook."

"She must have known how to cook a little."

He dipped the spoon in the broth. "Why? We had so much money, she didn't have to do anything." His bottom lip was still swollen, so he slurped louder than usual, trying to get the liquid in his mouth. He must have gotten some because he made a sound of approval. "Mmmm."

"It's delicious, right?"

"Aren't I supposed to say that?"

I smiled. "I'm confident of my chicken soup. That and chicken enchiladas. Those are two dishes I always serve if I'm trying to impress someone."

He avoided my gaze. "I see."

I shifted. "I'm going to head over to the station. You okay here all alone?"

"Of course. Alone is my thing."

I frowned but didn't take the bait. "After I interview Charity and Fred, I'll probably hang around the station and work the case."

He finally looked up. "Royce, do what you need to do. I don't need a babysitter."

"I know. I'm just trying to tell you where I'll be."

"I don't care where you'll be. It's not important."

Gritting my teeth, I forced a smile. "Someone's mighty grumpy."

He set the spoon down and sighed. "I just mean you have a killer to catch. Don't worry about me."

I moved to the door. "I'm not worried," I lied. "I'm simply keeping you informed. I'll let you know when I'm heading home."

"Okay."

"Have a good day," I said brightly, heading out of his room. I grabbed my gear from my bedroom and left the house. I tried to shake off the gloomy thoughts about Maxwell leaving town. He was right—I had a killer to catch. I needed to give that a hundred percent of my attention. Nothing I said or did would change Maxwell's mind. He'd do what he wanted to do.

Once at the station, I made a few phone calls while waiting for my deputies to return with the Bells. So far, Fred Bell was looking more and more like my guy. He'd definitely had motive to murder Bob. Charity carrying Bob's child must have been a huge slam to his ego. He must have wanted to kill Bob every time he looked at him.

Then there was the attack on Maxwell. The puka shell necklace could be key. Anytime I'd seen Fred at one of Charity's shows, he'd always worn that puka shell necklace and a Hawaiian shirt. Would he have his necklace on today? If not, that was pretty damning.

Of course, it was possible Charity had murdered Bob without Fred's knowledge. She'd probably hated Bob as much as Fred for the way he'd tricked and used her. She certainly hadn't been the one who attacked Maxwell, but she could have slipped that hatpin into Bob's chest all by herself. Or maybe they were both in on it together. I hoped to get some clarity once I sat them down today, armed with new evidence. I looked forward to hearing their excuses.

I knew the minute Charity and Fred Bell arrived at the station. Fred was bellowing in the hallway, and Charity sounded like she was trying to calm him down. I'd already decided I was going to interview them separately this time. I didn't want Charity looking to Fred for her answers.

Deputy Juan looked relieved to see me as I sauntered toward them. "I'm starting to think I should have arrested them. Maybe then they'd have been more cooperative," he grumbled.

"What in the world possessed you to send your people to come get us?" Fred roared when he spied me.

"I told you two not to leave town. Did it slip your mind?"

Ignoring my question, he said, "Do you have any idea how humiliating that was for Charity? Dragging her out of a paying gig, just so you could do some more bullshit questioning?"

"I'm sorry you feel solving a murder is bullshit. But I have a duty to uphold." I held his angry stare, noticing he had bruising under one eye and a cut lip. Trying not to overreact and accuse him of attacking Maxwell, I calmly asked, "What happened to your face, Fred?"

He wouldn't meet my gaze. "I got in a fight with an overzealous fan last night at Charity's show."

"Is that right?" Next I scanned his neck but found no sign of his usual puka shell necklace. Seething, I did my best to contain my emotions. I wanted to punch him in his fucking face, but that would only get me in trouble. "You got in a brawl with one of Charity's fans?"

"Yeah, you got a problem with that?"

Oh, I have so many problems with you, asshole.

Charity had her hand clamped on Bob's arm. "Now honey, remember about your blood pressure."

He gave her an impatient look. "I'm not gonna let you get pushed around by some small-town sheriff just trying to close his case."

"I'm not looking for an easy solution, Fred. I'm searching for the killer." I gave him a cold look. "But I also don't give a damn who it is. I won't go easy on someone just because I know them."

"Is that right?" he growled.

Ignoring him, I addressed Deputy Juan. "Did you read them their rights?"

"I did. I thought it was prudent in case they blurted something out on the drive back." He glanced at Fred, who looked like a teapot about to boil. "I didn't arrest them because they decided to come back with us of their own free will."

"Okay."

"Our own free will?" Fred gave a harsh laugh. "That's a joke."

Deputy Sam scowled. "You said you were willing to cooperate."

Fred curled his lip. "What was I supposed to say? You pulled this shit in front of the people at that party. You think I wanted you dragging my wife out in handcuffs?"

"Do you want to cooperate or not, Fred?" I studied him. "Because right now, I just need to ask you some questions, but we can do it your way too. We can arrest you both if that makes you more comfortable."

"I don't want to get arrested, Fred." Charity looked panicked.

"Ain't nobody arresting you, Sweet Pea." Fred gave me a hate-filled look.

I crossed my arms, doing my best not to sneer. "So how should we play this, Fred?"

"Fine," Fred spat out. "But if the questions get too intense, we're leaving."

"Whatever you say, Fred." I glanced at Deputy Juan. "Take Fred to interview room one, and Deputy Sam, will you please escort Charity to interview six?"

"Wait just a minute," Fred said, his face mottled. "Why are you separating us?"

"I'd like to hear what each of you has to say, when the other one isn't there. It's standard procedure."

Charity swallowed hard. "But you didn't separate us last time."

"This is a more formal interview, Charity."

"This is bullshit, that's what it is," roared Fred. "This is an outrage."

"Calm down, Fred," I warned, moving closer.

"I won't let you separate us. No fucking way. You'll confuse Charity, and she'll get herself in trouble."

"Not if she tells the truth," I rumbled, almost enjoying how enraged he looked.

"Charity didn't do a damn thing."

"Then there's no harm in talking with her, now is there?"

His face quivered. "You leave her out of this bullshit case."

"You know I can't do that, Fred." I gave a pleasant smile, fully aware that would annoy him even more.

Fred put his fists up, his eyes wide and filled with anger. "You want to take a swing, Sheriff? Come on, you must get tired of always playing the easygoing pussy cop. How about you be the bad cop for a change?"

"I don't think you really want to go down that road with me, Fred."

"Come on, hit me," he goaded. "I know you want to."

You have no idea.

"Nah, that would be unprofessional."

"Why are you harassing my wife? Are you in a bad mood because your faggot boyfriend got beat up? Oh, boo-fucking-hoo."

Anger shifted through me at his brazen statement. "If you were out of town, how would you know about that?"

He pushed his face toward me. "How do you think?"

"Did my deputies tell you?"

"Nope." He popped his *P* loudly.

"What are you saying, Fred?" I held back the angry words that wanted out. Hopefully, if I gave him enough rope, he'd hang himself.

"It was bad enough we had one of you in town, then he showed up. You perverts make me sick."

Charity gasped. "Fred. Don't you dare talk like that."

"Why not? It's about time someone said what the whole town is thinking."

"No." Charity shook her head, looking at me. "That's not even close to true, Sheriff."

I gritted my teeth. "Whether it is or not, the fact remains I need to question you two, and it's happening separately." I'd heard homophobic slurs before and had little doubt I'd hear them again. It didn't change what my job was.

Fred snarled, "I'll bet it hurts knowing you weren't there to protect your little pansy boyfriend. He got his ass kicked real good."

"Are you saying what I think you're saying, Fred?" I asked in a gravelly voice.

"Fuck yeah. You two are an embarrassment to the community, and I decided to do something about it."

It was almost anticlimactic having him spill his guts so easily. "To be absolutely clear, you're confessing to assaulting Dr. Thornton?"

He sneered. "What are you going to do about it, *pussy*?"

I met Deputy Juan's alert gaze, and I reached for my handcuffs. The deputy moved forward at the same time, and together we grabbed hold of Fred. Swearing, Fred started punching wildly, and Charity screamed like something out of a horror movie. Deputy Sam joined in, and the three of us managed to get the big man facedown on the ground. Breathing like I'd run a marathon, I slid the cuffs on his thick wrists.

"Fred Bell, you're under arrest for assault and attempted murder," I panted, clicking the cuffs into place. I had no idea if he'd killed Bob or not, but he'd literally admitted to being the person who'd tried to kill Maxwell.

Charity was crying and watching the events with an expression of horror. "Fred. Fred. What are you doing?"

"It's all right, Sweet Pea. You'll be all right now," Fred mumbled, struggling against the restraints.

I scooped my hat off the ground and directed my deputies to drag Fred to interview room one and to keep a watch on him. When I turned to Charity, her face was stained with tears, and little sobs escaped her lips. She looked bewildered, and I figured now was probably a good time to interview her. She wouldn't be thinking straight.

Giving her a stern look, I said, "What about you, Charity? Are you willing to talk to me? Or do I have to arrest you too?"

"Arrest me?" She bugged her eyes. "But why would you arrest *me*?"

I moved toward one of the interview rooms, hoping she'd follow instinctively, and she did. I pushed open the door and said, "Have a seat."

"Am I under arrest too?" she squeaked.

"Not at this time." I sat down, still breathing hard. Fred Bell had been hard to handle with my two deputies along for the ride. I couldn't imagine how terrified Maxwell must have been going up against him alone.

She wiped at her eyes, looking shell-shocked. "I don't understand what's happening. Why did Fred go crazy like that?"

I ran my hand through my hair and settled my hat back on my head. "I'm hoping you can help me figure that out."

She swallowed. "All I know is, I was at my gig, and then those deputies came and told us we had to come back to Rainy Dale." Her voice wobbled. "It was so embarrassing."

"I sent them to come fetch you for a good reason, Charity."

"But why?" She sniffed. "We already talked to you."

"Yeah, you did. But I've since found out you lied to me too." I pursed my lips, watching her reaction.

Her face tinted pink, and she stared at the table. "When?"

"When I asked you about the hatpin."

"It was just a white lie."

"It was a huge lie. You said you'd never seen the hatpin that killed Bob."

She winced. "Fred said it would look bad if you knew it was my pin."

I frowned. "Not necessarily, but it sure looks bad that you lied."

"Well, the second he found out it was a hatpin that killed Bob, Fred told me to forget about that pin. Just put it out of my mind, as if I'd never seen it."

"And you didn't think that was odd?"

She shrugged. "He's my husband. He always looks out for me."

"So, when I showed you the photo of the murder weapon, you didn't think that maybe you should come clean?"

"I did, but Fred was adamant that I keep my mouth shut. He can be very persuasive, and plus, he knew you'd immediately think I killed Bob."

"Charity, I have no idea yet who killed Bob. I simply wanted to ask you why you lied to me about the pin."

"Oh." A line formed between her light brows.

"It's the lying that makes you look guilty."

She widened her eyes. "But I'm not guilty. I couldn't kill anyone. Especially that way. Sticking a hatpin through someone's heart? I… I just couldn't." She looked a bit queasy.

"You had a show at the Red Lantern last night, correct?"

She nodded.

"What time did you perform?"

Charity seemed to perk up at the mention of her gig. "My set started at 11:00 p.m. and went until 12:30 a.m. I was the headliner, so I went last." She looked excited, showing no resemblance to the girl weeping five minutes ago.

"Did Fred do sound for you?"

"Oh, goodness no." She gave a little laugh. "He only has to do that at private parties. The Red Lantern has a stage and a sound guy. It's a real show venue."

"Uh, that's great."

"It really is." Her eyes were glazed with delight. "I hope they have me back again."

"Did you see Fred during your set?"

"Oh, I get so into my performance, I don't see anyone." She sighed. "But I'm sure he was around in the back. Fred watches everything like a hawk. He'll do just about anything to make sure things go smoothly for me."

That's what I'm afraid of.

"Was Fred there at the end of your set?"

She frowned. "Um... yes. Although he was a little late coming to help me down off the stage. He's usually always there. I had to have some other guy help me." She sounded a little annoyed. "I really did not appreciate that at all. So when he finally showed up, I gave him the cold shoulder. Just to teach him I won't tolerate that sort of thing from my man."

It was becoming very obvious the only thing Charity Bell really cared about was Charity Bell. As we spoke, her husband was sitting in handcuffs, and I suspected it was all because he was trying to protect her. Yet all she was thinking about was her show last night.

Her self-centered attitude bugged me so much, I decided to shake her up a little. "Does Fred know you're pregnant?"

Her expression changed instantly, and the blood drained from her face. "What?" she hissed.

"Does your husband know you're carrying Bob Cunningham's baby?" I took childish pleasure in the horror that swept over her pretty features. Her husband had possibly murdered a man, and tried to murder another, simply to protect her. She didn't get to act like none of this was real.

"How... how do you know that?" Her eyes filled with resentment. "Did Dr. Thornton tell you my business?"

"He kept your confidence until he discovered you'd had an affair with Bob. Then he realized you and Fred had plenty of motive to kill Bob. Patient confidentiality doesn't count when you could be a danger to others."

"We're no danger," she whispered. "Or, at least, I'm not."

Her willingness to throw Fred under the bus was disgusting. "You didn't answer my question. Did Fred know about the baby?"

She shook her head. "No way. Heck, I... I didn't really even know for sure until last night. I took two home pregnancy tests, but Dr. Thornton confirmed I'm probably pregnant."

"How do you know Fred doesn't know?"

Blinking at me, she seemed muddled. "Well, I hid the boxes in the trash, and if he knew, he'd say something, wouldn't he?"

"Maybe he didn't want you to know that he knew."

"Fred doesn't keep secrets from me." She gave a confused laugh. "We're married, silly."

"You don't keep secrets?"

"No sirree." She looked self-satisfied.

"I see. So, when you slept with Bob to further your career, Fred knew about that?"

She swallowed. "Well, no. Not at first."

"But he found out."

"Yes. And when he asked me, I told him the truth."

"So then, you keep secrets from Fred, but you don't think he keeps them from you?"

"Right. Wait… no." She pressed her fingers to her temple. "You're getting me all twisted up. All I know is, Fred loves me, and… and… I love him."

I leaned back in my chair, crossing my arms. "You know what I think, Charity?"

"What." She squinted at me.

"I think you only love yourself."

Her face flushed. "That's not true."

"So if Fred goes to prison for murdering Bob, you'll stand by him?" I watched the different emotions play over her features. I suspected Charity Bell wasn't the kind of woman who stood by her man. She'd probably sink her claws into some other sugar daddy as fast as possible.

"Of course I'd stand by my man." She lifted her chin.

"Through the entire trial?"

"N… naturally."

"You'll stay by his side, even with all the negative publicity?"

Her gaze flickered. "Why would there be negative publicity?"

"Because your husband may have killed a man. The father of your baby, in fact."

She looked physically ill. "Even if Fred did kill Bob, nobody needs to know about the *baby*. I'm… I'm not keeping it."

"That won't matter."

"But… that's my personal business."

"All that private stuff comes out in a trial."

She leaned forward angrily, her innocent little girl act slipping. "But that would destroy my career."

"A man died, Charity," I drawled. "Shouldn't that be the main thing on your mind?"

Wrinkling her brow, she said, "But I've worked so hard."

"I'm sure you have. Bob worked hard too when he was alive. He deserves justice."

She chewed on her bottom lip, her gaze suddenly shrewd. "If there's a confession, does there need to be a trial?"

"So now you'd prefer Fred just takes the fall for everything, quietly?"

"He wouldn't want this to hurt my career. He's worked as hard as me on it."

I sighed. "Charity, don't you get that Fred doesn't give a rat's ass about your career? He only cares about you. Keeping you happy. He's probably done all sorts of horrible things just to protect you."

She blinked at me. "You're wrong. He wants me to be famous."

I shook my head because it was hard to believe she was that clueless. One thing was clear, if Fred confessed to murdering Bob and trying to kill Maxwell, she wasn't going to be around to comfort him. She wouldn't want to be known as the singer with the murderous husband in jail. She'd probably find some younger, richer guy who fit the image she wanted to project.

"I'm going to talk to Fred next. Is there anything you want to tell me before I go in there?" I studied her, taking in her flushed cheeks and pretty blue eyes. She looked harmless, but that just made her twice as dangerous.

She shook her head. "Nope. All I know is, I didn't kill Bob. And… and last night, I was either onstage or with other performers the entire time. I had no part in that horrible attack on poor Dr. Thornton."

Yeah, she was already preparing her exit strategy. If I didn't dislike Fred so much, I might have felt sorry for him. "So, do you think Fred killed Bob?"

Her gaze flickered. "Well, no, but you're the expert."

I narrowed my eyes. "Fred would take a bullet for you, and that's the best you can do?"

"You said yourself it was odd of him to tell me to lie about the hatpin."

"So he's on his own."

She lifted her chin. "Fred didn't get himself arrested so that I could incriminate myself."

I chuffed. "That's probably the first candid thing you've said all day." I stood and moved to the door. "You're free to go for now, Charity. We'll be talking again real soon. Don't leave town. I mean it. I won't be so lenient the next time."

"Okay," she said meekly, standing.

I found it telling she didn't ask about getting Fred a lawyer or about bail. She asked none of the questions a concerned spouse would generally ask. Instead she gathered her things and hurried out of the room, striding in the direction of the front lobby as fast as possible. I'd seen rats abandon sinking ships slower.

It was times like these I wished I had a bottle of whiskey stashed in my desk. I wasn't looking forward to questioning Fred. Not even a little. But it had to be done, so I went into the restroom, splashed some cold water on my face, and headed to interview room one.

Both Deputy Sam and Deputy Juan were in the interview room with Fred. I had Sam go outside but kept Juan in the room, just in case Fred decided to go loco again.

Fred's eyes were dark and angry, his face beet red. "It's about time you showed up, asshole," he snapped.

"I was having a nice chat with your lovely wife." I forced a smile and sat down across from him.

Deputy Juan gave me a sympathetic look. "He's a real charmer, Sheriff. He's been calling me lots of inventive names."

"Never met a cop I liked," Fred grumbled.

"Now come on, Fred. Since when are you such a handful?" I asked calmly, hoping he'd settle down enough to answer my questions. "We've never had any trouble with each other in the past."

He narrowed his eyes. "You never tried to arrest my wife before."

"You're the one in cuffs, not her."

At the moment.

"Pfft. Yeah. I had to do something. I know how you cops think. She's easy to confuse, and you thought you had an easy way to solve your case."

"Nothing about this case has been easy," I muttered. "So, why'd you get so upset earlier, Fred?"

"You know why."

"Not really. It's normal during a murder investigation to ask questions. I'm not sure why that's so hard for you to grasp."

His mouth thinned. "How about we cut the bullshit and be real with each other, okay?"

"Fine by me."

"You need someone to pin the murder of Bob Cunningham on, so I'm confessing."

I narrowed my eyes. "The evidence has to support your statement. You need to make me believe you killed him."

"He slept with my wife. Isn't that reason enough?"

"Not really. He slept with a lot of people's wives. Plenty of them were probably at the party too."

He shifted, wincing a little as if the cuffs were bothering him. "I assume you've ruled out most of them. You still wanted to talk to me and Charity, so you haven't ruled us out."

"Fair enough."

"How about you go ahead and rule Charity out? I killed Bob, and I tried to kill Dr. Thornton. I picked last night to go after the doc because Charity was at her show. You can check on that. It was easy for me to sneak back to his place. I can move in and out of her shows effortlessly, but she can't." He shrugged. "And I murdered Bob because of good old-fashioned jealousy. I told Charity that I forgave her affair, but seeing Bob again at that party, I just snapped."

"Really?" I frowned.

"Yeah, he was holding court, laughing and acting like he was some big deal. He only got where he was, lying and cheating people. Same way he lied to Charity. Promised her the fucking moon and couldn't deliver."

"Did you know ahead of time she was going to sleep with Bob?"

His face flushed. "Hell, no. I found out after. She's not a very good liar. I can always tell when she's trying to keep shit from me." He smiled, as if he found her deceitfulness adorable. "But she can't keep anything from me for long."

I leaned toward him. "Does that include her pregnancy?"

A muscle worked in his cheek, but he smirked. "So you know about that, huh?"

"Yep."

"If you're hoping for a big gotcha moment, I'm afraid you're out of luck. I found the pregnancy tests in the trash where she put them. She was acting weird, and I knew she was up to something."

"Interesting. She assumed she'd hidden the pregnancy."

He laughed. "I know. She didn't. She snuck out last night to go see your boyfriend. I followed her. I listened outside the examination room to their whole conversation. Then after she left, I snuck out too."

"Dr. Thornton thought he heard someone creeping around."

"He did."

I crossed my arms. "So then what? You went back?"

"When he confirmed her pregnancy, I was a little in shock. I mean, I knew she was knocked up, but hearing him say the words, it made me sick."

"Because you can't have sex anymore." It wasn't a question.

His mouth hardened. "I'm still more of a man than you, faggot."

I sighed. "Fred, could you cool it on the name-calling? I've heard every slur there is. It doesn't affect me, it's just annoying."

He smirked. "That works. I love annoying you."

I rolled my eyes. "So, you knew your wife was pregnant. How do you know it was Bob's child?"

"Like I said, Charity can't hide shit from me. I know he's the only guy she fucked. If there were others, I'd know."

"So the knowledge that she carried Bob's child enraged you?"

"I certainly didn't want anyone else knowing. I knew Charity would terminate the pregnancy first chance she got. I also knew the only way news of her pregnancy got out was through Dr. Thornton. He knew something he didn't need to know. But I had to act fast. Apparently, since you know, it wasn't fast enough."

"That's where you fucked up, Fred. Dr. Thornton only told me about the baby today, because you attacked him. He had no idea who Charity had slept with. If you hadn't assaulted him, we'd never have talked about Bob's affair with Charity. He'd never have felt compelled to tell me about her pregnancy."

He shrugged. "Oh, well. Either way, his death would be no big loss."

Anger coiled in my gut. "You're a piece of work, Fred."

He just gave a surly laugh.

Struggling to control my temper, I said, "You find your ED embarrassing?"

"Wouldn't you?"

"Not enough to kill."

He shrugged. "Well, it wasn't just her being pregnant I cared about. I really didn't want anyone knowing she was pregnant with *Bob's* baby. How humiliating. How that old fat bastard got her pregnant, I'll never know."

"Hey, insult him all you want, but he did what you couldn't." Maybe that was a low blow, but the fucker had tried to murder Maxwell.

He gritted his teeth, giving me a murderous look. "Fuck you."

Now it was my turn to laugh.

He didn't speak for a few moments, and then he said coldly, "There were numerous reasons that information needed to die with Dr. Thornton." He sighed. "Unfortunately, that little prick put up a much better fight than I'd expected." His eyes were vacant as he continued. "But he'd have died if you hadn't shown up."

A chill went through me because he wasn't wrong. I cleared my throat, pushing away grim thoughts that wanted to take root. "So that's how you got your face banged up? It wasn't a bar brawl."

"Right."

"Let's go back to the day of Bob's murder. I thought you were outside the whole time?"

His gaze flickered. "Mostly. But at one point, I went inside to get a cold drink. That's when I did it."

"How did you know he wouldn't cry out or make a noise?"

He frowned, looking confused. "What?"

"Stabbing someone isn't usually silent. That's only in the movies."

"Right." He scrunched his face. "Uh, I drugged him."

"With what?"

He grimaced. "I don't know the name of the drug. He had a condition… fuck, I forget the name. Charity told me about it."

"And you just happened to have some of that medication to drug him with?"

"Charity had it." He looked smug suddenly. "Yeah, that's right. He kept it in a vitamin bottle. He had that sleeping disorder, you know where they fall asleep all the time."

He actually had more details than I'd expected. Maybe he really was the killer. At first I'd assumed he was just shielding his wife, but it was beginning to seem more and more like he was the murderer. There was no doubt in my mind he was the one who'd *tried* to kill Maxwell.

"So you went in to get a drink and on the way stabbed Bob?"

"That's right. He was laughing, and it made me infuriated."

"How did you come to have the hatpin?"

He frowned. "Yeah, uh, Charity didn't have her hat on, and I slipped the pin in my pocket."

"It's an interesting murder weapon for a man." I narrowed my eyes.

His gaze flickered with anger. "I felt it was fitting that the fucker to die with the gift he'd given my wife. He was a piece of shit, and I'd do it again in a heartbeat."

I stiffened at the raw hatred in his voice. "So, no remorse?"

"My only regret is using the hatpin cast suspicion on Charity. She had nothing to do with any of this. I didn't think that hatpin thing through. I thought it was a poetic gesture to murder him with something he bought, but in the end it just caused us trouble."

I think I'd almost hoped he wouldn't convince me he'd killed Bob. I didn't like that he was falling on his sword for Charity, especially knowing how little she appreciated it. "You're willing to sign a sworn statement to all of this?"

"Absolutely."

I stood and moved to the doorway. Before leaving, I stopped and faced him. "I hope you don't expect Charity to wait for you."

He wrinkled his brow. "What?"

"She's hoping you'll just take the fall and it won't go to trial. That's how much she cares about you, Fred. She just doesn't want any of the shit to stick to her."

He shrugged. "You think I've been married to her for this long but don't know her, Sheriff?" He gave a hard laugh. "She'll probably serve me divorce papers before I can plead to the murder in front of a judge."

I scowled. "And that's fine by you?"

"It's just how she is. She's like a feral cat. I've never really owned her."

"But you did all of this because you love her."

His laugh was harsh. "Hey, what's that saying? If you love someone, set them free, or something?"

Baffled by his blind devotion to such a narcissistic woman, I studied him. He looked smug, as if he'd won the war. I'd wait until he wrote out and signed his statement before informing him that falling on his sword wasn't going to keep Charity out of jail. I planned on charging her with obstruction of justice. She'd willingly cooperated with him in hiding the truth from me. She'd helped him confuse and interfere in my investigation, and I wasn't letting her get away with it.

He'd no doubt think that by arresting his wife, I was just being vindictive. Truthfully, I did relish the idea of slapping cuffs on Charity. But mostly that was because I was offended at the Bells' lack of reverence for human life. Both of them had lied and twisted the facts simply to further Charity's career. One person had died, and another almost perished, simply because of one woman's insatiable drive for fame.

Usually when I wrapped up a case, I felt a sense of euphoria. That was missing this time around. Even with Fred's full confession, something nagged at me. Maybe it was the hours of paperwork ahead of me that had me depressed. The work didn't end for me just because I had my suspect in custody.

Or perhaps my unrest had nothing to do with the case, and everything to do with Maxwell. Once I handed off the case to the courts, I'd have more free time again. If Maxwell decided to return to LA, that free time would be drudgery. Before he'd come to Rainy Dale, I hadn't really noticed how lonely I was. I'd taken my job seriously and never allowed myself to think too much about the fact I had nothing else in my life.

Odd though Maxwell was, he'd filled that void nicely. I'd made the mistake of thinking I did the same for him. That had apparently been a miscalculation. I needed Maxwell, but he didn't need me. It hurt to face that fact, but you couldn't swim against the rapids forever. Eventually, the white water pulled you under and you drowned. Smart people let the current carry them along, not fighting the inevitable.

I suppose that was why I was depressed. I was no quitter, but even I knew better than to wage a losing battle.

Chapter Fifteen

Maxwell

My aching body and throbbing skull made for a restless night. Grumpy groaned every time I moved, which was both annoying and amusing. I hadn't invited the puppy to sleep with me, but I actually sort of enjoyed his little body pressed to mine. When I woke from a nightmare near morning, tangling my fingers in his soft fur soothed me.

The rosy dawn spread across the small room, giving me the sensation of still dreaming. The house was so quiet, I didn't think Royce was home yet. As much as I hated to disturb the puppy, eventually my bladder wouldn't be ignored. I climbed from the bed and made my way to the bathroom.

I hadn't eaten much yesterday, and I decided whether I was hungry or not, my body needed fuel to heal. I went into the kitchen and opened the fridge, noticing a big Tupperware container labeled *Chicken Soup*. Soup for breakfast was an odd choice, but I knew it was a nourishing option. I grabbed the container and hunted down a ladle. Once I had a bowl filled, I popped it in the microwave.

As the soup heated, I thought about how down I'd been yesterday. The pain medication in my system had sent me into a depressing spiral. I'd said some things that bothered Royce. He'd looked really dejected when he left for work. After a night of sleep, I was feeling more optimistic. I wasn't ready to leave Rainy Dale or Royce yet. Did I worry I'd never be what Royce needed? Absolutely. I had very valid fears. But my feelings for Royce were way too strong to just toss him aside and run back to LA. My life was here for now. I couldn't say I'd stay forever, but I still wanted more of Royce in my life. He made me happy. Well, as happy as I ever seemed to be.

The microwave beeped, and I carefully took the steaming bowl out of the appliance. I was sitting at the kitchen table eating when I heard the key in the front door. My pulse immediately picked up, but I pretended to be unaffected as Royce entered the kitchen. "Good morning," I said, spooning soup into my mouth.

He gave a weary smile. "Morning." His voice was husky, and he had lines beneath his eyes. "I have cereal in the cupboard. You didn't have to have soup again." He picked up Grumpy, who was jumping up on his legs, whining.

"Soup has better nutritional value than Cheerios."

"I see." He nuzzled the pup. "Hey, fella. Happy to see me?" The dog's tail wagged furiously in response. After a few moments, Royce set the puppy on the ground. He moved to the coffee maker and began to prepare some coffee.

I mentally chided myself because I should have thought to make him coffee. Of course, I hadn't realized he was coming home yet. "You didn't call me."

"What?" He glanced over his shoulder, looking puzzled.

"Not that you had to call me, but you said you'd let me know when you were on your way home." Hopefully he didn't think I was lecturing him. I was just stating a fact. "I'd have made you coffee. That's the point I'm trying to make."

"Oh." He sighed. "I didn't want to wake you in case you were asleep."

"I see." I pressed my napkin to my mouth. "So, how did it go with the Bells?"

He didn't answer right away, but then he turned to face me, leaning on the counter with his arms crossed. "Fred Bell confessed to everything."

I raised my brows in astonishment. "*Everything*?"

He nodded. "Yep. He admitted he killed Bob and attacked you."

"Holy hell," I rasped.

"I suspect he confessed to keep Charity out of jail, but I'm going to arrest her too for obstruction of justice. He knew enough details I kind of have to believe he's my guy." He sighed. "What a despicable couple they are."

I blinked at him, wondering why he didn't look happier. Was that my fault? "You seem down. I'd expect you to be thrilled you caught the bad guy."

He shrugged. "I'm beat. I need sleep."

My gaze flicked to the hissing coffee brewer. "Then why are you making coffee?"

He glanced at the coffeepot. "Because I'm on autopilot."

He'd been working almost nonstop since Bob's murder. My chest tightened with compassion and also concern. He truly looked worn-out. "Don't drink that coffee. Go get some sleep instead."

He sighed. "I don't think I can sleep. My mind is still buzzing."

"Coffee won't help that."

He gave a grudging smile. "No."

I cleared my throat, trying to think what a normal person would do in this situation. "Do you want to talk? Maybe that will help you unwind?"

He rubbed his face roughly. "I don't know."

He always took care of me, it was only fair I did the same for him. I patted the seat next to me. "Come on, sit. Tell the doctor all your troubles."

He laughed gruffly and moved toward me. With a groan, he sat sideways in the chair, his legs brushing mine. I liked the physical contact and wanted more. I grabbed his hand, and while he seemed surprised at the demonstrative gesture, I didn't care. I couldn't not touch him. He seemed so down, it made my stomach hurt.

His thumb swept over my knuckles, and he frowned at the scrapes.

"They don't hurt," I volunteered.

He glanced up, studying my face. "How are you feeling? I didn't even ask."

"Better."

"The swelling is down even more."

I nodded. "Good. Yes. I still have a headache, but I'm on the mend."

He clenched his jaw. "It took all my self-control not to punch Fred Bell in the face."

I grunted in surprise. "Royce, that's unexpected."

He dropped his gaze. "He was completely unapologetic. Fucker."

"He's a Neanderthal. What did you expect?"

Glancing up, his brown eyes buzzed with anger. "Some human compassion? Just a *hint* of guilt or regret would have been nice."

"You've been sheriff a long time—how often do you get that from a suspect?"

He sighed. "Hanna was sorry for what she did."

"Sure, but Liam wasn't. Most criminals aren't remorseful, you know that. They're generally selfish. They think the end justifies the means."

"Yeah." He winced. "I know you're right."

"The important thing is you got the person who murdered Bob." I hesitated. "And attacked me. Rainy Dale can rest once more, knowing their fearless sheriff saved the day."

I'd hoped he'd smile, but his face remained tense, his mouth a grim line. He kept his gaze down, and it was obvious something weighed on him. I wanted to ask him what was wrong but wasn't sure I wanted to hear the answer.

He swallowed hard. "I… uh… know you prefer the guest room, but would you be willing to lie down with me? Just for a bit?" He glanced up, his gaze hopeful.

A lump rose in my throat because it was painfully obvious he needed comfort. Of course he did; he wasn't a machine. He was always the one who reassured me, but he had needs too. He'd had a stressful, traumatic night, and he wanted to know someone cared. I needed to show him I cared.

"Yes. Of course," I said softly. "Whatever you want, Royce."

Some tension left his features. "Yeah?"

I stood. "Come on. Let's get you to bed. You've had a horrible week. What you need is sleep."

He didn't argue; he let me lead him to his room. Grumpy followed, looking curious about what we were up to. I had Royce sit on the bed, and I took control of the situation.

"Reach for the sky," I ordered.

He laughed but obeyed, and I tugged his shirt off over his head. Seeing him smile made my heart warm, and I knelt down to pull off his boots. He watched me, studying me with a serious expression. I was self-conscious because I knew my face was still bruised and ugly, but he didn't look repulsed. He looked alert.

I was in no condition to have sex, but God, I wanted him. Just being near him, inhaling his clean scent and feeling the heat of his body, was intoxicating. His breathing was slightly elevated, and I got the feeling he was in the same mood as me, exhausted but horny.

"Where do you keep your pajamas?" I asked.

"Dresser. Third drawer from the bottom."

I nodded. "How about you take off your pants, and I'll get them?" I turned my back on him, hearing the sound of his zipper lowering. I opened the drawer and grabbed the first pair of pajamas I saw. Facing him, I found him sitting on the edge of the bed, wearing nothing. I tried to ignore all the tanned, bare flesh and moved to him.

Think of him as a patient.

It was a nice plan, but since I'd had sex with him many times, I knew the pleasure that could be found in his arms. Pretending he was just a random person didn't work. I forced myself to hand him the pajamas, and he took them. I moved around to the other side of the bed, while he slipped on the silky clothing. I pulled back the covers, and we both got in the bed. Instinctively we moved closer, and he put his arms around me gently.

"Am I hurting you?" he asked softly.

"No. Feels good," I whispered. It did feel good. Too good. His lanky body pressed to mine had me hard within seconds. I told myself to calm down, that what he needed was rest. I meant that too, but my dick didn't seem to understand. My hips seemed to move of their own volition, and he let out a long, shaky breath.

"Take your bottoms off, Max." As he spoke, he kicked off his.

Unable to say no, I slipped them off, unsure of what he had planned. I was still bruised and sore, so the idea of his weight on me made me nervous. But when he simply tugged my body to his, I relaxed. He began to flex his hips, and I did the same. The friction of his cock rubbing mine made me moan and press closer.

I pressed my face to his throat, glad he wasn't trying to kiss me. I'd have been way too self-conscious to enjoy it. His fingers dug into my hips as we ground our erections together. What we needed from each other wasn't romance; we both just needed to get off. We craved release, pure and simple.

"Can't wait to fuck you again," he grated, moving faster.

I moaned, shivering with need. His dick against mine was good, but yeah, I'd have killed to have him inside me. My climax came quickly, body trembling, dick throbbing and spilling between us. I cried out, gnashing my teeth at the intense pleasure flushing through me, and he groaned and came too.

"*Fuck,*" he growled, his breaths coming in harsh, short bursts. His dick jerked and sticky warmth painted my abs. He kept thrusting, gripping me so tight, it was hard to breathe.

We moved together for a few moments more, seeking every last drop of relief owed us. Then we held each other, panting. He kissed my hair and stroked his fingers down my spine. I shivered and pressed my lips to his throat, tightening my arms around his waist. I never wanted to let go. My eyes stung with emotions I didn't understand. My need for Royce was like a hunger that could never be satiated. It was terrifying to need someone so much.

"Sorry," he said. "I didn't mean for that to happen."

"I wanted it as much as you." He didn't know that?

"Okay."

He let go of me and grabbed tissues. He handed me some, and we cleaned off in silence. Then we got back under the covers and faced each other. His gaze was guarded, not something I was used to with Royce. I hated that I couldn't read his emotions like usual. It made me uneasy.

"You should be proud of yourself," I said. "You caught Bob's killer."

"Yes." His smile appeared strained.

I sighed, feeling frustrated. "You seem different."

"Do I?" He dropped his gaze. "Sorry."

"Are you mad at me?"

He glanced up, looking surprised. "What? No. Why would I be mad?"

"I don't know. You just seem… withdrawn."

He reached out and stroked my good cheek. "Everything is okay, Max. I'm just tired."

I didn't believe him. I'd seen him tired plenty of times—this felt different. "Would you rather I go back to the guest room?"

He scowled. "No."

His response was so heartfelt, it relaxed me a bit. Maybe he really was just bone-tired.

He patted his chest. "Come here."

I moved closer, laying my head on his chest with a contented sigh. I teased my fingers over the bare skin of his stomach, and he shifted as if it tickled. I smirked and did it again.

He grabbed my hand, laughing. "Stop it."

"I didn't know you were ticklish."

He grunted. "Just a little."

There were probably lots of things about him I didn't know. Things I'd never find out if I left Rainy Dale. I didn't think I could give him what he needed, but I was way too selfish to let him go just yet. "I said some things yesterday… I think they bothered you."

"It's okay. You can't help how you feel."

I winced. "The thing is, I don't… want to leave Rainy Dale… Well, honestly, I could leave Rainy Dale in a heartbeat." I sighed. "I don't want to leave you."

He stilled. "Really?"

"Yeah."

He let out a shaky breath. "God, that's good to hear, Max."

"Is it?" I felt relief at his happy reaction.

"I thought you'd probably bought your one-way ticket by now." His arms tightened. "I'm awfully glad to know you want to stay instead."

"We've just been kind of floating along. I'm not sure what we are. I think it unsettles me. I work best with structure."

"Structure, huh?"

"Yes." I kissed his skin, inhaling his scent and letting it settle inside of me. Sometimes I felt as if Royce was a drug, and I was an addict. "I don't know the rules of what we are. It makes me uneasy."

"Uh… we're whatever you need us to be."

I frowned. "I guess I don't understand why that's okay with you. Why don't you make demands? Everyone makes demands. Everyone wants things their way."

"Now you sound like you're mad I don't make demands." He sounded confused.

I grimaced. "No, but that's just how everyone is."

He shrugged. "I'm not everyone, and I just like being with you."

"Without strings?"

He hesitated. "I don't want you to see other people. That's my only string. If you start seeing other people, I'll cut you loose."

I raised my brows. "Cut me loose? What am I, a kite?"

He didn't laugh, and his voice was gravelly as he said, "It's just something I won't put up with."

Feeling breathless, I said, "I'm not interested in anyone else."

"Good. Me neither."

"Okay, then."

He sighed. "Any other rules we should abide by?"

"Well… I don't want to move in together."

"Not ever?"

"Certainly not anytime soon." I uneasily waited for his response.

There was amusement in his voice as he said, "I had no plans to ask you to move in, Max. I know you like having your own space to run back to when you need a break from humans. Truth be told, I like having my space too." He cleared his throat. "For now."

"For now?"

"Well, if you stay in Rainy Dale, and we keep going strong, yeah, eventually I'd probably want to live with you. But I'm talking way down the line."

"You're far more optimistic than me. I've no illusions that I'm an easy person to be in a relationship with. I worry we won't last a year."

He lifted his head, looking annoyed. "Now, don't go putting an expiration date on us, like we're a pack of corn dogs."

I found myself laughing, possibly because I suddenly felt a little giddy. If he wasn't going to put a bunch of pressure on me, maybe I wouldn't feel the need to run away. "Mark my words, eventually you'll tire of me."

He sounded drowsy as he muttered, "I doubt it. I have a high tolerance for pain."

****

A few weeks later, I finally returned to work. I slipped the key in the door of my clinic, but it opened suddenly and Girdy stood there. She gave me an uneasy smile, and she had a funny look on her face. "Welcome back, Dr. Thornton."

"Hello, Girdy." I frowned and stepped over the threshold.

There were several loud *POP. POP. POP* sounds, and colored confetti flew in my face. I grabbed my chest, letting out a decidedly unmanly squeal, and a crowd of people broke into applause. Blue and yellow streamers were hung from the ceiling, and Penelope Granger, Royce, and numerous other townsfolk stood looking at me expectantly.

My mouth fell open, and I took a step backward, considering making a break for it.

Girdy grabbed my arm. "Oh no you don't. You can't run away," she hissed. "This party is for you."

"But… I don't want a party." I glanced over her shoulder to find Royce mouthing the word "Sorry."

Girdy laughed nervously and whispered, "I know you hate surprises, Doc, but you need to buck up." In a louder voice, she said, "Isn't it wonderful? Mayor Granger wanted to make sure you knew how much she appreciated your help in her father's murder case. She insisted we throw you a Welcome Back party."

"Oh. How… how nice." I hadn't done much of anything, other than manage to get beat up. But I assumed that was probably a tactless thing to say. I forced a smile, feeling as if my face would crack, and muttered, "It was nothing."

Literally.

Penelope walked up to me, holding a giant bouquet of daisies. "Dr. Thornton, how can I ever thank you?" She sniffed, wiping at her eyes. "If not for you and Sheriff Callum, my father's murder might never have been solved."

The people behind her started clapping again, and I wanted the floor to open up and swallow me. The one good thing about this impromptu welcoming committee was it did take away some of the dread I'd felt at returning to my clinic. The last time I'd been here, Fred Bell had been trying to murder me, so this was certainly a distraction from those negative memories.

As the crowd of people closed in, I felt as if I couldn't breathe. I met Royce's gaze, and he must have seen the panic in my eyes. He pushed through the crowd and put his arm around my shoulders.

"Okay, everybody, let's back up a little and give Maxwell some air." His authoritative tone worked, and everyone stepped back.

"Sorry." I tugged at my tie, loosening it. "I... I don't like crowds."

Penelope nodded sympathetically. "Oh, you poor dear."

One older man patted my back. "We're glad to have you back, Doc. We missed you."

"Really?" I raised my brows in surprise.

A red-haired woman in the crowd nodded. "We got used to having a doctor again. Two weeks without you reminded us we'd better make sure we don't lose you to the big city."

"Well, isn't that nice?" I mumbled. Apparently Fred Bell almost murdering me was good for business?

A lanky, bearded guy I remembered giving a checkup to recently said, "Your bedside manner could be better, but you're a damn fine doctor."

"Uh... thank you?" I felt like I was in an episode of *The Twilight Zone*. For the last month I'd taken a lot of flak from the people of Rainy Dale. It seemed perhaps the tide was turning.

"I haven't had a chance to come see you and thank you personally." Penelope sighed. "I don't know what I'll do without Dad around. He was the light of my life."

Her husband, Gerald, pulled her in for a hug. "There, there, honey."

"He was the most wonderful man ever born," Penelope wailed, dabbing at her eyes with a tissue. "A saint among men."

Gerald gritted his teeth, and I had no idea what to say. I'd never even had a conversation with Bob, and all I'd ever heard about him were terrible things. I knew there were words of comfort I should give in this situation but had no idea what they were.

"He'll be missed," Royce said smoothly, rubbing my back. "Isn't that right, Maxwell?"

I nodded, relieved he'd stepped in. "Most definitely."

"When I think that I had that dreadful woman sing at my birthday party, and the whole while they planned on murdering my father." She fanned herself. "Well, I just about lose my will to live."

I frowned. "Well, don't do that."

"Who wants cake and coffee?" Girdy called out, and everyone swept in her direction like a wave.

Relieved I was no longer the center of attention, I slumped. Royce leaned in and gave me a kiss, and that helped distract me from my nerves. When he lifted his head, he smiled and my stomach flip-flopped.

He winced. "I'm sorry. Girdy swore me to secrecy."

"Now I know where your loyalties lie." I sniffed.

He laughed. "Don't be mad."

"Just wait until it's your turn," I muttered.

"Oh, they already ambushed me at the station." He grinned.

I frowned. "Why wasn't I invited?"

"They were afraid you'd figure out you were next." He smiled. "Consider yourself lucky. I didn't even get a cake."

"No?"

"Nope. They had frozen banana pops." He grimaced.

"Yikes."

A middle-aged man in a very expensive suit approached. His hair was jet-black, and his eyes were so green, I suspected they were contacts. "Sheriff, I wanted to apologize for not being able to make our second appointment a few weeks ago." He gave a gruff laugh. "I guess it all worked out, since you nabbed the culprit."

Royce shook hands with him, and shrugged. "I simply wanted to follow up on a few things that had come to light."

"Is that right?" The man turned to me. "Hello, Dr. Thornton, I don't believe we've met. I'm Larry Stephanopoulos."

"How do you do?" We shook hands.

Rocking back on his heels, Royce said, "Yeah, I wanted to talk to you after I spoke to Patrice O'Malley. She let the cat out of the bag about you two."

Larry laughed, looking confused. "I'm sorry?"

Royce glanced around and lowered his voice. "She told me about you hiring her to spy on Bob."

Widening his eyes, Larry sputtered, "She said what?"

"It's okay. Water under the bridge. But you really should have come clean. It made me wonder why you hid that from me."

"But..." Larry scowled. "Sheriff, I never hired anyone to spy on Bob."

Clenching his jaw, Royce leaned forward. "Larry, there's no point in lying. I'm not going to arrest you. The case is basically closed."

I wasn't privy to the details of Royce's case, but it seemed obvious to me Larry had no idea what he was talking about.

"I'm afraid I'm a bit lost." Larry laughed.

Royce scowled. "Patrice O'Malley. She was Bob's secretary. Surely you remember her?"

"Well, I've met her, but..." Larry shrugged.

Looking skeptical, Royce said, "She came to me a few days ago. She was telling me how you hired her to find dirt on Bob. In fact, she was concerned maybe you killed Bob."

Larry bugged his eyes. "She said that to you? What in the world?"

"She was worried about you," Royce murmured. "Or at least, that's what she said."

"Sheriff, I'm not sure why she said anything like that to you, but I barely know the girl." Larry wheezed a little, sounding agitated.

Royce's entire body tensed. "Seriously?"

"I used to know her dad a little. You know, enough to shoot the shit if we were stuck in an elevator together for five minutes. But I wasn't close to the family." Larry looked baffled. "She actually told you she was working for me?"

"Yeah. Said you wanted revenge on Bob because you two had tangled recently over a piece of real estate. You wanted to prove he was a fraud."

"Tangled recently?" Raking a hand over his black hair, he looked even more bewildered. "I hadn't spoken to Bob in years. I avoided the bastard. I don't know why she'd lie about that."

Royce's cheeks were flushed, and he looked shell-shocked. "Jesus Christ. I had you scheduled to come in, to follow up, but then Fred confessed, so I dropped it."

"I swear, I have no personal ties to Patrice. She seems like a nice enough girl, but that's about all I know of her."

"I wish now I'd brought you in regardless." Royce scowled. "I could have sat you two down together and figured out which one of you is lying."

Larry raised his brows. "It's not me."

"But of course you'd say that."

"Fair enough." Nodding, Larry said, "You want to call my secretary and ask her if I've had any dealings the last few years with Bob? She knows my schedule backwards and forwards. She's worked with me for years. She's at the office right now. She works Saturdays. Just call my office."

Royce studied Larry and then said, "You have a card on you?"

"Sure do." Larry reached in his suit jacket and tugged out a business card. He handed it to Royce. "Swear to God, I'm on the up-and-up, Sheriff."

Royce took the card and wandered a few feet away.

Larry and I stood in awkward silence while Royce spoke quietly on the phone. After a few moments, he hung up and returned to us.

"Well?" Larry looked hopeful.

"Sorry to accuse you of lying, Larry. I had to be sure." Royce's jaw was hard.

Larry slumped with relief. "No problem. I have no idea what game Patrice is playing, but she didn't play it with me."

Royce held out his hand to the older man. "No hard feelings?"

Larry grabbed his hand, looking relieved. "Not at all. You're just doing your job."

Royce moved toward the door, and I followed. "Hey, where are you going?" I sounded a little more panicked than intended.

He glanced at me, looking distracted. "I think I need to have a chat with Patrice O'Malley."

"Now?" I glanced around at the milling people, sweat breaking out on my brow.

"Yeah, now." His tone was irritable. "She lied to my face about her relationship with Larry. Many times. That's not okay."

"Right, but do you have to go right now? Can't it wait?"

He scowled. "No it can't wait. I'm pissed."

I put my hand on his arm. "Then take me with you."

"What?" He laughed gruffly. "All these people are here for you."

"Yeah, exactly." I swallowed hard. "Please, take me with you."

"Max, you can't leave your own party." He squeezed my shoulder.

"I didn't come in today to see patients. I was going to do some paperwork and get caught up. I wasn't ready to see people today, and now I'm stuck? No way. That's not fair." I scowled. "I didn't ask for a damn party."

"But…" He grimaced. "It's weird if you leave."

"The whole town already knows I'm weird. Who cares?" I dug my fingers into his arm. "I'm begging you to take me with you. All these people care about is the cake, let's be real."

His lips twitched. "For goodness' sake, Max, you're never going to fit in if you do strange things like leaving your own Welcome Back party."

"Fitting in isn't in my future. We both know that," I muttered. "I promise I'll stay in the car."

Skepticism rippled through his gaze. "Your track record on staying in the car isn't a good one."

"I'm aware, but I double promise. Just please don't leave me here. I'll end up saying something I shouldn't. I wasn't ready to be the center of attention. That's the sort of thing I need to work up to. You can't just throw me into this sort of thing and not expect there to be trouble."

Laughing grudgingly, he said, "Fine. Let's sneak out quickly while they're all ogling the cream cheese frosting."

Relief flooded me. "Oh, thank God. Yes. Let's go."

Royce moved stealthily toward the front door, and I held on to the back of his shirt. Thank goodness he'd taken pity on me. Without him there to cover for me, I'd have put my foot in it for sure. Plus, it was kind of exhilarating to sneak out with Royce, and I smirked gleefully as the door closed behind us.

Chapter Sixteen

Royce

Of course I should have verified Patrice's version of events with Larry. I'd intended to, but when Fred had confessed to Bob's murder, everything had seemed to wrap up so nicely. Possibly too nicely. Fred had known enough details he'd convinced me he was the killer. He still very likely was the killer. However, I had to at least ask Patrice why she'd lied about her relationship with Larry.

Perhaps she simply had emotional problems, and she enjoyed pretending she was adored by certain men. Maybe she had daddy issues. Maybe she thought it was funny to mess with an ongoing murder investigation. Without talking to her, I had no idea why she'd weave such an outrageous lie about Larry.

Maxwell's thoughtful voice cut into my musings. "You say Patrice actually tried to implicate Larry in the murder of Bob?"

I gripped the steering wheel. "She did. She came to me, under the guise of concern, and basically accused Larry of killing Bob." I grunted. "She was convincing too. I genuinely believed she cared about Larry."

Maxwell shivered. "That's so creepy."

"I even saw her at the Squeaky Wheel, and she continued the charade. She said she was buying Larry a pair of cufflinks for his birthday." I scowled. "She seemed so harmless anytime I spoke to her."

"She might *be* harmless. Just because she's nuts doesn't mean she's violent."

"True." I nodded.

"Her lies might have absolutely nothing to do with Bob's murder. She might simply be looking for attention. It's not uncommon for people to insert themselves into police investigations, right?"

I frowned. "It happens. The part that bothers me is she tried to throw Larry under the bus. That seems more malicious than wanting attention."

"Hmmm. Yes." Maxwell stared out the window.

I parked in front of Patrice's yellow one-story home, noticing a tricycle on the lawn. Did she have kids? I'd gotten the impression she was single and lived alone. I turned to Maxwell. "You're staying in the car, right?"

He nodded. "Of course."

I chuffed. "You're zero for two, Max. I'm telling you to stay put. Do you understand?"

He shrugged. "You already told me I had to stay in the car. There's nothing wrong with my hearing."

"No, just your listening," I murmured.

He sighed. "Just go talk to the girl. I'm dying to know what her reason was for lying to you." He clasped his hands in his lap. "I'll be right here waiting."

"You'd better be," I growled, climbing out of the car. I strode up the path to the door, taking in the perfectly trimmed hedges and Home Sweet Home sign hung over the front door. I rang the doorbell, feeling agitated.

When the door opened, Patrice stood there in a ruffled pink dress and pigtails. She looked like a little girl, and I was momentarily taken aback. "Patrice?"

She smiled. "Sheriff Callum? Well, what a nice surprise."

I cleared my throat. "I had a few questions for you. Just some housekeeping stuff with the case."

Blinking, she nodded. "Oh, okay. Come in."

I stepped in warily, scanning the small living room. There didn't seem to be anyone else with her. I kept my eye on her and moved farther into the room. "Do you have kids?"

She closed the door behind me. "I have a little boy. He's sleeping."

"I see."

"Too bad too. He'd love to meet a real live police officer." Her eyes were bright. "He wants to be a police officer when he grows up. I guess all little boys do."

I smiled, trying to relax. "I actually wanted to be a fireman when I grew up. Somehow, I ended up a cop."

She laughed and gestured to the couches. "Would you like to sit?"

I took the couch across from her. She sat down demurely, smoothing the ruffles of her dress. Her home was cozy, with lots of family photos on the walls.

She leaned forward. "So, what exactly do you need to clarify with me? I thought the case was all wrapped up."

"It is for the most part. There were a few inconsistencies I need to address—"

"Oh!" She jumped up. "I just made some fresh lemonade." She looked excited. "Would you like some? I'm going to have a glass, so it's no trouble at all."

"Uh…" I didn't really want lemonade, I just wanted to get to the questions.

"It's fresh-squeezed." She sighed. "Sorry, I don't have visitors that often. It's fun to play hostess."

"Okay, sure." Maybe once she got the lemonade, she'd sit down and focus.

"I'll be right back." She hurried into what I assumed was the kitchen.

I glanced around the room, taking in the fluffy pink pillows on the couch and colored blocks strewn on the floor. There was a stack of children's books on the coffee table: *Goodnight Moon*, *Green Eggs and Ham*, and *Are You My Mother?*

She came out of the kitchen with a tray and two glasses filled with ice and lemonade. "I hope it's sweet enough. You know how homemade lemonade can sometimes be too tart?" She set the tray on the table. "Help yourself."

I reached out and took the glass closest to me. She sipped her drink and then watched me expectantly. I took a sip and nodded approvingly. It was on the salty side, which seemed odd, but actually tasted pretty good. "That's delicious."

Her cheeks tinted pink. "I'm so relieved."

I was actually kind of thirsty, so I took a few more gulps and set my glass down. Clearing my throat, I said, "So, anyway, I needed to clear up a few things that you told me."

"Is that right?" She tilted her head.

"How come you told me Larry Stephanopoulos hired you to spy on Bob?"

I expected her to deny it, or make an excuse, but instead she smiled sheepishly.

"You finally talked to Larry?"

"Uh, yeah."

She laughed again and sipped her lemonade, the ice clinking against the glass. "I've expected you to come every day, but you never did. To be honest, it was kind of stressful waiting and waiting for the knock on the door."

I frowned. "You admit you lied?"

She winced. "I felt kind of bad throwing poor Larry under the bus. He's a nice enough man, but I had no choice."

"You had no choice?"

She shrugged. "Well, you're a good detective, Sheriff. You were slowly but surely making your way toward me."

"And you have something to hide?"

"Come on, you must know I do."

"But… lying like that, you could have sent an innocent man to jail."

She pushed her lip out in a pout. "Don't be mean about it, Sheriff. I'm not proud about it."

"Then, why'd you do it?"

"To confuse you."

"So, you confess to trying to interfere with the investigation?" It was a bit warm in her house, so I had another sip of the ice-cold lemonade. Running a finger under my collar, I blew out a shaky breath. She seemed to have her heater up awfully high for October. Clearing my throat, I continued speaking. "Interfering in a murder investigation is a crime."

"Is it?" Her eyes were wide.

"Of course."

She fingered one of the ruffles on her skirt. "You've always been so nice to me, Sheriff. You treated me with kindness each time we met."

"Well, sure. Why wouldn't I?"

She glanced up. "Many men aren't like you. So many of them are… ugly."

"Ugly?"

"Yeah, ugly. Bad. You know." She nodded. "Bob was bad. Very, very bad."

I narrowed my eyes. "Did that make you angry with him?"

Wrinkling her forehead, she said, "Yes."

My pulse felt unusually slow, and I shook my head, trying to clear my mind. "Did you do something to Bob? Is that why you wanted to confuse me?"

She didn't answer my question, just gave a little shrug.

I studied her, trying to gauge whether she was trying to admit to something or just venting about her unpleasant boss. "You can tell me the truth, Patrice. I'm already here. I already have suspicions."

"I know."

"Why don't you tell me what you've been up to?"

She covered her face, giving a funny laugh. When she lowered them, her cheeks were pink, and her eyes glittered. "Sorry. I sometimes giggle when I'm nervous. Men in power make me nervous."

"I remember you said that before." My tongue was oddly sluggish, and I still felt hot. I was also breathing at a quick, shallow rate, which was making me light-headed.

She narrowed her eyes. "You okay? You look a little flushed."

"I'm feeling a bit overheated." I unbuttoned the top buttons of my shirt, hoping that helped.

"I see."

"Uh, where was I?" I wiped perspiration from my upper lip.

"You were telling me you had suspicions about me because I lied."

Nodding, I said, "That's right. You shouldn't have lied."

"I know." She chewed her pink fingernail, a funny look on her face. "My dad was a bad man like Bob."

I blinked at her. "Was he?"

"Yeah." Her mouth thinned. "Why do men with power think it's okay to lie and cheat? Don't you think it's weird how men in power so often aren't nice?"

As a wave of nausea swept over me, I grunted and tried to stand. It was becoming obvious to me that what I felt wasn't normal. I wasn't just overheated; I felt drugged. I glanced at the lemonade she'd given me and then at her. Her expression was odd. Guilty. "Patrice," I rasped. "What did you do?"

"I'm sorry," she said softly. "You really are a nice man."

Once on my feet, the room seemed to shift. I grabbed onto a nearby chair and growled, "You can't drug a cop. That's assaulting a police officer."

"Really?" She bit her lower lip.

"*Shit,*" I rasped, stumbling backward and bumping into the couch. I sat quickly, because it was that or fall down. I shook my head, trying to clear my head, but it was no use. "You're making things worse for yourself."

She stood and came closer, studying me like a butterfly stuck with a pin. "You really gave me no choice."

My response was to wheeze and slump back against the couch. I watched her warily, trying to decide my next course of action. I wanted to get my phone in hand so I could dial 911, but my fingers felt like sausages. Plus, she was watching me intently. For whatever reason, it hadn't occurred to her that I had a gun. It was on my hip, covered by my jacket. My biggest problem was a complete lack of coordination. If I tried to grab for my gun, I'd probably miss, and then she'd know I had a gun.

I decided to ask questions. If I could keep her talking, maybe the drugs would wear off enough for me to do something to help my situation. Or perhaps I'd be able to think of what to do. Maybe I could talk some sense into her. "Why'd you murder Bob?"

She winced. "It sounds so brutal when you say it out loud."

"Murder is brutal."

"Yeah." She nodded. "But isn't the world a better place without him in it?"

"That's not for you to decide."

"Why not?" She frowned. "He hurt so many people. Someone had to stop him."

"How'd you do it?" I slurred.

"You really want to know?"

"Yes."

"Well, at first, I was just going to kill him with his GHB. I got him a drink at the party, and I put a ton of it in." Her gaze flickered. "Way more than I gave you, Sheriff. Don't worry."

I stared at her, not sure how to respond.

She grimaced. "Then I found Charity Bell's hatpin on the floor. It felt like God was sending me a sign."

"You think God wanted you to frame Charity Bell for Bob's murder?" I scowled.

"All I know is, the pin was right there next to Bob. The sun was glinting off it, and it was like God himself was shining a spotlight on it." She shivered. "It gave me goose bumps."

"Why would God want that?"

"Why?" She widened her eyes. "You've met the Bells. They're horrible people. She had sex with Bob! Can you believe that?" She looked nauseous, and she clutched her throat. "Right there in the office. It was disgusting."

"God wouldn't want you to murder anyone."

She scowled. "Oh, people always say nonsense like that. God killed bad people all the time in the Bible. He has no problem with punishing evil. You should know that, Sheriff. You punish evil people too."

"I'm upholding the law."

She lifted her chin. "Well, I'm... I'm... upholding God's law."

My lids were getting heavier, and I was afraid I'd pass out. What would she do to me then? I needed to stay awake, but I was so damn sleepy. "You gonna kill me too?"

Gritting her teeth, her expression was strained. "I don't know what to do about you. Would you be willing to just let me go?" She sounded like a little girl. "Fred already confessed—you could just go with that. After all, he did try to kill Dr. Thornton."

"You know I can't do that, Patrice."

She slumped. "I just knew you'd say that."

"It'll be a lot harder to kill a cop and get away with it."

Nodding, she said, "I know. But if you won't cooperate, it really is you or me, right? I mean, if you're going to be stubborn." She moved closer. "I knew you'd come eventually. I even searched the internet on how to dispose of bodies. But I don't think I can chop a body up into little pieces." She seemed to gag. "Stabbing that pin in Bob was horrible enough."

A chill went through me, and I tried to sit up.

She took a few steps back. "There's really no point in trying to escape, Sheriff. I gave you enough GHB to take down a giraffe." She glanced at my half-full glass and frowned. "You need to finish your drink. Then you won't feel any pain. I don't want you to feel pain."

A floorboard creaked behind me, and Maxwell's voice came to me. "Ms. O'Malley, I suggest you step away from Sheriff Callum right this minute."

Shocked at the sound of his voice, I twisted my body and found him standing behind me, holding a can of pepper spray. "Max?"

Patrice's eyes were wide. "Dr. Thornton? What are you doing here? You can't just walk into my house without permission."

Scowling, I growled, "God damn it, Max, I told you to stay in the car."

"Looks like it's a good thing I didn't," he mumbled, taking a step closer. "Okay, I'm going to take Royce and go. If you try and stop me, I'll spray you."

"What?" Patrice's eyes glittered with anger. "No." She stomped her foot. "You're ruining everything."

"Royce, can you get up, please?" Maxwell asked, his voice wobbling. "Who knows what this psycho will do next."

"Psycho?" Patrice sounded insulted.

"Not sure I can," I said, leaning forward. The room spun, but I managed to tip forward onto my feet. I stumbled sideways but stayed upright.

"Come around the couch toward me," Maxwell coaxed.

"Easier said than done." I inched along the sofa, holding on to the back.

"Are you drugged?" Maxwell scowled, giving Patrice an angry glare. "What did you give him?"

"None of your business." Patrice looked miffed.

"GHB." I rounded the corner of the couch and took a step toward him. "I'm really dizzy."

Patrice clutched her head. "I won't let you leave. This can't be happening."

I pointed at her. "You have the right to remain silent."

"Do you have handcuffs? Should I make a citizen's arrest?" Maxwell sounded completely serious.

Blowing out a shaky breath, I grabbed hold of him. He put his arm around my waist, still pointing the pepper spray at Patrice. If I left her here, she'd take off. But I was in no condition to restrain her. Perhaps with the help of Maxwell and his pepper spray, we could at least keep her here until help arrived?

Trying to fight off the impending loss of consciousness, I mumbled, "Max, call the station. Tell Deputy Juan to get over here."

"Uh, okay." He let go of me, and I swayed alarmingly. His arm returned. "Anchor yourself onto something Royce, or you're going to go down like a redwood."

I grabbed the back of the couch, leaning so far forward, I thought for one second I was going to topple over and land on the floor, face-first.

"Steady," Maxwell said, grabbing the back of my jacket.

"I'm good," I lied, clutching the leather sofa.

I was far from good.

Patrice strode over to the fireplace and grabbed an iron poker. Then she moved back in our direction, holding it above her head in a threatening manner. "I'm not letting you two leave. No way. No. No. No."

"Do you seriously think you can beat two men to death with that?" Maxwell gave a startled laugh, raising his can of spray.

"Oh, you ruined my whole plan!" Patrice wailed and tossed the iron at us.

It bounced off my chest, just missing my face, and Maxwell shouted angrily. Patrice bolted for the front door and scrambled out of the house, shrieking.

"*Fuck,*" I hissed, taking a step after her. Unfortunately, my legs buckled, and I fell face-first onto the carpet with a loud *OOF*.

Above me I heard Maxwell practically shouting into his phone. My face was numb, and breathing was becoming a chore. Patrice wouldn't get far. She stood out a lot with her pink ruffled dress and pigtails. I was confident my deputies would catch her, so I closed my eyes.

Max knelt above me, turning me over. His face was blurry, and I reached out to touch his cheek, but I got his nose. "Don't go, K?" I mumbled.

"I'm here. Don't worry."

I scowled. "No, I mean, don't go *ever*."

He didn't speak.

"Stay with me, please," I whispered, my vision closing down to a dark pinpoint. Was I dying? Were these my last moments with Max? If so, there were so many things I'd want to say to him. My chest ached, and even though it was almost impossible to form words, I managed to say, "Love you."

I had no idea what his response was. Maybe he said he loved me too. Or maybe he recoiled in horror. But for me, everything simply faded to black.

Chapter Seventeen

Maxwell

While Royce's heartfelt declaration startled me, I was acutely aware that people often said crazy things when drugged. And Royce was very much drugged. Judging from how incapacitated Royce had been, that bitch Patrice had probably put enough GHB in his glass to incapacitate an army. Thankfully, he hadn't finished his drink.

Instead of sending Royce for an hour-long ride in an ambulance, I brought him to my clinic. There was no magical antidote for GHB, and no one would take care of him better than me, since I had a vested interest in his well-being. Besides, my clinic had everything needed to treat him for an overdose, and the sooner I began treatment, the better his chance of survival and recovery.

Once I had him in a makeshift bed in my office, I monitored his blood pressure and heart rate and started an IV to help flush the drugs from his system. He was breathing on his own, so I didn't want to intubate him unless absolutely necessary. There was always a danger of damaging a patient's trachea or vocal cords when going that route. Unless he suddenly went downhill, I'd let him keep breathing on his own.

One good thing about GHB was it didn't stay in the system very long. Within three to five hours, most of the drug's effects would be eliminated from the body. The next few hours, I sat next to Royce, watching him closely for any signs his condition was deteriorating.

Don't go ever.

I was well aware Royce wanted me to stay in Rainy Dale, so that declaration hadn't been a huge shock. The thing about loving me had thrown me a bit. If I was honest, it simultaneously made me nervous and exhilarated. Love wasn't anything I had experience with, but I suspected what I felt for Royce was the closest I'd ever been to loving another man. Not being able to leave him behind in Rainy Dale was the biggest clue of all.

There were times when I fantasized about once more living in the city, where dust wasn't stuck in every crevice, the scent of cow manure didn't hang in the air, and food delivery was at my fingertips. I missed one-hour dry cleaning, the occasional play at the Mark Taper Forum, and organic produce. But I also realized that all of that paled in comparison to the pleasure I got just spending an evening with Royce. The feel of his hand in mine and his husky laugh did the strangest things to my heart.

When I'd walked in on the scene at Patrice's house, for one awful moment, I'd thought Royce was dead. He'd been so still as that madwoman stood over him menacingly. When I'd figured out he was alive, I'd have done anything to get him out of there. Even now, I felt annoyed I hadn't been able to douse that stupid woman's face with pepper spray. If anyone had deserved it, she did.

Royce groaned, and I stood to check on him. His eyes opened, and confusion shifted through his gaze. "You're okay," I said quietly. "I'm taking care of you."

His gaze darted around the room. "Where am I?"

"My office."

Relief replaced the confusion. "Good."

I took his arm and placed my fingers on his wrist. "Just checking your pulse."

He nodded and held still, watching me. Once I felt confident his pulse was close to normal, I relaxed. "How do you feel?"

"Tired."

I smiled and brushed a lock of blond hair from his forehead. "You'll be happy to know your deputies have Patrice O'Malley in custody."

"Yeah?" He raised his brows.

"She was hiding behind the library building."

He frowned and cleared his throat. "Her son. Did someone get him from the house?"

"Her son?" I wasn't sure what he was talking about.

"Yeah, she said her little boy was sleeping in the house."

"Uh, I believe Deputy Sam searched the house, and there wasn't anyone else inside."

"What?" He scrunched his face. "She said she had a kid."

I shrugged. "Well, if so, he wasn't at her house."

"But the tricycle and the children's books?" He struggled to sit up.

I put my hand on his arm. "Calm down, Royce. I'm sure if there was a child in the house, your deputies wouldn't have missed him."

"Did she make it up?" He rubbed his face roughly. "Why would she?"

"I don't think she's mentally stable. Surely you know that?" I laughed gruffly.

"Sure, but…" He looked bewildered.

I crossed my arms, studying him. "She's in custody. You'll have plenty of time to question her tomorrow."

"Tomorrow?" He scowled.

"You can't seriously think you're going to rush down to the station and demand answers from her?"

"Well…"

"Right now, you're my patient. You're not going anywhere."

His jaw tensed, and I assumed he'd argue, but then he suddenly slumped. "Yeah, okay. I do feel pretty weak."

"Can you walk?" I asked.

"Honestly, I don't know."

I bit my bottom lip. "I only ask because I think you'll be much more comfortable in my bed."

His glum expression brightened. "Yeah?"

I shrugged. "I changed the sheets and everything. Just for you."

He grinned, and it made him look younger. "Are you trying to take advantage of me, Doc?"

I glanced at my watch. "Not for another three hours."

He rubbed his head, laughing. "Yeah, I wouldn't be any good to you. Why do people take GHB? It's horrible stuff."

"Patrice gave you way more than normal. You didn't get any of the fun parts everyone raves about. You jumped straight to the *almost kill you* part."

He shuddered. "I think I'll stick to alcohol for my fun times."

"Give your liver a rest and don't do any drinking for a few weeks."

"Deal." He sighed. "So if Patrice killed Bob, I guess Fred didn't. He must have thought Charity killed Bob and was covering for her."

"He still tried to kill me."

He grimaced. "Oh, I don't feel sorry for him. I'll just have to amend the charges."

"What will happen to Patrice?"

"She'll be charged with murder, but it's up to her lawyer what her defense will be. I think she's loopy as a Froot Loop, but it's not up to me." He kept his gaze down. "Uh… the last part of my encounter with Patrice is a bit of a blur."

I studied him. "How much do you recall?" Did he remember his declaration of love? I couldn't tell from his expression.

"I remember you coming in…" He glanced up. "You're zero for three, by the way."

"This one shouldn't count. If I hadn't disobeyed, you might very well have died," I said huskily. "You were taking so long, I just wanted to see what was going on."

He nodded, his eyes dark and serious. "Yeah. I misjudged her. I didn't suspect a thing when she got the lemonade because I hadn't really asked her any questions yet."

I couldn't help myself, and I grabbed his hand. His fingers curled around mine, warm and strong. "That was a close call. There are too many of those lately. For both of us."

"Yes." A muscle worked in his cheek. "Does this make you want to run back to LA again?"

I hesitated. "Not really."

"No?" His brows rose.

I smirked. "Who would watch out for you? It's obvious your skills are slipping in your old age."

A little smile settled on his lips. "You want to look out for me, Max?"

I leaned down and kissed him gently. Then I straightened, my chest tight with emotion. "It would seem so."

His thumb rubbed over my skin. "That's progress."

Whether he truly didn't remember saying he loved me or was too embarrassed to admit it, I wasn't sure. But I decided not to bring it up if he wasn't going to. I was surprised I didn't hate the idea he might be falling in love with me. Just a few months ago, the thought of that would have sent me running for the hills. Or the city.

But not now.

"Come on, Sheriff. Let's get you upstairs." I lowered the railing on the side of the bed.

"Okay." He hung his legs over the edge of the bed, resting a hand on my shoulder.

"Test your legs, make sure they'll hold you."

He did as instructed, looking relieved when his legs were stable. "I could probably just go home."

I frowned. "Would you rather go home?"

"No."

"Good." I gave a sharp nod. "Because I want you here."

His gaze flickered. "That's *definitely* progress."

My face warmed. "Okay, well, enough of that sappy stuff. Upstairs with you. Chop. Chop."

"Whatever you say, Doc. Hey, if I'm a good boy, will you give me a sponge bath?"

I sniffed. "I don't have a sponge. They're disgustingly unhygienic."

He grinned. "Even better."

****

Having taken a few weeks off after my assault, getting back into the swing of things was grueling. The first few days it seemed everyone in town wanted to make an appointment, in case something happened to me, and they had to go without a doctor again. Thankfully, Girdy was excellent at weeding out those who were truly ill and those who were just making stuff up so they could get an appointment.

One of the lucky few who did get past Girdy was Herman Harrison. He was from out of town, complaining of stomach pains. Herman was in his thirties, with red hair and jade-green eyes. The moment he sat down across from me, I knew he wasn't faking. Sweat gleamed over the pale skin of his face, and his eyes were bright and feverish-seeming.

"What can I do for you, Mr. Harrison?" I asked, watching him closely.

"Well, I've had a headache for days now, and I just don't feel right." He grimaced.

"Any vomiting or diarrhea?"

"Yep." He nodded. "I can't seem to keep anything down."

His speech was slightly slurred, nothing too severe, but enough I wondered if perhaps he'd been drinking. "Are you taking any medications? Alcohol?"

He frowned. "Oh, I don't drink, Doc. And I'm not on any medications at all. I'm usually healthy as a horse."

"Hmmm." I stood. "How about we examine you?" I led him to the examination table and had him get up on it. "Take your shirt off, please."

He did as instructed, but it took him longer than it should have, as if his coordination was off. I ended up helping him because the cuffs were stuck to his wrists, and he seemed confused about how to get them off.

"I'm just so tired," he muttered.

I placed the blood pressure cuff around his upper arm. "Just sit still. The cuff will tighten on your arm. It might be uncomfortable, but just let it do its thing, please."

"Okay."

The reading was on the high side, so I took it two more times to be sure. His pressure was definitely up. His breathing was also elevated, which gave me some concern. "I'll need to take blood and urine. Your body is certainly exhibiting signs of stress."

"It's so weird how it just came on so quickly." He rubbed his stomach.

I went to grab the items needed for drawing blood. "You don't live in Rainy Dale?"

"No. Well, I used to. I came into town for work."

"I see. What do you do?"

He sighed. "I'm a solar specialist."

"A what?"

"I sell solar energy." He glanced around. "It's the future."

"Right. I suppose it is."

He sighed. "My ex-wife, Lola, lives here. We share custody of Sparky. He's our chocolate Lab."

His comment made me think of Grumpy. "Labs are great."

"Yeah. Do you have a Lab?" He looked interested.

"Oh, no. My, uh… a guy I know… he has one. A puppy."

"Ahh, yeah. I see. They're great dogs."

I finished taking his blood and labeled the vials. Then I got him a specimen cup. "There's a toilet behind that door. Please leave the urine sample in the little window, and my receptionist will collect it."

"Oh, sure." He slid off the table and headed into the tiny bathroom.

After washing my hands, I went to my laptop and ordered a few additional tests for Herman. When he came out of the bathroom, he pulled on his shirt and sat back in the chair in front of my desk.

"Are you staying in town?" I asked.

He nodded. "Yeah. I leave Saturday. I'm staying over at the Dusty Steer."

"That's a nice enough hotel."

"So far, so good."

"I've ordered a chest X-ray for you, Mr. Harrison. You'll have to drive to Dallas for that test. If that's inconclusive, we'll move on to more invasive tests."

"Okay. I live in Dallas, so that's fine. I can go home and pick up some more clothes while I'm there." He nodded. "I probably should have come in to see you sooner. Lola thinks I'm being a hypochondriac, but I'm telling you, something just ain't right. I feel like I'm dying."

"Well, at least you're here now." I stood, signaling the appointment was over.

"Yeah. That's true." He rose and scowled. "God, I'm so damn dizzy."

I frowned. "You can sit a while longer, if needed."

"Nah. I have a bunch of calls to make."

"Maybe you should just rest today. You are sick after all."

"My bosses would kill me." He smiled weakly and held out his hand. "Thanks for your time, Doc."

"Of course." I resisted the urge to wipe my hand because his was so sweaty.

He left my office, and I stared after him. He was awfully young for any kind of heart issues, and he didn't drink or smoke. He only had a very low-grade fever, so that seemed to rule out the flu. I was a bit stumped as to what might be bothering him. Hopefully the chest X-ray and blood work would shed some light on his condition.

I sighed and pressed the intercom, letting Girdy know I was ready for my next patient.

Epilogue

Maxwell

Madam Woo's Chinese Restaurant was a new and welcome addition to the cuisine available in Rainy Dale. The little eatery had just opened a few weeks ago, and so far the reviews were stellar. The *Town Tattler* had given it five out of five spurs. I'd always been a fan of Asian cuisine, but even if I hadn't been, I'd have been thrilled to have something new to eat. A man could only consume so many burgers and falafels.

Royce and I were seated at a corner table at the front of the small restaurant. The ceiling was decorated with brightly colored paper umbrellas painted with Chinese characters, the tables adorned with pink cloth coverings and white tea lights.

An older Asian woman was at the front, greeting all the guests as they entered the restaurant. I assumed she was Madam Woo herself, although I had no proof of that. Our waitress was a young Asian girl who seemed bored as she took our order. I wondered if perhaps she was Madam Woo's granddaughter and she'd been roped into working in the family restaurant against her will.

I ordered the Woo Street Noodle dish, a meatless entree with sesame paste and peanut soup base. Royce went for the Big Plate Chicken, a dish with braised chicken, potatoes, and hand-pulled flat noodles. To drink, I went nonalcoholic and had fresh watermelon juice, but Royce had a Tsingtao lager.

Once the ordering was out of the way, Royce said, "So I had a chance to interview Patrice O'Malley today."

"Really?" I raised my brows. "How'd that go?"

"She wasn't happy to see me." He laughed. "I guess she doesn't think I'm such a nice guy anymore."

"How rude of you to not let her kill you."

"Right? I'm such a spoilsport." He swept the tip of his finger through the condensation on his beer stein.

"Did you figure out why she had all that children's stuff at her house?"

"She thinks she has a son." He glanced up, frowning. "All those family photos on the walls? They're all fake."

"Really? That's odd."

"Her parents are deceased. She has no siblings." He sighed. "I hope she goes the mental illness defense route. She's definitely mentally ill. I truly think in her mind, she was doing the right thing by killing Bob."

"What about when she wanted to kill you because you got in the way?"

"Maybe she wouldn't have gone through with it."

I shook my head. "Compassion has no place in your line of work, Royce."

"That's not true." He scowled. "Compassion has a place in every job."

"Oh really? What about assassins? Should they have soft, fuzzy feelings?"

He laughed. "Be quiet. You know I mean regular jobs."

"Perhaps we should trade occupations. You be the doctor, and I'll be the sheriff." I smirked, sipping my juice.

"The jail isn't big enough. You'd arrest everyone in town your first day."

"Not necessarily." I smirked. "Are firing squads still in use?"

"Geez."

I laughed. "I'm kidding. Perhaps I'd arrest everyone, but you'd probably kill everyone."

"Yes. But only with kindness." He grinned.

I rolled my eyes.

We fell silent, and then he said, "There's some red-haired guy at the front staring at you."

I frowned and followed his gaze. Herman Harrison was there, waving in our direction. I lifted my hand in response, gritting my teeth when the man approached. I was simply hoping to enjoy a night with Royce and didn't want to think about work.

"Hey, Dr. Thornton." Herman stopped at our table. He looked worse than yesterday. His skin was sallow, and his breathing was elevated. There was a slight blue discoloration around his lips, and his speech was slurred.

"Herman, you don't look so good." I found it impossible to pretend I wasn't alarmed. He'd definitely gone downhill since I'd last seen him.

"I know. I feel worse." He mopped his forehead with a handkerchief. "Lola wanted to try this place, so she sent me over to pick up some food." He winced, rubbing his stomach. "I'm not hungry though. I'm in too much pain. I'll just get her something."

"Perhaps you should call an ambulance to take you to the hospital, Mr. Harrison." I frowned.

"Nah. I'm sure it's just the flu."

"Hmmm. I don't think so."

Royce cleared his throat. "Sorry to hear you're not feeling well. I'm Royce, by the way."

"Oh, hi." Herman smiled. "I'm Herman. I'm a patient of Dr. Thornton's."

"Royce is the sheriff of Rainy Dale," I announced.

Royce looked embarrassed. "Not that that is relevant."

"Are you really the sheriff?" Herman's gaze sharpened.

Royce shrugged. "I don't usually declare that the minute I meet people, but yeah."

Glancing around uneasily, Herman lowered his voice. "Do you think maybe I could come in and talk to you tomorrow?"

"Uh, sure." Royce nodded. "Is something wrong?"

Herman shuddered and leaned his hand on the back of my chair. His breathing was ragged as he said, "I saw something I wasn't supposed to."

"Is that right?" Royce suddenly had his cop face on.

"Yeah, I've had a few weird text messages, warning me to keep my mouth shut." He grimaced and clutched his chest. "Hey, Doc, I… I don't feel so good." As he finished speaking, he crashed forward onto the table.

Royce and I jumped to our feet as our drinks went flying and the china dishes crashed to the floor. A woman at a nearby table let out a shrill scream, and Herman's body rolled from the table to the floor with a thud.

"What the hell?" Royce growled, kneeling down beside Herman.

I did the same, grabbing Herman's wrist, feeling for a pulse. There wasn't one, and I met Royce's stunned gaze. "I can't get a pulse."

Royce's eyes were wide with shock. "Jesus."

"Call 911." I adjusted my position and began CPR. Despite his young age, I'd have been willing to believe Herman had simply had a heart attack, if not for his cryptic statement right before he'd collapsed. "You heard what he said, right? About someone threatening him?"

"Yeah, I heard him."

I kept telling myself it wasn't possible and that I had to be imagining things. Herman Harrison had simply died of natural causes, but in my soul I knew that wasn't true.

Unbelievable as it seemed, yet another murder had occurred in the sleepy little Texas town of Rainy Dale.

Book Three

Arsenic and Old Lies

Coming April 27th

Other Books by S.C. Wynne at:

www.scwynne.com

Hard-Ass is Here

Christmas Crush

Hard-Ass Vacation

The New Boss

Guarding My Heart

The Cowboy and the Barista

Up in Flames

Until the Morning

Falling into Love

The Fire Underneath

Kiss and Tell

Hiding Things-Rerelease coming soon!

Damaged Heart

Assassins Are People Too #1

Assassins Love People Too #2

Assassins Save People Too #3

Assassins in Love Series

Believing Rory

Unleashing Love

Starting New

The Cowboy and the Pencil-Pusher

Memories Follow

Shadow's Edge Book #1

Shadow's Return Book #2

Shadows Deceive #3

My Omega's Baby (Bodyguard & Babies Book #1)

Rockstar Baby (Bodyguard & Babies Book #2)

Manny's Surprise Baby (Bodyguard & Babies Book#3)

Bodyguards and Babies Boxed Set

Strange Medicine (Dr. Maxwell Thornton Mysteries Book #1)

Doctor in the Desert

Redemption

Married to Murder

Crashing Upwards

Other Books Continued

Single Omegas Only

Omega Kidnapped Book One

Omega Tricked Book Two

Home to Danger

Secrets From the Edge

Mistletoe Omega

Footsteps in the Dark Anthology

Reality Bites (Book #1 Hollywood Detective Mysteries)

Painful Lessons

Scalpels & Psychopaths

Book Two Dr. Maxwell Thornton Mysteries

Printed in Great Britain
by Amazon

75333826R00159